CHOCOLATE LOVERS, REJOICE!

JoAnna Carl first gave readers a taste of her Chocoholic Mystery series in the short story "The Chocolate Kidnapping Clue." And in the words of *Publishers Weekly:* "This satisfying appetizer will leave fans hungering for the main course, Carl's upcoming novel, *The Chocolate Cat Caper.*" The wait is over.

The cat got her tongue— and everything else!

I walked past Clementine Ripley's kitchen and into the huge, cold reception room. And there I stopped, because six people were looking in my direction in horror.

For a moment I wondered wildly what I had just done. Then I realized that they weren't looking at me. They were looking over me. All six of them were staring at something over my head. And whatever it was, it was making a horrible choking sound.

I quickly took six steps forward and whirled to see what they were looking at, what the ghastly noise was.

I looked up just in time to see Clementine Ripley tumble over the balcony rail. She hit the floor in front of the bar, landing all splayed out, like a beanbag doll. She didn't move. But something round and white rolled toward me and stopped at my feet.

It was an Amaretto truffle from TenHuis Chocolade. . . .

The Chocolate Cat Caper

A Chocoholic Mystery

JoAnna Carl

SIGNET
Published by New American Library, a division of
Penguin Putnam Inc., 375 Hudson Street,
New York, New York 10014, U.S.A.
Penguin Books Ltd, 80 Strand,
London WC2R 0RL, England
Penguin Books Australia Ltd, Ringwood,
Victoria, Australia
Penguin Books Canada Ltd, 10 Alcorn Avenue,
Toronto, Ontario, Canada M4V 3B2
Penguin Books (N.Z.) Ltd, 182–190 Wairau Road,
Auckland 10, New Zealand

Penguin Books Ltd, Registered Offices:
Harmondsworth, Middlesex, England

First published by Signet, an imprint of New American Library,
a division of Penguin Putnam Inc.

First Printing, March 2002
10 9 8 7 6 5 4 3

Printed in the United States of America

Dedicated to the wonderful folks at Morgen Chocolate, Dallas, with thanks for explaining how to make fine bonbons, truffles, and molded chocolates and for allowing TenHuis Chocolade to copy their product line. And with special appreciation to Rex Morgan, Andrea Pedraza, Mark VanGiles, and Betsy Peters.

Acknowledgments

This book could never have been written without the help of many friends and neighbors from the shores of Lake Michigan, including: Judy and Phil Hallisy; Tracy Paquin and Susan McDermott; Ellie Bellone; boatbuilder Tom Bolhuis; Ellen Clark, Saugatuck City Clerk; and Michigan lawman Bob Swartz. In addition, Lucy Zahray, poison expert and friend to the mystery writer; Claire Carmichael McNab, writing coach; and Inspector Jim Avance, of the Oklahoma State Bureau of Investigation, helped with advice and information, as did David Frost and David Hovell, breeders of Birman cats.

Chapter 1

"Every town has a crooked lawyer," I said. "But even crooks have the right to buy chocolate."

"Clementine Ripley isn't our town's crooked lawyer," Aunt Nettie said scornfully. "Clementine Ripley is just a crooked summer visitor. And I'd be a lot happier if she kept her crookedness elsewhere."

"We can't refuse her business."

"We can refuse if we're not going to get paid."

"Oh, I'll make sure we'll get our money before she gets her chocolate."

Aunt Nettie knotted her solid fists on her solid hips and stood solidly on her solid legs. Solid is definitely the word for Jeanette TenHuis. Even her thick hair, blond streaked with gray, with its natural curl firmly controlled by a food-service hairnet, looked substantial and dependable—hair that wouldn't stand for any nonsense. She is five-foot-four and may weigh 175, but she doesn't look fat. She looks like a granite statue hewn by a sculptor who got tired of chiseling all the excess stone off a big block, so he just whacked a little around the edges, then polished the whole thing smooth and shiny.

But if I compared Aunt Nettie to one of the delectable chocolates she makes, I'd say she was a Frangelico truffle (described in her sales material as,

"Hazelnut interior with milk chocolate coating, sprinkled with nougat."). In other words, she's firm outside, but soft at the heart and has a slightly nutty flavor. When I left the guy I sometimes refer to as Rich Gottrocks and gave up my career as a trophy wife, all my other relatives told me how stupid I was. Aunt Nettie offered me room, board, and a job running the business side of her chocolate shop and factory while I studied for the CPA exam.

Of course, after a couple of days of working on her books, I saw she wasn't being merely philanthropic. My uncle's death eighteen months earlier had thrown her into a financial hole I hoped was temporary, and she needed a cheap manager. But I needed a place where nobody knew my ex-husband, a place to lie low and gather energy for a new attack on life. So we made a good pair.

Soft center or no, Aunt Nettie was quite capable of refusing to sell chocolates to Clementine Ripley, even if it cost her money. It was my job to keep her from doing that, so I spoke firmly. "Listen, Aunt Nettie, when you brought me back to Warner Pier, you said the business side of TenHuis Chocolade was my responsibility. And the business side can't stand for you to snub a two-thousand-dollar order. That would buy a bunch of all-natural ingredients. So load those chocolates up."

She rolled her round blue eyes, and I knew I'd won. "All right, Lee," she said. "But you'll have to deliver them. I won't speak civilly to Clementine Ripley."

"Sure."

"And you'll have to use your minivan. Because of the air-conditioning."

"I'll be glad to," I said. "Maybe I'll get a look inside that house."

"And make sure we get our money!"

"Cross my heart."

I watched while Aunt Nettie loaded six giant silver trays with handmade truffles and bonbons and with fruits dipped in chocolate coating for Clementine Ripley. Candies in dark chocolate, milk chocolate, white chocolate; strawberries and dried apricots half covered with dark chocolate; fresh raspberries mounted on disks of white chocolate and drizzled with milk chocolate—she arranged them into swirling designs of yummy. Each type of truffle or bonbon was decorated in a different way or came in a different shape. A dark chocolate pyramid was coffee-flavored. The white-chocolate-covered truffle with milk chocolate stripes was almond-flavored, its milk chocolate interior flavored with Amaretto. The oval bonbon, made of dark chocolate and decorated with a flower, had a cherry-flavored filling. This went on through sixteen different kinds of truffles and bonbons.

When I'd worked behind the counter as a teenager, I'd known them all. Now I could identify only a few, but that didn't matter. All were genuine luxury chocolates—no jellies or chewy caramels or hard centers—and every flavor could lift me into a state of ecstasy. Aunt Nettie's chocolates were guaranteed to wow the guests at the fund-raiser Clementine Ripley was sponsoring for the Great Lakes Animal Rescue League. It was a big event, or so the Warner Pier weekly had claimed. Guests were coming from Chicago and Detroit—all carrying big checks for the Rescue League.

I snagged an Amaretto truffle Aunt Nettie hadn't placed on a tray yet and bit into it, savoring every sweet, almond-flavored morsel. Every TenHuis Chocolade employee is allowed two free chocolates each working day—a perk I found more pleasant than a company car would have been.

When the first tray was completely filled, Aunt Nettie covered it with plastic wrap, and I picked it up and carried it toward the alley, where I had parked.

"Start the air-conditioning!" Aunt Nettie said.

"I will, I will! I'm not taking a chance on having a couple of thousand dollars' worth of chocolate melt all over my van."

Warner Pier's summer weather is usually balmy. People come here to get away from the heat elsewhere in the Midwest. Most Warner Pier folks don't bother to have air-conditioned cars, and many—including Aunt Nettie—don't even have air-conditioned houses, though she keeps the chocolate shop and workroom chilly. But the lakeshore does have a few really hot muggy days each summer, and this happened to be one of them.

In Texas, we've all given up trying to live without air-conditioning and it's installed everywhere—in houses, offices, industrial plants, cars, trucks, and tractors. My used van had a Texas tag and enough Texas air-conditioning to keep chocolate from melting in any temperature the Great Lakes region was likely to hand out.

I went back and forth out the back door, sliding the trays onto the floor of the van, making sure each tray was wedged firmly. Aunt Nettie didn't get a lot of orders for trays already arranged, but when she did, she wanted them to look artistic. She always arranged them herself, without the help of any of the "hairnet ladies," who were also bustling around the workroom.

These chocolates looked gorgeous. Aunt Nettie carried the last tray out, and I put it in the floor of the front seat. Then I looked at the array and sighed. "They're almost too beautiful to eat."

Aunt Nettie gave a satisfied snort. "They'll eat them," she said. "Now I'll get the cats, and you can go."

While Aunt Nettie went to the storage room, I

popped into the rest room off the break room and freshened up. I had to duck to see the top of my head in the mirror; I got a tall gene from both the Texas side and the Michigan Dutch side of my family, so I'm just a shade under six feet. I tucked my chocolate-brown shirt with the TenHuis Chocolade logo into my khaki slacks. I rebrushed my hair—whitish-blond like the Michigan side—and clipped it into a barrette on the back of my neck. Then I added the merest touch of mascara, tinted faintly green like my Texas hazel eyes. I wiped my mouth and put on a new coat of medium pink lipstick. It was nice to look like myself again. Mr. Gottrocks, whose name was actually Richard Godfrey, always liked me to wear bright red lipstick and big hair, but I'd left the glamour behind with my wedding ring.

As I came out Aunt Nettie was arranging the last of Clementine Ripley's special order of cat-shaped candies onto a smaller silver tray. I admired these, too. Each about three inches high, they were made of solid white chocolate, formed in a mold specially ordered from the Netherlands. They had been hand-detailed with milk chocolate glaze and colored chocolate, so that the blue eyes and the light brown markings of the cats mimicked the photo Clementine Ripley had provided of her Birman male, Champion Myanmar Chocolate Yonkers. To a non-cat-fancier like me, Yonkers looked as if a Siamese cat had decided to let his hair grow. He had immensely fluffy Persian-like fur, but had the delicate light brown paws, ears, nose, and tail of a Siamese.

Even to a non-cat-fancier, Yonkers was a beautiful creature, and his chocolate replicas looked scrumptious on their silver dish. "Gorgeous!" I said.

Aunt Nettie wrapped the dish with a huge sheet of food-service Saran, then picked up a small white box tied with blue ribbon from the table behind her. "Here are the samples," she said.

"Samples? For me?"

"No! For Clementine Ripley. I don't want my display ruined. So I packed a few extra chocolates for her to sample. I wrote her name on top."

I laughed. "Maybe you'd better send an extra cat, so she won't get into those either."

"There's a cat in there. Amaretto truffles are her favorite, though. She buys those every time she comes in. So I sent a half dozen. But I'd better get my money!"

"No check, no chocolate. I talked to her assistant—Ms. McCoy?—and she assured me she'd have the money ready."

"Good girl!"

I shook my finger at Aunt Nettie. "And unlike some other people—I'm sticking to it. Not a chocolate comes out of the van until I have that check."

Aunt Nettie smiled sheepishly. She's much too understanding and patient. A year earlier she had let Clementine Ripley have chocolates for her big benefit party on credit. But in the offhand way of the really rich, Ms. Ripley neglected to pass on the invoice in a timely manner to the person who paid her bills. It was several months before Aunt Nettie got her money. This year we weren't going to let that happen.

I'd insisted that Clementine Ripley use a credit card, but that hadn't worked either. Now I'd arranged to get a check when the chocolates were delivered.

I checked to be sure I had the invoice, slung my purse over my shoulder, and took the tray of cats to the van. I was settled behind the wheel when Aunt Nettie ran out, waving. "Wait! Take these."

I rolled down the window, letting out valuable air-conditioned air, and took what she handed me—a dispenser box containing a few pairs of plastic food-service gloves.

"In case any of the chocolates shift, use these to move them back in place."

"I'll drive slow and steady," I said. "And I'll try not to say anything stupid, either."

Aunt Nettie laughed. "You're not stupid, Lee," she said. Bless her heart. I hope she's right, but not everybody agrees with her. She waved as I drove off.

Nothing's very far away from anything else in Warner Pier. Clementine Ripley's overly dramatic showplace home on the cliff at Warner Point was only two miles from TenHuis Chocolade, located on Fifth Street between Peach and Pear Avenues.

I pulled out of the alley and very gently turned onto Peach Street, then followed that a block to Dock Street, the pride of Warner Pier. Dock Street has been turned into a real attraction—a mile of marinas, all crammed with boats and yachts in the summer. And dividing the street from the marinas is a mile-long park—a narrow series of green spaces, gazebos, and wooden walkways. Boaters can dock at a Warner Pier marina, then walk across the park to reach a business district filled with good restaurants, antique and gift shops, art galleries, trendy and expensive clothing stores—and the occasional specialty shop like TenHuis Chocolade. It's pretty neat, or so we Warner Pier merchants think. I followed Dock Street, driving slowly because of the chocolates and because of the tourists who roamed the streets, until I was out of the business district.

The older residential neighborhoods of Warner Pier were designed by Norman Rockwell in 1946. At least, my mother always claims she grew up on the cover of an old *Saturday Evening Post* magazine. The town looks as if it's under a glass dome. Just shake us, and it snows on the white Victorians, Craftsman bungalows, and modified Queen Anne cottages and on their lush, old-fashioned gardens.

Warner Pier lies along the Warner River, not far

upstream from the spot where the river enters Lake Michigan. In the 1830s, settlers—some from the Netherlands and some from New England—saw a chance to make money by cutting down all the native timber. With those trees gone, the next generation planted replacements, but they concentrated on fruit trees, and Warner Pier became a center for production of "Michigan Gold," which was the early-day promoters' nickname for peaches. By 1870 Warner Pier had become a town of prosperous fruit growers and ship owners—solid citizens with enough money to build the substantial Victorian houses that today are being gentrified into summer homes or into bed-and-breakfast inns. Warner Pier is still a fruit-producing center, but today a lot of the area's "Michigan Gold" comes from tourists and summer residents.

I followed the curves of Dock Street to the showplace home of Clementine Ripley, one of Warner Pier's most famous summer visitors. Most summer people come for the beaches and Victorian ambiance, but Ms. Ripley seemed to have come seeking seclusion. Several years earlier she had acquired ten acres of prime property on top of a bluff overlooking the Warner River, right at the point where it entered Lake Michigan. She built a low stone house that appeared to be about two blocks long, with a tower slumped at one end. That tower was apparently based on an abstract idea of a lighthouse—or maybe planned as a squatty version of the Washington Monument. It was known to boaters up and down the lake as "the sore thumb," because that's what it stuck out like.

The house might be highly visible from the lake, but it was not inviting. Signs warning boaters and swimmers to keep away were posted along the shore. Guards and a high brick wall kept Clementine Ripley private and protected from the land side.

Clementine might well need protection, and from more than prying eyes. Her office was in Chicago, but she had a national practice in criminal law. As one of the nation's toughest defense lawyers, she'd kept a series of high-profile clients out of prison on charges that ranged from fraud to murder. Not a few people—witnesses she'd shredded on the stand, prosecutors she'd made look like circus clowns, former clients and their victims, plus the tabloid press—had it in for Clementine Ripley. Even sainted Aunt Nettie, who loved everybody else in the world, didn't like her. She hadn't told me why, but her feelings seemed to be deeper than a payment problem.

So Clementine Ripley might need her guards, I told myself as I drove up to the metal security gate. The gate was probably eight feet high, and its grill seemed to snarl. I wouldn't have touched it on a bet; the thing looked as if it would carry thousands of volts of electricity. I stopped by the intercom mounted on a post and punched a button on its face, feeling as if I was about to order a hamburger and fries.

A disembodied voice answered, "Yes?"

"Lee McKinney, with a delivery from TenHuis Chocolade."

"Just follow the drive up to the house," the voice said.

The gate slid sideways, and I drove on in, almost frightened of what might happen once I was behind the brick wall and in the area controlled by Clementine Ripley.

There was nothing scary in there, of course, unless you find deep woods threatening. But the undergrowth in these particular woods was largely cleared out, and ahead I could see the long stone house, its tower leaning like a drunken troll. I drove on slowly—still remembering my fragile cargo—and I coasted around the circular drive and came to a halt in front of the wide flagstone steps.

On the steps was a hulking man—broad and tall.

He had a shaved head and a thick upper lip that curled into a snarl. He wore a gray uniform, and the patch above his shirt pocket read GRAND VALLEY SECURITY SERVICE. He motioned for me to lower my window.

When he spoke, his voice surprised me by being a high-pitched squeak. "Ms. McKinney? I'll unload the delivery here."

I told myself not to say anything stupid. Then I took a deep breath and spoke. "Do you have my check?"

He spoke curtly. "Check? No, payment is handled by Ms. Ripley's personal assistant, Ms. McCoy."

"I told Ms. McCoy we had to have payment before we delivered the chocolates."

"It will be taken care of." The gray-uniformed man went to the back of the minivan.

I jumped out, leaving the motor running, and went after him. *Keep calm and speak carefully,* I thought.

"I can't allow the chocolates to be unloaded until we are paid."

Gray Uniform reached for the handle to the back door. "You'll be paid," he squeaked, but he still sounded curt.

I stepped between him and the door. I was taller, but that didn't give me any real edge, since he was broader. "I'm sure we will be paid, but I need the password today."

Rats! I'd done it. Said something stupid.

The security guard looked puzzled. "Password?"

"Payment," I said. There was nothing to do but go on. "I need payment. I explained to Ms. McCandy."

That ripped it. Now Gray Uniform was grinning, obviously amused. Darn! If I'm going to have a speech impediment, why can't I lisp? People recognize a lisp as a problem. This saying the wrong word business simply makes me sound like an idiot.

I tried again, speaking slowly and carefully. My

insides were twisting up to match my tongue. "I can't unload the chocolates until I receipt the check. I mean, receive! Receive the check."

Gray Uniform's grin became patronizing, and he gave a clumsy wave, as if he were going to brush me out of the way. "Now listen, young lady . . ." Then his eyes widened, and he looked behind me, obviously surprised.

Could it be the famous Clementine Ripley? I whirled to see.

It wasn't. It was a tall man—at least two inches taller than I am. He had dark hair and was wearing navy-blue pants and a matching shirt. Sunglasses seemed to cover his face from hairline to upper lip.

"What's the problem, Hugh?" His voice boomed. Definitely a basso.

The guard squeaked in reply. "Joe! How did you get here?"

The mouth of the tall guy shaped into a sardonic grin. Somehow that grin seemed familiar. "I tied up at the boathouse and walked. Why? Have you got orders to run me off?"

"No, no!" Gray Uniform sputtered, but the newcomer cut off his excuses.

"What's your problem here?"

Gray Uniform stumbled through an explanation, while the dark-haired man and I eyed each other warily. Or I think he eyed me behind his sunglasses. I kept trying to place him. Who was he? I was sure I'd met him, but I couldn't figure out where or when.

Gray Uniform's mouth began to run down, and the tall man scowled. "Sounds like Clemmie hasn't been paying her bills. Where's Marion?"

"Out on the terrace, but—"

The man's head turned toward me. "I'll take you around."

"Let me get the invoice." I opened the driver's door and retrieved my purse and the small box of sample chocolates Aunt Nettie had sent. I checked to see that I had my extra car keys; then I locked the door and slammed it.

The tall guy spoke again. "You left the motor running."

"Air-conditioning," I said. "I can't let the chocolates melt."

"Oh." He turned and led the way along a flagstone walk that circled the house. I tried to keep up.

"I do appreciate this," I said. "The security man seemed determined to unload the chocolates, and I promised my aunt—"

He stopped and turned toward me. "Your aunt? Are you Jeanette TenHuis's niece?"

"Lee McKinney." I put out my hand.

He took the hand. Then he took off the sunglasses and hung them on his shirt pocket.

I gave a gasp. "You're Joe Woodyard! I thought you looked familiar, but I didn't recognize you with clothes on."

I'd really done it this time. Joe's smile almost turned into a glare. I spoke quickly. "I used to hang out at Warner Pier bitch when you were a lifeguard." I decided to ignore turning "beach" into "bitch" and kept talking. "I always saw you looking down from that high chair."

"Yeah, Joe Lifeguard, lording it over the beach." He started walking again. I trailed him. "I remember you."

Joe Woodyard had been the head lifeguard at the Warner Pier beach the year I was sixteen, the year my parents divorced and I was packed off to work for Aunt Nettie and Uncle Phil in the chocolate shop. I'd made a few friends among the local girls who had summer jobs in the downtown businesses, and we'd spent our off hours at the beach, flirting with the Warner Pier guys (dating a summer visitor could ruin your rep) and drooling over Joe Woodyard.

He'd been the best-looking guy in Warner Pier in those days—dark curly hair, dark brows, long lashes, and vivid blue eyes, not to mention great shoulders. He was three or four years older than we were, and he had an air of dangerous arrogance. To the sixteen-year-old mind he had been the epitome of cool, but intimidating.

He had been a sharp dresser, too. But now I recognized his matching shirt and slacks as "work clothes," the kind you buy at Kmart. And he wasn't as good-looking now. Or maybe he was good-looking in a different way. At twenty he'd been almost too handsome; now he looked tougher, more rugged, sadder—as if he'd had a few rocky nights and rough days.

Joe spoke again. "What are you doing back in Warner Pier?"

"Working for Aunt Nettie. I'm planning to commute to Grand Rapids and take the CPA review course. What are you doing now?"

Joe's smile twisted into its sardonic version, but before he could speak, a new voice sounded from in front of us. It was a deep, throaty voice, a voice with vibrato that could make a stone shudder—or at least sway a jury.

"Don't you know?" the voice said. "Joe is the former Mr. Clementine Ripley."

Chapter 2

I recognized her, of course. *Sixty Minutes*, the *Today* show, *Dallas Times-Herald, Time* magazine—Clementine Ripley and her photograph had been everywhere during the prominent cases she had worked on. After Thomas Montgomery's estranged wife was found beaten to death, for example, nobody had believed even the Montgomery millions could keep him off death row. But Clementine Ripley had done it. When rock star Shane Q. was accused of burning down his record producer's house, the evidence looked damning. But Clementine Ripley kept him out of jail. And the fee from either case—or from any of a dozen others she had handled—could have paid for the house in Warner Pier.

Clementine Ripley would have drawn attention even if her photo hadn't been plastered over the world's news media. She was an attractive woman, but there was nothing showy about her looks. She simply looked competent. If I'd had a small country that needed running, I'd have hired Clementine Ripley for the job on sight, never mind the references.

Then she came out of the house, down a step, and I was surprised to see that she wasn't very tall. She had a full figure—no skinny lightweight could look as reliable as Clementine Ripley looked—but she wasn't plump. She wore casual pants in light blue denim with a matching man-tailored shirt, but the embroidered trim showed that the outfit hadn't come off the rack at Penney's. Her hair was blond—bottled, but not brassy—her features symmetrical, her makeup subtle. Her skin was outstanding—fine-textured and smooth, but with lines around the eyes.

She was at least fifteen years older than Joe Woodyard, I realized.

"Meow." The comment made me jump guiltily, for my cattiness. Had Clementine Ripley read my mind?

Then Ms. Ripley emerged from behind a bush that had partially hidden her, and I saw that she was holding a cat, an enormous ball of white-and-minky-brown fur.

The cat spoke again. "Meow."

"Oh!" I said. "Is this Yonkers?"

Ms. Ripley caressed the cat with a gesture as sensuous as Aunt Nettie's chocolate cream. "Yes."

"He's beautiful!"

Champion Myanmar Chocolate Yonkers accepted my admiration as his due, and Ms. Ripley ignored it. She looked at Joe Woodyard. "Joe, are you going to introduce me to your attractive friend?"

She managed to make the last word almost objectionable, and I spoke quickly, before Joe could react. "I'm Lee McKinney, from TenHuis Chocolade. Mr. Woodyard showed me the way back here. I'm here to deliver your order."

Ms. Ripley's eyes narrowed like the cat's. "I'm sure that the security guard can help you unload the chocolates. You can go back the way you came."

She was beginning to unnerve me, and that always had a bad effect on my tongue. "I was told I could find your personal assailant here." Oops! I went back and tried the remark over. "I need to talk to your personal assistant."

The catlike eyes blinked twice, and Ms. Ripley

called out. "Marion!" She looked into the room behind her. "Someone wants to talk to you!"

She turned around and put the cat inside the house, then slid a screen door shut, imprisoning him. Champion Yonkers immediately leaped onto the screen and climbed, using his claws as pitons and grumbling deep in his throat. The screen was speckled with enlarged holes; apparently the cat made this climb frequently. At any rate, both Joe Woodyard and Clementine Ripley ignored his stunt.

The real cat reminded me of the candy one. I lifted the white box and thrust it toward Ms. Ripley. "My aunt sent these."

She eyed the box suspiciously. "Your aunt?"

"Jeanette TenHuis. She's the chocolate expert. She wanted you to see one of the special order cats. She sent several Amaretto truffles as well."

I kept the chocolates extended, and Ms. Ripley took them. She slid the blue ribbon off the box, opened it, and pulled out the white chocolate cat. She smiled. It was impossible not to smile at the chocolate version of Champion Yonkers.

"Delightful!" She held the cat up for Joe Woodyard to see. "Isn't it lovely, Joe?" She sounded slightly sarcastic when she spoke to him.

"Just dandy," Joe said. "I need to talk to you. Where's Marion?"

"I'm coming," a woman's voice answered. "I was upstairs."

The woman who came toward us, sliding the door open only a few inches and making sure the cat didn't get out, was frankly middle-aged. Or maybe she was much the same age as Clementine Ripley, but not as well kept. Her hair had been allowed to stay its natural gray, and she didn't seem to be wearing makeup. She had on polyester pants and a loose, sloppy T-shirt. She was almost as tall as I am, and she was thin. Not slender, not svelte, not slim, but something close to skinny. Her skin had been weathered by the sun.

She stopped a few feet away from Clementine Ripley and stared at Joe Woodyard. "What's he doing here?" she said.

Ms. Ripley ignored her remark. "It's the chocolate delivery," she said. "This woman says she needs to talk to you."

Marion McCoy glared at me. "The security man could have called me to the door."

"I'm sorry to bother you," I said. "But you promised to have a check—"

She cut me off before I could finish the sentence. "Just come this way." Still glaring, she brushed past her employer.

"Wait a minute," Ms. Ripley said. She put her hand on Ms. McCoy's arm and stopped her, but she looked at me. "Did you say you were to receive a check?"

I nodded unhappily.

"But I thought I put the chocolates on my Visa card."

"I'll take care of it," Ms. McCoy said firmly.

"Please wait, Marion. Let this young woman answer me. Didn't I give you my credit card number?"

I glanced at Joe Woodyard, standing with his arms folded, and at Marion McCoy, who was glaring. I didn't want to have to answer that question.

"Have you stopped taking credit cards?" Ms. Ripley was insistent. "Someone asked for one when I called the order in."

"Oh, we still take them! It's just that—well, there was some discrepancy. The card was dejected." Oh, I'd done it again. "It was rejected," I said.

Ms. Ripley stood there deadpan, then gave her slow, catlike smile again. "Rejected?"

Joe Woodyard gave a barking laugh. "You're maxed out, Clem. Is that why you've gone back on our deal?"

Clementine Ripley turned on him, and now she looked like a cat who was ready to claw. I spoke quickly, before she could attack either of us. "There are a lot of possible explanations," I said. "We may have taken down the wrong number over the phone, for example. But Ms. McCoy assured me—"

"Yes, I'll write a check on the personal account," Marion McCoy said. She shook her employer's hand off her arm and moved toward me.

Ms. Ripley was back in control of herself, but her eyes were still narrow. "You do that, Marion," she said. "And we'll discuss this later." Then she reached into the little white box of chocolates, but she didn't offer to share. She pulled out the chocolate cat and took a bite. She chewed and swallowed, made a satisfied "ummm" sound, and popped the rest of it in her mouth. Then she slid the blue ribbon back around the box, effectively reserving the chocolates for herself.

"Here, Marion," she said. "Take these into the house, please. Just put them in my room. I'll eat them later."

Marion snatched the box ungraciously, then walked off without another word. I followed her. Behind me I heard Ms. Ripley speak. "So, Joe—why are you here?"

"I want my money," Joe said.

I didn't hear any more. I didn't want to. I didn't know just where Joe Woodyard and Clementine Ripley stood. Maybe they were in the middle of their divorce. Or maybe they were divorced already. Maybe Joe was asking for alimony. And maybe the credit card "dejection" meant Ms. Ripley had more serious money problems than a bill from TenHuis Chocolade.

I followed Ms. McCoy along the flagstone terrace,

which overlooked a broad lawn dotted with trees trimmed carefully to avoid blocking the view of Lake Michigan. It wasn't as hot or muggy here on the lakeshore. The sky was blue, the clouds fluffy, a fresh breeze teased the water into rhythmic lines of whitecaps.

"This is beautiful," I said.

Ms. McCoy ignored me. She certainly wasn't friendly. She led me past a long row of windows, then through a French door and into a paneled office. I stood by while she dug a big flat checkbook out of a drawer in the walnut desk that centered the room. She took the invoice I handed her and wrote the check.

As she gave it to me, she glared. "There was no need to bother Ms. Ripley about this."

"I didn't intend to. Joe Woodyard happened to pop up as I arrived, and he told the security goon—I mean, he told the security guard that he'd take me out to the terrace to find you." I could feel myself blushing. Goon! Had I really said that? I went on quickly. "How do I get back to the drive where I left my van?"

Without a word Ms. McCoy led me across a hall, through a utility room, and out a door. We emerged behind some bushes, turned a corner, and were back on the circular drive. My minivan and the security guard—he did look and act like a goon—were right where I had left them. Another vehicle, a sporty vintage Mercedes convertible, had been parked behind me. Its driver—a tall man with a beautiful head of gray hair—got out, waved at Marion McCoy, and went up the steps to the front door.

I unlocked the van, and the security man and Ms. McCoy unloaded the chocolates, turning down my offer to help. The security man managed to tip one of the trays, of course, and all the chocolates slid to one side. I offered to rearrange them, but they again refused my offer. So I handed Ms. McCoy the food-service gloves and advised her to use them to rearrange the chocolates. Then I got in the van and drove away.

I met only one more crisis. When I got to the massive gate, I slowed, wondering how to open it. It slid back on its own, and I found myself hood to hood with a police car.

A pair of sunglasses and a head of dark hair sprinkled with gray poked out the window of the police car, and its driver called out, "I'll back up!"

He backed onto the street, and I drove out the drive. I waved as I passed him, to acknowledge his courtesy, and he gave me an answering wave and a friendly grin. If he was on official business, it didn't seem to be anything serious. In fact, his grin was the only genuine one I'd seen since I left TenHuis Chocolade.

"Whew!" I said aloud as I turned toward the Warner Pier business district. "What a bunch. Rude secretary. Officious security man. Family fight. Everybody at everybody else's throat." It would be nice to get back to the chocolate shop, where Aunt Nettie kept all her employees happy. And where I could absorb the news that Joe Woodyard, the guy the sixteen-year-old me had thought was so cool, was trying to squeeze money out of his ex-wife.

But as I turned onto Peach Avenue, I realized I hadn't seen the inside of the house. I refused to count the office and the utility room as a view of a show-place home.

When I came through the back door of TenHuis Chocolade, I could see Aunt Nettie standing at a stainless-steel worktable, using a big metal lattice to cut a sheet of lemon canache into diamond shapes. Canache—it rhymes with "panache"—is a thick filling, stout enough to stand up on its own, but not as solid as a jelly. Pieces of this are "enrobed," or covered with chocolate, and turned into a type of bonbon I think is actually more like a truffle.

Aunt Nettie was talking to a woman whose back was toward me. All I could see of her was shoulder-length brown hair.

Aunt Nettie beckoned. "Lee! See who's here!"

The woman turned around. "Lee!" She held her arms out.

I yelled at her, "Lindy Bradford! I mean, Lindy Herrera!"

We hugged each other enthusiastically and made good-to-see-you-again noises. Lindy had worked for TenHuis Chocolade the same summers I did. The two of us had lazed on the beach and ogled the local guys on our days off. I'd always thought Joe Woodyard was the coolest, but Lindy had had her eye on Tony Herrera even then.

Lindy still had a sweet dimpled face. She'd gained a little weight since high school, of course, but she looked great.

"Aunt Nettie says you have three kids now," I said.

"Right. And I hope you're ready to look at pictures!"

Everybody who comes into TenHuis Chocolade gets a sample, so Lindy picked a strawberry truffle ("White chocolate and strawberry interior coated with dark chocolate"). Then we went into the office, where I admired the pictures of three cute, dark-haired kids. Lindy had married Tony a year after we graduated from high school. I'd been working in Dallas and hadn't had the time or money to come for her wedding. Aunt Nettie hadn't been too optimistic about the marriage. Tony and Lindy were "too young," she had said. Tony had been working for his dad's catering business when they got married.

"Is Tony still working for his dad?"

"Oh, no! He hated that, you know. He went to school, became a machinist."

"Does he like that better?"

"He did—until he got laid off a month ago."

"Ouch! Has he found anything else?"

"They're supposed to call everybody back in the fall. For now he's doing what he can find—helping Handy Hans repair cottages, painting houses. He's been working with Joe Woodyard some."

"I guess it's reunion week," I said. "I ran into Joe out at the Ripley house."

"Joe! What was he doing there?" Linda leaned close. "He and the Ripper split up two years ago."

"I guess they had some business to discuss." I might be disappointed in Joe for trying to get money out of his ex, but I decided I didn't need to spread the word around Warner Pier. It would spread fast enough without my help. Warner Pier is a town that size.

"Tony says Joe's having some business problems," Lindy said.

"What does Joe do?"

"Well, he used to be a lawyer. But now he's restoring antique powerboats."

"Antique powerboats?"

"You know. Wooden speedboats and such."

"He quit practicing law to do that?"

Lindy shrugged. "His mom was mad as hops. She was real proud of her son the lawyer. But when Joe walked out on the Ripper, he dropped out of law, too. He bought the old Olson shop at the far end of Dock Street. It caused a lot of conversation in the local coffee klatches."

I laughed. "I guess so. When I was in Warner Pier Joe was definitely tagged as 'most likely to succeed.' "

"Oh, yeah. Joe's kept the town on its ear since he was state high school debate champ and state wrestling champ in the same year. Then he organized the student Habitat for Humanity chapter for Michigan. He won all kinds of scholarships. And apparently he did real well in law school, ran the—what do they call it?—law review."

I nodded. "That's quite an honor."

Lindy went on. "His mom was bragging about all the big law firms that offered him high-paying jobs, but he went with one of these outfits that help the poor. Legal Aid? That was in Detroit. Then he married big, and his mom started bragging again. But two years ago he left the Ripper and quit law completely."

"Money isn't everything."

Lindy rolled her eyes. "Wish I had enough of it to say that."

"Money." I opened my purse, produced the check, and leaned out into the workroom. "Tah-dah!" When Aunt Nettie looked around I waved the check.

She smiled sweetly. "Oh, good!"

I turned back to Lindy. "Mission accomplished. I delivered a huge order of chocolates to Clementine Ripley, and this is the check for them. But I didn't get to see the inside of the house."

"It's ugly as sin. I get to see it several times a year."

"How do you rate? Are you an Animal Rescue League supporter?"

"No, I'm a waitress! Tony quit his dad, but I've been working for him sometimes—Mike Herrera's Restaurant and Catering. We do all of Clementine Ripley's parties." Her dimples deepened, and her face lit up. "Do you really want to see the inside of the house?"

"Sure. But what excuse do I have to go back?"

"Waitress! You waited tables when you were in college, didn't you?"

"I did it more recently than that. When I walked

out on Rich it was the only job I could get in a hurry. Rich nearly had a fit."

"Why?"

"He was telling all his friends I was out to take him financially. Then I showed up on the lunch shift at his favorite Mexican restaurant. Running my feet off. It made it sort of obvious that I hadn't taken a lot of his worldly goods with me. Waiting tables is hard work."

"Well, the Ripley parties are a snap. It's just circulating with a tray and picking up dirty napkins. And Papa Mike's been looking all over for an extra waitress for tonight. If you really want to see the inside of the house, I'll call him and see if he's found anybody."

I thought about it a second. "What do you wear?"

"Black slacks, white shirt. Mike will furnish the vest and tie."

"It might be easier to wait until the house is in *Architectural Digest*."

"Come on, Lee, do it!" Lindy said. "It'll give us a chance to talk without the kids underfoot."

I considered for a long moment before I spoke. "Sure. I'll do it. Call."

It wasn't until after Mike Herrera had agreed to take me on and after Lindy had gone home that Aunt Nettie heard about the plan. Her reaction amazed me. She looked horrified.

"Oh, no!"

"What's wrong?" I said. "It's just a chance to talk to Lindy."

"I just don't like the thought of you working for the woman who was responsible for your uncle's death!"

Chapter 3

I stared at Aunt Nettie. When Uncle Phil, my mother's brother, had died eighteen months earlier, that left Aunt Nettie as sole owner of TenHuis Chocolade—an expert on chocolate, but a little hazy on the business side. Uncle Phil had been killed by a drunk driver. But the guy had been tried and sentenced to jail, and this was the first time I'd heard that Clementine Ripley had anything to do with it.

"What do you mean, 'the woman who was responsible for Uncle Phil's death?' "

"That was the reason I didn't want to do all that chocolate!"

"But you had the chocolate cat mold."

"Oh, I ordered that two years ago, and it got here too late to use. When Clementine Ripley called the order in, it was your first day. I wasn't here, but I guess somebody told you about the cat mold."

"Yes, I asked one of the ladies, and she said the special mold was available. But what's this about Clementine Ripley's connection with the wreck that killed Uncle Phil?"

"She kept that terrible Troy Sheepshanks out of prison."

"Troy Sheepshanks? Wasn't that the driver?"

"Yes! He killed your uncle Phil. But it was the

second time he'd been involved in a fatal accident. The first time he hired Clementine Ripley, and the district attorney wouldn't even file charges."

"Then the evidence must not have been good."

"It would have been good enough if Troy had had any other attorney. The district attorney was simply scared to face her in court. So he dropped the case."

"That's terrible. But . . ."

Aunt Nettie sat down in an office chair and pursed her lips. She looked as solid as ever, and she hadn't burst into tears. Only someone like me, who'd known her a long time, would have realized that she was extremely upset.

"Because Troy Sheepshanks was never charged in that first case, he got his license back and was on the highway—drunk again—when he killed Phil." She sat back and folded her arms across her solid bosom. One lonely tear ran down her cheek. "I've always blamed Clementine Ripley as much as I blamed Troy Sheepshanks. If she'd been responsible at all, she would have seen that he shouldn't be driving. You don't know how often I've longed to kill that woman."

I was sitting in an office chair that was on rollers. So I dug in my heels, grabbed the end of the desk, and scooted across the floor until I was knee to knee with Aunt Nettie. Not graceful, but I got there. "Why didn't you tell me all this?"

She shrugged, sniffed, and shook her head silently.

"If I'd known, I'd never have urged you to fill that order for chocolates."

"No. You were right. We can't refuse to sell chocolates just because we don't like the customers who want to buy them." Aunt Nettie sniffed again, but this time she smiled. "I hate Hawaiian shirts, but I'm glad to sell chocolates to people who wear them."

"We could put up a sign on the door: 'Hawaiian shirts? No service.' " That made her laugh, just a little, and I gave her a one-armed hug. "Listen, I'll call Mr. Herrera and tell him I can't serve at the party after all."

"No! No! He's counting on you now."

I could have predicted that reaction, I guess. The Warner Pier business community is not large, and the merchants help each other out. "I won't make a habit of being backup help for Mike Herrera," I said. "But Mom didn't tell me a thing about all these problems with Clementine Ripley."

"She probably didn't know. For the last few years your uncle and I haven't had much contact with her. And you were having your own problems when Phil died."

That was true. Uncle Phil had died a month after I left Rich and when I was hitting my lowest point financially. My mom is notorious for never saving a cent. She is totally immersed in her work as a travel agent, though that has its good side. When Uncle Phil died, she was able to get us a standby flight. If she hadn't, neither of us would have even been able to come to Warner Pier for the funeral. But we had stayed only two days. Neither of us had been any help to Aunt Nettie.

Aunt Nettie took a tissue from her pocket and blew her nose. "I guess that's why I hate that big house of Clementine Ripley's so much. It's like a memorial to the injustice of Phil's death."

"What does the house have to do with Uncle Phil's death?"

"The first time Troy was accused of drunk driving, the Sheepshankses paid Clementine Ripley's fee by giving her that ten acres out on Warner Point. The city had been trying to get hold of the property, but Ms. Ripley ruined that."

We left the situation as it stood. Aunt Nettie didn't want either of us to have anything to do with Clementine Ripley, but I'd promised to help out one of

Aunt Nettie's fellow Warner Pier merchants, and she wouldn't hear of my backing out.

I dashed to the bank to deposit the check for Ms. Ripley's chocolates, making it into the main lobby before three p.m., when the bank closed for the weekend. I could have deposited the check at the drive-through, which would be open Saturday, but I was trying to establish rapport with Barbara, the branch manager. Then I went out to the house, changed into black slacks and a white shirt, and pulled my hair into a knot at the back of my head. Not glamorous, and not really required by the health department, but I hate waitresses who look as if they're shedding hair into the onion dip. At four-thirty, I picked up Lindy at her house—Tony had taken the kids to the beach, so I didn't see them—and I headed the minivan toward Clementine Ripley's estate for the second time that day. And this time I planned to see the inside of the place.

We were allowed through the gate and directed around the house by a service drive. We parked in a gravel area beside a four-car garage, next to the Herrera Catering van. The van was brand-new and had a classy logo painted on the side.

"Looks as if your pa-in-law is doing well," I said.

"He's really thrown himself into the business since Tony's mother died four years ago," Lindy said. "He's become a workaholic. Though recently we've caught a few hints that he's got some new romantic interest."

"How does that hit Tony?"

"Not very well. Of course, we both want Mike to be happy. But he's so secretive. We don't know who he's seeing. It makes us feel . . . worried."

I had the sense to nod understandingly and keep quiet.

Lindy took a deep breath before she spoke again.

"It sounds silly, but Tony's afraid he's dating an Anglo."

"So? Tony married one."

"I know. Maybe that's why he's trying so hard to hang on to his cultural heritage. Trying to teach the kids Spanish. Stuff like that." She smiled. "It all started when Papa Mike changed his name from Miguel."

The breeze had switched to the north, dropping the temperature and humidity from their earlier highs and promising a pleasant evening for Clementine Ripley's party. The terrace overlooking the lake faced west, so sun might be a problem on that side of the house, but the terrace on the river side was shaded by some big trees.

I greeted Mike Herrera. I barely remembered him from my teenage summers in Warner Pier; all I had was a vague recollection of a man with slicked-down hair and a little Latin mustache who was always cheerful. Now I saw that he'd changed his persona over the past twelve years, with a shave and a new hairstyle that turned him into a sort of heavyset Antonio Banderas. It was a surprising transformation. The twenty-eight-year-old me noted that he was an attractive man, something the sixteen-year-old me had missed.

Mike Herrera had been the first Hispanic to own his own business in Warner Pier—most Mexican-Americans in the area pick fruit—and I knew Aunt Nettie thought a lot of him. I felt sure he didn't remember me at all, but he pretended that he did. Every successful caterer is a born glad-hander, and Mike Herrera had the act down pat.

He smiled broadly as he took my hand in both of his. "Lee. The little Texas lady who stayed with Jeanette and Phil and worked in their shop. Welcome back to beautiful Lake Michigan." His accent was very faint.

"This time I plan to stay through the winter, Mr. Herrera. Do you think a Texan can stand the snow?"

"You'll grow to love it, Lee. Brisk! Invigorating! And the summers—ah, yes. Life without air-conditioning. You know I grew up in Denton? But I'd never go back to Texas now that I've discovered this beautiful place." He gave my hand a final pat, and a subtle change came over his face. When he spoke again I recognized it; Mike Herrera had moved from Warner Pier booster to businessman.

"I can't do your paperwork today," he said. "But I'll be in the office tomorrow. Can you bring your Social Security number by?"

"Sure."

"Hokay." He nodded. "Have you ever tended bar?"

"A few times. I can manage highballs and martinis. If they get into anything more exotic . . ."

Herrera smiled. "If they want anything more exotic, you'll ask Jason to mix it." He led, I followed, and I was finally inside the house.

I could see why Lindy had described the interior as "ugly as sin," but some interior designer had been paid a bunch of money to make it that ugly. The walls were white and completely bare. The ceilings were white, too, and they soared. The floor was bare wood, with a finish so dark it almost hit black. A stairway—dark wood risers with stark white balustrades—led to a balcony that loomed over the shortest side of the room. The south and west walls were lined with French windows, which showed off the views of the lake and the river. The windows were bare; no curtains, blinds, valances, or even lengths of fabric twisted around poles. If the room had a focal point—other than the views of river and lake—it was a severe stone fireplace at the narrow end. An unobtrusive area rug lay in front of that, and the fireplace faced a white leather couch—the kind you have trouble getting out of. All the other furniture was dark wood and looked spindly and uncomfortable.

I pictured the room in winter, with all that bare wood, no comfortable chairs, and nothing to block the view of icy river and lake outside. *Clementine Ripley must have to keep the thermostat set on ninety degrees,* I thought. The room was beautiful, in an austere way, but it was a visual deep freeze.

It was not a room I could imagine Joe Woodyard in.

A half dozen men, women, and teenagers in black pants and white shirts were bustling about, setting up tables and dressing them with white cloths and silver dishes. I spotted two silver trays of TenHuis chocolates.

Through a double door I could see a dining room—more dark wood and unadorned white walls. A man in a white undershirt was building a white linen nest for a steamboat round. I felt sure he'd put on a double-breasted jacket and a chef's hat before the guests arrived.

I hadn't ever waitressed at a party like this, true, but in my role as Mrs. Rich Gottrocks, I'd gone to hundreds of similar events. Boooorrring. At least I wouldn't have to make conversation this time.

The last person I expected to see was Clementine Ripley herself. She should have been upstairs soaking in the whirlpool or treating her beautiful complexion to a last-minute facial. But as Mike Herrera and I crossed toward the bar, she came in the terrace door, still wearing her casual denim outfit. Herrera nodded and smiled his caterer's smile.

"Hello, Mike," she said. "Everything looks fine."

"Thank you very much, Ms. Ripley. We wish to please in every way." Herrera would have moved on, but Ms. Ripley touched his arm, and he stopped politely, still smiling professionally.

Her voice was almost flirtatious. "Don't you approve of my home? Now that it's built? Isn't it better than an auditorium?"

"It is truly beautiful, Ms. Ripley."

She laughed. It wasn't a pleasant sound. Then she walked on.

Herrera moved on, too, but he muttered as he walked. He spoke in Spanish, but all Texas kids learn a few Spanish swear words in junior high. I was pretty sure I understood him. "Bitch," he said. "Bitch, bitch, bitch."

Herrera showed me to the built-in bar, which was about eight feet long. It was under the balcony and located between the kitchen and this big black-and-white whatever-it-was room—you couldn't call it a living room, certainly. A lifeless room, maybe?

Herrera introduced me to Jason, who was the head bartender. Around fifty, Jason had dark, dramatic eyes, but his hair was his most striking feature. He had a high forehead and a long tail of salt-and-pepper hair, which he wore just like I usually wore mine—in a clump at the back of his neck. The combination of bare forehead in front and long hair behind made him look as if his scalp had slipped backward. He smelled of some spicy cologne or aftershave. Jason asked me a few questions about my bartending experience, and while he talked, his hands kept busy arranging glasses. I went around the bar, knelt, and started handing him glasses from racks on the floor.

Herrera left us, and Jason leaned closer. "I saw the Ripper talking to Mike," he said. "What did she have to say?"

"Something about how she hoped he liked the house better than an auditorium. What did she mean by that?"

Jason rolled his eyes. "I'd better not say."

"Look," I said. "Is there something going on here that I need to know about?"

"I'd better shut up."

"Whatever you think," I said. Then I kept my mouth shut—a method I've found works like a charm when somebody says they don't want to tell you something. If you act as if you don't want to know—they'll tell you.

It took Jason thirty seconds to start talking again. "You know that Mike is mayor of Warner Pier?"

"No, Aunt Nettie never mentioned it."

"Warner Pier is too small a town to have a village idiot, you know. We all have to take turns."

I laughed. "So it's Mr. Herrera's turn to be mayor?"

"Yeah," Jason said. Or I think that's what he said. To a Texan, the Michigan "yeah" sounds a lot like the Dutch "ya." But they think I'm the one with an accent.

Jason was still talking. "Mike's been mayor for five years. Warner Point was one of the last bits of undeveloped land inside the city limits, and Mike had this great plan for it. He wanted to build a conference center that would attract business in the winter, as well as the summer."

"Get rid of the off-season slump?"

"It might have helped. A lot of us have to go on unemployment."

"But Clementine Ripley got the land instead?"

Jason nodded. "Oh, she'd owned the land for several years. She'd acted interested in selling it—Mike was about to propose a bond issue. Then all of a sudden she built this huge place. And she employs a grounds service, a housekeeping service, and a maintenance service—all out of Grand Rapids."

"Tough on Mr. Herrera's plan to increase year-round employment."

"If she just wouldn't keep rubbing it in."

Jason and I finished the glasses. Then he handed me a box knife, one of those gadgets that holds a razor blade, and told me to start opening cases of soft drinks and mixers. "This'll be a wine crowd," he said. "Maybe some beer. I don't think we'll have many requests for mixed drinks, but we'd better have several mixers out. Then you can slice the lemons and limes. Not too many. I'm going into the kitchen to chill wine."

I was kneeling on the floor, ripping open the first soft drink box, when I heard Marion McCoy's voice. "Here, kitty! Kitty, kitty, kitty!" I saw no sign of the cat, so I kept working with the box knife. Suddenly Ms. McCoy's face poked around the end of the bar.

"Oh!" I jumped up.

"Is that cat back there?" she said. Now I could see her dress. It was a basic black, and it hadn't come cheap, but it hung on her. She still looked weather-beaten and skinny, though she wasn't exactly flat-chested.

"No, Ms. McCoy. I haven't seen him."

She looked at me narrowly. "I know you—oh, you're the young woman from the TenHuis Chocolade. What are you doing here?"

I resisted the impulse to go into a detailed explanation. "Mr. Herrera needed an extra waitress."

"You're a waitress?"

"I was when I was in college. Now I'm an accountant. But all the Warner Pier merchants try to help each other out, and Mr. Herrera needed an extra set of hands. If I see the cat, I'll try to catch him."

"We wanted to shut him up in the office until he makes his appearance for the donors. He always jumps up on the tables and tries to get in the food."

I smiled, still determined, in my Texas way, to be friendly. But she was making me nervous. "I'll tell the others, and we'll try to keep him from sampling the bubbly—I mean, the buffet!"

Ms. McCoy sniffed, straightened up, and left. I heard, "Here, kitty, kitty," from the dining room.

I had the box open by then. So I stood up, leaned

over, and took two two-liter bottles of Diet Coke out of their box.

"Here. Lemme hep you."

A handsome, gray-haired man came around the corner of the bar. He took the bottles out of my hands, put them on the counter, then turned back with his hands out, ready for more bottles.

"Thanks," I said. I opened another box and handed him two club sodas, and he lined them up neatly at the left end of the work counter.

All the time I was trying to figure out who he was. He wasn't with Herrera Catering; I'd figured that out from his blue knit sports shirt. All us worker bees were wearing black and white. But he did seem familiar—a lean face with a grin that made him look rakish and with serious glasses that made him look reliable. But his most eye-catching characteristic was a gorgeous head of gray hair . . .

"Oh!" I said. "You were in the Mercedes convertible."

He looked at me narrowly, then smiled. "And yew were in the van." He definitely had a Texas accent. I had tried hard to get rid of my Texas accent, but this man had evidently tried to emphasize his.

"Right," I said. "And I think you're a guest, not an employee of Herrera Catering, so maybe you'd better get out from behind the bar before I get in trouble."

"Ah don't want yew to git into trouble!" He moved around the end of the bar. "I was about to ask for a favor, and I thought if I did one first . . ." He grinned, and it was a grin nobody could resist.

I didn't even try. "I do appreciate the help, and I'll be happy to do you a favor. Anything that's legal."

He leaned over the bar and dropped his voice. "I know you're not open yet. But do you hev any bourbon back there?"

"Sure. On the rocks?" I looked around for ice and

found none. "Actually, I don't have any rocks yet. But I can get some from the kitchen."

"Straight up will be fine. I kin git my own ice."

I found a bottle of bourbon—a very good brand—and used the tip of the box knife to break the seal. I found a shot glass, filled it, and poured it into an old-fashioned glass. Then I lifted my eyebrows and looked questioningly at the gray-haired gent. "Double?"

"Why not? I'm staying in Clementine's guest cottage, so I won't be driving, and I'm as dry as a west Texas toad frog." He stuck his hand over the bar in shaking position. "I'm a cosponsor of this wingding. Clementine Ripley is one of my clients. Duncan Ainsley."

"Oh, that's why you look famous!" Oh, God, I'd done it again. "I mean, I mean"—I was stammering—"I mean, familiar! You look familiar. I read an article about you in *Business Week,* Mr. Ainsley. I should have recognized you from your pictures."

Now he was the one who seemed surprised. "You read *Business Week*?" He kept holding my hand.

"I have a degree in accounting. Someday I'll take that CPA exam."

"Don't want to spend your whole life behind the bar? Good fer yew! And many thanks." He squeezed my hand, grinned again, and moved toward the kitchen.

Well, this might turn out to be an interesting party. Duncan Ainsley! Investments weren't my specialty, but the things I'd read about him sounded fascinating. Colorful Texan famous for his parties. Investment counselor to stars of stage and screen. And apparently to Clementine Ripley, too. No wonder she could afford the house at Warner Point.

Now I understood his accent. If Duncan Ainsley was operating out of Dallas or Houston, he'd try to sound like he'd been to Harvard. Since he was a

Texan operating out of Chicago, he used his Texas talk to make himself stand out from the crowd of Harvard MBAs. The thought of Duncan Ainsley kept me pepped up while I sliced the lemons and limes, then put olives and cherries in little dishes on the bar.

In a minute I scented Jason's spicy cologne, and I looked up to see him walking toward me. Then there was a flash of white fluff, and Jason screeched as he was attacked by a giant ball of fur.

Champion Myanmar Chocolate Yonkers had jumped down, apparently from the balcony, and landed on Jason's shoulder, barely missing the long queue. Using Jason as a springboard, he bounced on over to the bar.

It was hilarious, but I tried not to laugh. Jason didn't look amused, for one thing, and for another, the cat was now reaching a languorous paw out toward the dish I had just filled with olives.

"Oh, no!" I said. "Those are not for cats. Even gorgeous champion chocolate cats." And I grabbed.

I guess Champion Yonkers didn't expect to be denied his little treat. Anyway, he didn't dodge in time, and I was able to scoop him up. He gave a low snarl, and he kicked, but I had him.

"Into the office with you, fella," I said. "If I only knew where it was."

I carried the enormous cat out from behind the bar and started looking. I assumed Ms. McCoy had meant the office I had visited earlier that day, somewhere at the east end of the house. So I went past the kitchen and into a hall that seemed to lead in the right direction. At least I'd get to see a few more rooms of the house.

Almost immediately I found myself in a covered corridor, maybe forty feet long, with windows on both sides and a room at the far end. A parabola? Pergola? I was a little hazy on the name of this architectural feature. I was beginning to figure out that the house wasn't really one big building. It was a series of little buildings strung together. I'd heard a couple of people call it "the village," and that name was close to the feel of the thing. The tower—the "sore thumb"—was a sort of village church steeple.

As I entered the room at the end of the passageway, I called out, "Ms. McCoy!" She didn't answer.

This was obviously not one of the public areas of the house. It was too pleasant and homey, with some comfortable-looking chairs and a couch covered in a nubby fabric in front of a rustic-looking fireplace. The color scheme was still severe, but it had texture. I could remember my Dallas decorator talking about "texture." Texture is good.

"Ms. McCoy?" Still no answer.

I was sure the office had been at this end of the house. I spotted a hall with doors on either side of it. I opened one and peeked through. "Ha!" It was the utility room I had gone through when Ms. McCoy showed me out. That meant that the room on the left should be the office.

I knocked at the door. No answer there, either. Champion Yonkers yowled and kicked.

"Sorry, Champ," I said. "I think this is where you're supposed to be." I opened the door and found myself facing the big walnut desk. Marion McCoy was sitting behind it. We both jumped.

"Oh!" I said. "Is this where you wanted the cat?"

"Yes! Give him to me."

I handed him over, and Ms. McCoy held him at arm's length, apparently trying to keep the cat hair off her basic black. But Yonkers saw prison on the horizon, and he wasn't happy. He yowled and kicked, and he managed to draw blood from her wrist.

"Ouch! Let me help you," I said. "Bad cat!" I quickly closed the door behind me, then looked around the room and spotted a box of tissues on an end table. I plucked one and held it out to her.

Ms. McCoy put Champion Yonkers down. He ran under the desk and knocked over a small wastebasket, then looked at us proudly.

"You're a naughty cat," I said. Ms. McCoy was pressing the tissue to her arm. "You should put something on that. Cat scratches can be dangerous."

"Yonk never roams through garbage cans," Mrs. McCoy said. "Just the office trash."

I knelt and started scooping papers back into the wastebasket.

"I can take care of that," Ms. McCoy said. She was glaring now. I didn't understand why she should be mad. She certainly was acting oddly. "I'm sure you need to get back to the bar."

I was dismissed. I stood up. And as I did Champion Yonkers jumped out from under the desk. He capered about, knocking some wadded-up papers around like balls.

"You're a character," I told him as I edged toward the door. "And you were right, Ms. McCoy. He jumped down onto the barker—I mean the bartender—I guess from that balcony. The he tried to eat the olives."

"Jumping down like that is one of his favorite tricks. Thank you for bringing him back. You can go now."

"Certainly." But before I could open the door, something shot out across the floor and hit my foot. Champion Yonkers chased it, still capering around. I looked down, but Ms. McCoy moved casually, and her foot almost touched mine. Something crunched.

Startled, I looked around. "Did something break?"

"It's that cat," Ms. McCoy said easily. Her glare had softened into a watchful look. "I'll clean it up. Would you mind taking those two glasses on the coffee table back to the kitchen?"

I nodded. In a chair near the door, I saw a wad of plastic, and I recognized it as a pair of the plastic gloves used by food-service workers. "How did these get here?" I said. I scooped them up and stuck them in my pocket. Then I picked up two glasses from the coffee table. One smelled strongly of bourbon. "Sorry about the scratch," I said, and I left.

I went back through the sitting room and down the corridor or pergola or whatever—suddenly I remembered. "Peristyle," I said. "It's a peristyle."

Well, I was glad I hadn't tried to say *that* in front of Marion McCoy. It would probably have come out "parachute" or "percolator."

Why did the woman intimidate me so much? I wondered all the way down the peristyle, past the kitchen, and into the huge, cold reception room.

And there I stopped, because six people were looking in my direction in horror.

For a moment I wondered wildly just what I had done. Then I realized that they weren't looking at me. All six of them were staring at something over my head. And whatever it was, it was making a horrible choking sound.

I quickly took six steps forward and whirled to see what they were looking at, what the ghastly noise was.

I looked up just in time to see Clementine Ripley tumble over the balcony rail.

She hit the floor in front of the bar, landing all splayed out, like a beanbag toy. She didn't move. But something brown and white rolled toward me and stopped at my feet.

It was a half-eaten Amaretto truffle.

CHOCOLATE CHAT

HEALTH

- Chocolate is only figuratively "to die for." Modern nutrition has found many health benefits in the luscious stuff. Chocolate contains antioxidants, a substance that protects cells. A 1.4-ounce piece of milk chocolate typically has four hundred milligrams of antioxidants. A piece of dark chocolate the same size has twice as many, but white chocolate—which contains cocoa butter only—contains none.

- Chocolate does contain caffeine. But even a dark chocolate bar contains from a tenth to a third of the caffeine found in one cup of coffee.

- But isn't chocolate fattening? Not in moderation. In Switzerland, where the annual consumption of chocolate is twice that of the United States, the obesity rate is half as high.

- While chocolate may not harm humans, it can be lethal to dogs and cats. Both the Cat Fancier's Assocation and the American Veterinary Medicine Association warn against allowing either species to have chocolate in any form.

Chapter 4

I reached down to pick up the Amaretto truffle, just on general principles of neatness. But before I could grab it, Mike Herrera stepped in front of me, blocking me like an opposing guard jumping in front of a top scorer. He didn't single me out, but shooed all of us into the kitchen.

The Warner Pier hospital closed several years ago, so the village relies on a team of volunteer EMTs, and someone called them pronto. While we waited, Jason, who turned out to be Herrera Catering's official first aider, did what he could. Of course, there was nothing anyone could do for Clementine Ripley. All of us who had seen her fall knew that. I felt sure she had been dead before she fell over the balcony rail. She certainly hadn't moved after she hit the floor.

The speculation in the kitchen was that she'd had a stroke. "My grandmother dropped over just the same way," Lindy said. "Got up to answer the phone and died before she could get into the living room." Everybody nodded wisely and muttered about Clementine Ripley's heart.

But the chef who'd been preparing the nest for the steamboat round laughed harshly and spoke under his breath. "What heart?" he said.

The paramedics arrived within ten minutes, and

Jason came into the kitchen with the rest of us. He was shaking his head, and his aftershave was almost overpowered by sweat. "God, Mike," he said. "I was afraid to touch her much. The way she fell—her neck . . ."

"I do not think eet is of importance," Mr. Herrera said. Excitement had brought out his accent. "Eet's hokay."

Jason shook harder. "If Greg just wasn't on duty—"

"Everybody knows hee's an idiot," Herrera said.

Lindy and I were leaning against the sink. She snorted. "Oh, no! Not Greg Gossip!"

I spoke in an undertone. "Greg who?"

"Gregory Glossop," Lindy said. "You remember, Mr. Glossop at the Superette pharmacy? He's a creep."

"All I remember was that Aunt Nettie always insisted that her prescriptions be filled at Downtown Drugs."

"That's because Gregory Glossop is such a blabbermouth. I bought some prenatal caps in there the day I found out I was pregnant with little Tony, and the phone was ringing when I got home. My mom's club had already set a date for the baby shower."

"What's Mr. Glossop doing as a paramedic?"

She shrugged. "He took the training and all. I think he just hates to miss anything."

We stood silently, and in a minute I heard a loud voice coming from the cold room where Clementine Ripley was lying on the cold floor. It was a prissy, high-pitched tenor, and its owner had projection. The voice carried into every corner of the kitchen.

"Well! I'm willing to stake my reputation on it." The tenor's voice was filled with pleasure.

Lindy grimaced. "There he goes. Greg Gossip."

A deeper voice, a baritone, muttered, but I couldn't catch the words.

The tenor squawked again. "You're going to have to call in the state police!"

The baritone made soothing sounds, but the tenor didn't calm down.

"Well! I believe that piece of candy killed her!"

A piece of candy killed her? One particular piece? That was the most ridiculous thing I'd ever heard. What could a single chocolate do? Send her into some kind of diabetic fit? Or was it one piece too many—a chocolate last straw, as it were—and it laid down the final piece of plaque on a key artery, giving Clementine Ripley a heart attack? How could the guy—whoever he was—say a piece of candy could kill anybody?

While I was thinking all that, the lower voice rumbled again. Then the tenor answered, even higher than ever.

"Chief, this is cyanide poisoning! I can smell the scent of almonds."

Well, that did it. The tenor was claiming that one of my aunt's delicious chocolates had contained poison. I wasn't going to stand for it.

I walked to the kitchen door, pushed past Mike Herrera, crossed the dining room, and entered the room where Clementine Ripley had died.

"Of course, that chocolate smells like almonds," I said loudly. "It's an armadillo truffle!"

That stopped everybody in the room in their tracks. Two paramedics kneeling by Clementine Ripley swiveled their heads toward me, and two uniformed cops, both very young, swung around to see who this fool was. But I focused on the two men who were facing each other in the center of the room. They had to be the tenor and the baritone who had been arguing. They had also whipped their heads in my direction when I spoke up.

I walked closer to them before I said any more. "I mean, Amaretto. It's an Amaretto truffle," I said. "I work for TenHuis Chocolade. We furnished the chocolates for the party, and Nettie TenHuis sent an extra half dozen Amaretto truffles for Clementine Ripley personally."

Both men stared at me. The taller man seemed familiar, and in a moment I realized he was the man who had backed up his police car and let me out of Clementine Ripley's driveway that afternoon. Standing up, he looked like Abraham Lincoln with a shave and a buzz cut. His features hinted that he'd been in several fights over the years, but he didn't look tough or angry. In fact, he was peering over the top of a pair of half glasses, and the angle of his head gave an impish look to his soft brown eyes. He looked humorous, somehow, but dependable.

He spoke calmly, repeating the key word. "Amaretto?" I recognized the deep voice I had heard from the kitchen.

I nodded. "Yes. It's an almond-flavored liqueur. Aunt Nettie uses it in that particular chocolate."

The second man sputtered again. "Well! I don't care what flavor the chocolates were," he said. "I still think Ms. Ripley was killed by cyanide."

This man was several inches shorter than I am. He was chubby and almost completely bald, and he had light-colored eyelashes and eyebrows. The combination managed to give the impression that he had more skin than the rest of us. His pouty little mouth was pursed into a disagreeable little circle.

"It's not up to me to say how cyanide could have gotten into the candy," he said. "That will be up to law enforcement authorities. But I'd be derelict in my duty if I smelled that almond aroma and said nothing."

"We wouldn't want you to be derelict in your duty," the tall man said. He spoke deliberately. "And now, miss, I gather that you're Mrs. TenHuis's niece."

"Yes. I'm Lee McKinney."

"I'm Hogan Jones. I'm chief of police for Warner Pier. And I gather that you know something about the chocolates."

"I delivered them."

"Tell me about it."

I told him. About how Aunt Nettie had taken the bonbons, truffles, molded chocolate, and fruits from the workroom storage and loaded them onto the silver trays that Clementine Ripley had sent. And how she had prepared a small box with samples.

"Did you see her put the chocolates in that box?"

"No. She did it while I was combing my hair. But I'm sure someone saw her. There's nothing sneaky about Aunt Nettie. And she's very proud of the quality of her chocolates."

The tenor—he wore an EMT jacket—sniffed. "Well! She may be proud of her candies, but we all know she had a good reason not to like Clementine Ripley."

I turned on him. "I've only been back in Warner Pier a week, and I've already heard all kinds of bad things about Clementine Ripley. She was supposedly crooked. She beat the city out of this land and hurt the community economically. Plus, every news magazine in the country has had some story about how she kept some guilty clinic—I mean, client!—out of prison. Who did like her?"

"I used to."

The words came from behind me, near the French doors. I whirled toward the speaker.

It was Joe Woodyard. He was standing in one of the doorways that led out to the terrace.

I could have died on the spot. Not only had I been speaking ill of the dead—I'd been doing it at the top of my voice in front of the dead's ex-husband. I expected Joe to tear into me about the way I'd been talking about Clementine Ripley.

But he didn't pay any attention to me.

"Hi, Joe," the police chief said. "This is bad business. How'd you find out about it?"

"Hugh called me."

"Ah." The chief nodded.

Hugh? Wasn't that the security guard? I didn't ask the question. In fact, I stood as still as a rabbit with a coyote nosing around outside its hole. I didn't move. I didn't speak. I didn't do anything that might call anyone's attention to me.

Joe Woodyard walked around the three of us, zigzagged past the uniformed cops, and knelt beside Clementine Ripley's body. I couldn't see his face. He reached out and touched her hair gently. Then he stood up and turned toward the police chief. He looked pretty serious.

"I assume you'll do an autopsy."

Chief Jones nodded. "We'd have to, Joe. Unattended death. You have any objection?"

"It wouldn't matter if I did. I've been out of the picture for two years, remember?"

"How come you're here?"

"Clementine and I might not have been able to live together, but I didn't wish her any harm." Joe nodded toward me. "Like the lady says, Clementine was pretty short on friends. And she didn't have any family. Except maybe Marion. And Hugh said Marion took off for Holland right before somebody called the EMTs."

"We're looking for Ms. McCoy now," the chief said. "Joe, I'd appreciate it if you'd hang around awhile."

Joe nodded. He pulled a spindly Windsor chair away from the wall, moved it toward Clementine Ripley's body, and put it down several feet from her head. "I'll be here," he said. "I'll stay until they take her away."

He sat down in the chair, and though he didn't

snap out a salute, bark out orders, or even sit up straight—actually, he leaned over with his elbows on his knees, clasped his hands, and stared at the floor—it was clear that he was standing guard over his ex-wife.

The EMTs brought in a sheet and laid it over Ms. Ripley. Gregory Glossop helped them, but he didn't say another word. The chief conferred quietly with his two uniformed officers. I made a quick retreat to the kitchen and slunk into my spot beside Lindy.

She leaned close and spoke in my ear. "What happened?"

I shook my head. I didn't want to describe either my stupidity or Joe Woodyard's behavior.

Why had Joe married Clementine Ripley? She was a lot older than he was. She was also a lot richer, and he'd been asking her for money earlier that day. The conventional opinion around Warner Pier would probably be that he married her for money—just as most of Rich's friends had thought I married him for his money—or to advance his career as an attorney. But somehow I thought Joe's relationship with Clementine had been more than that.

Whatever Clementine Ripley had been, she was definitely not a fool. She must have known that "everyone," whoever that is, would have thought she bought Joe as a boy toy, a plaything. I couldn't imagine a woman with the ego Clementine Ripley must have had allowing her friends to laugh at her over her choice of a husband. Unless Joe had fooled her completely, and his behavior now was another act. I'd never know. It was, I reminded myself, none of my business.

The catering crew huddled in the kitchen until we got the word that we could pack up and leave. Mike Herrera came in, smiled, and told us we were all wonderful employees, and he appreciated our calmness. The food, he said, was to be donated to the homeless shelter in Holland. He didn't explain who made that decision.

I didn't quarrel with that—obviously, the party was off—but it made me wonder about Marion McCoy. I couldn't believe she wasn't out there giving orders. If she'd gone to Holland—which was an odd thing to do right before a party—hadn't she taken a cell phone? Had anybody even told her that Ms. Ripley was dead?

And Duncan Ainsley? Where was he? If he was a house guest—he'd told me he was staying in "the guest cottage"—you'd think he'd show some concern over the death of his hostess.

All the Herrera Catering employees bustled around, putting the glasses, plates, and silverware back into their racks, wrapping rolls, refolding tablecloths, and stuffing napkins into sacks. I tried to help—I expected to be paid and wanted to earn my wages—but somebody had to explain everything about the routine to me.

When the new excitement began I was in the dining room concentrating on refolding tablecloths. The others on the crew were nudging each other and whispering before I caught the raised voices from the big room and realized something was going on.

"You've got to be wrong!" It sounded like a scream from a tortured animal. I had to listen to the second scream before I could identify the voice as coming from Marion McCoy.

"I only ran into Holland for a few minutes! Clementine can't be *dead*!"

A low rumble answered her. It could have been either the police chief or Joe Woodyard. But whatever was said didn't mollify Marion.

"No! No! It can't be true!"

Then I heard Greg Glossop's whiny tenor. "She may have been poisoned," he said. He sounded self-important.

"Poisoned!" Marion was still out of control. "That's impossible!"

Another voice tried to calm her. Was it Duncan Ainsley.

Then Marion again. "It must have been natural causes! No one would have wanted to hurt Clementine!"

That's not the way I'd heard it, of course. I kept folding, resisting the temptation to look around. But I admit I was listening hard.

"Nobody would have wanted to hurt Clementine." Marion said it more quietly. Then she gave a gasp. "Except—except you!"

Then I did look around. Marion was pointing at Joe Woodyard.

"Don't be silly, Marion," Joe answered her calmly. "I know you and I never got along, but Clem and I had settled our differences two years ago."

"Oh, is that true? Then why were you arguing with her just a few hours ago?"

"We didn't have an argument."

"Didn't you? You were here asking for money."

Joe didn't answer, and when I looked through the archway that separated the dining room from the living room, I saw that his face was like a thundercloud rolling in over the lake.

Marion McCoy evidently thought she was winning, and she pressed her advantage. "He was here, Chief Jones. And he did ask for money." She looked around, her face furious and excited, and her eyes rested on me.

"I can prove it, too," she said. "There was another witness. That woman from TenHuis Chocolade!"

She pointed at me, and everybody in the room turned in my direction. The chief, Joe, and Marion—all of them stared at me.

"Lee McKinney!" Marion McCoy said. "She can back me up. She heard every word Joe said!"

Chapter 5

I didn't do the first thing that occurred to me—turn and run out the kitchen door. I stood still, looking at everybody looking at me.

I'm not a fast thinker. If I hadn't become aware of this on my own over the years, I have plenty of friends and family who tell me about it. So I compensate. I don't act in a hurry. Rich used to yell at me over it. "Why are you just sitting there? Say something!" But I've found out from sad experience that, when I pop off and do or say the first thing that comes into my head, it usually lands me in a worse mess than I was in to begin with. As the old saying goes, it's better to keep quiet and be thought a fool than to say something and remove all doubt.

So after Marion McCoy yelled at me, I just stood there, and Marion, Joe Woodyard, Chief Jones, Duncan Ainsley, and two members of the Herrera Catering crew all stared at me.

Then Marion McCoy spoke again. "Well? You heard him, right? You heard Joe Woodyard demanding money from Clementine. If I heard him, you must have heard him, too. So tell the chief about it!"

After that, I knew what I wanted to do—the opposite of whatever Marion McCoy wanted me to do. So

I picked up the tablecloth I'd been told to put away, and I matched up the right and left corners and shook it out, ready to fold again. Then I turned toward Marion McCoy, and I said, "I'm sorry, but if there's some sort of quarrel going on out here, it's none of my affair. I will be happy to answer any questions Chief Jones has for me, but for now I don't think I'll make any comment."

Marion McCoy looked as if she were going to explode. Joe Woodyard gave a barking laugh—just one *Ha!*—and Chief Jones looked over the top of his glasses and grinned.

Duncan Ainsley patted Marion's shoulder awkwardly. His hands were shaking. "Now, Marion," he said. "The chief will be taking statements from all the witnesses. Why don't you go back to your apartment? You prob'ly feel like the ragged end of a misspent life."

I had to admire the guy. He could keep up the colorful Texan act even when he seemed shook up himself. He escorted Marion past me, into the hall that led to the office where I'd taken the cat. He was all attention as he walked with her, patting her arm, very much the friend who was helping her cope with the death of her employer.

There was just one odd thing. Right before he led Marion McCoy past me, as he reached a point when only I could see him, he nodded and winked at me.

What did that mean?

Of course, an investment counselor—even a famous one—is basically a salesman. That sort of gesture, designed to build rapport, was second nature to a man like Duncan Ainsley. There was no way he could have a personal interest in me.

Not long after that Mike Herrera told Lindy and me that we were finished, and the police chief didn't seem to have any more interest in us, though he warned that we might have to make formal statements later. The phrase "after we know the cause of death" was left unsaid.

So Lindy and I left. I was surprised that there was no crowd outside the heavy security gate. I guess I lived in a big city too long; I'd expected a lot of reporters to be gathered there, but the street was empty. I reminded myself that Warner Pier is a long way from major news agencies. As for the expected guests, Clementine Ripley had died two hours before the benefit was scheduled to begin, so apparently somebody—maybe Mike Herrera—had known whom to call to announce that the party was canceled. The security guard—Hugh?—would have turned away any guests who showed up.

I will say, however, that as we drove back toward the main part of Warner Pier we saw an unusual number of people sitting on their screened-in porches; it was a warm evening, and maybe they didn't have air-conditioning. But they all seemed to be paying close attention to the vehicles driving by. Warner Pier wasn't ignoring Clementine Ripley's death, whatever had caused it.

Personally, I was betting on natural causes.

It wasn't dark yet—just after eight o'clock. Ten-Huis Chocolade would be open another hour. I dropped Lindy off at her house and declined her halfhearted invitation to come in. Tony came out to the car and we spoke briefly; I wouldn't have known him as the skinny kid who used to flirt with Lindy over a limeade at the Downtown Drugs soda fountain. He'd grown five or six inches and gained forty pounds in the ten years since I'd seen him.

I saw what Lindy meant about his trying to get in touch with his Hispanic heritage. When we'd been in high school, Tony had tried hard not to look Mexican, while his father had been definitely Latino. Now his father just looked like a dark-haired American, and Tony had grown a mustache and sideburns.

I drove back to the chocolate shop and parked in the alley. As soon as I walked inside, Aunt Nettie ran to meet me. "Lee! Are you all right?"

"Of course. What are you doing here? You were supposed to go home at four."

"I had to make sure you were okay. I went out to Clementine Ripley's house, but they wouldn't let me in. What happened?"

I told her the story, but I slurred over the chocolates and the accusations that Gregory Glossop had made about one of them containing cyanide. I told her he had suggested cyanide poisoning, but I didn't specifically say that he'd accused an Amaretto truffle of being responsible for her death.

As I finished, Aunt Nettie shook her head. "Terrible, terrible. Such a thing to happen. And that Gregory Gossip! He's terrible, too."

"Then you don't trust his opinion on the cause of death?"

"Of course not. Greg always wants things to be as bad as possible. Nobody would poison anybody in Warner Pier. It's just a little place!"

I was torn. Should I tell her the rest, prepare her for the worst? Or let well enough alone? Which cliché applied?

Before I could decide, the phone rang.

I answered. "TenHuis Chocolade."

"Oh! Are yew open?" The voice on the phone was startled, but it still sounded Texan.

I checked my watch. Eight-thirty. "We close in half an hour."

"Ah see. Is this Lee McKinney?"

"Yes." The accent made the caller's identity plain. "Is this Mr. Ainsley?"

He laughed. "Shore is. I guess it's impossible for me to hide up here in Michigan. But if I try to talk different, it's like putting a high-dollar saddle on a jackass."

Why on earth was he calling? I wondered, but I tried to be polite. "My Texas grandma would have said your accent sounds as nice as a cotton hat."

"I'd better watch you, young lady. A Texas gal can tell when I'm bullin'. But when I called I was expectin' an answerin' machine. Do y'all work round the clock?"

"The shop is open from ten a.m. until nine p.m. My aunt comes in at eight, since she's in charge of making the chocolates. I come in at noon and work until the place is closed and the cleanup finished. Why? Did you need chocolates tonight?"

Ainsley chuckled. "An emergency chocolate attack? No, I just wanted to tell you I'm sorry Ms. McPicky"—his voice was scornful—"tried to put you on the spot, and to tell you that you handled her as smart as a tree full of owls."

"Thank you, Mr. Ainsley." I assumed he was trying to explain the wink. "I know Ms. McCoy's really upset."

"She is, as we all are, so we have to make allowances. But she shouldn't have asked you to make a statement discrediting your friend."

"You mean Joe Woodyard? I really can't claim him as a friend. I was one of the girls who used to hang around on the beach when he was a lifeguard. That was twelve years ago. I doubt he even remembered me, except as a face in the crowd."

"Oh, then you're not seeing him—socially?"

"Oh, no! I hadn't thought of him in years. When we ran into each other this afternoon, it took me a few minutes to figure out who he was."

"I see. Well, in that case . . ." He paused for a moment, then spoke again. "Well, before I go back to Chicago I just wanted to assure you that you shouldn't be upset over Marion's actions, and to say you handled the situation as slick as a peeled onion."

"Thank you, Mr. Ainsley."

"Please call me Duncan."

Well, that was peculiar. What did it matter what a peon like Lee McKinney called a man like Duncan Ainsley? He wasn't coming on to me, was he? Back when I'd been a beauty queen, that had been known to happen. But now that I had gone in for the natural look . . . Ainsley mystified me.

"I appreciate your call," I said lamely. "Then you're leaving tonight?"

"The police asked me to stay overnight. It's kind of awkward, being a house guest when the hostess dies. It's not as if we were even close friends. Clementine just asked me to stay because I was a cosponsor for this event that didn't come off. But I'm assuming the police will let me go in the morning, after they get this druggist fellow's stupid ideas straightened out."

"Then you don't take the cyanide charge seriously?"

"Of course not! From what Marion said, I guess this man and Clementine had had some sort of disagreement earlier. But the thought of someone poisoning Clementine is plumb silly."

"I thought she had a lot of enemies."

"Well, yes. If a disgruntled client shot her—but to poison her in her own house? That's ridiculous. Anyway, I do want to keep on top of the situation. Could I call you again?"

The request surprised me, and I reacted with my usual aplomb. I gasped and said, "What for?"

Ainsley chuckled. "You're a bright young woman. Perhaps I might at least call on you for local knowledge as the situation develops?"

I was even more surprised at that idea. And right then another strange thing happened. I looked out into the shop—as I said, the office had glass windows that overlooked the workroom where the chocolates were made and the little retail shop—just as the street door opened.

Joe Woodyard walked in.

He looked through the several thicknesses of glass that separated us, and he glared at me.

I stood holding the phone, completely silent, until I heard Duncan Ainsley's voice again. "Lee? May I call you? For local background?"

Suddenly I was very nervous. "I'll be happy to help in any way I can," I said. "But I'm not really a yokel." And I hung up.

I stood there, feeling like a complete fool and staring at Joe Woodyard. This was all too strange. First a call from Duncan Ainsley. Then a visit from Joe Woodyard. I couldn't believe my personal magnetism was suddenly attracting all the men I'd met that day.

Like other Warner Pier retailers, Aunt Nettie hired the children of friends to deal with the summer trade, and now Joe was talking to the teenager behind the counter, a girl with brown hair tucked into a stringy ponytail. She was no dippier than I had been the summer I was sixteen and worked for TenHuis Chocolade for the first time. She gestured behind her while she spoke to Joe. Then she came to the door to the shop and beckoned to me. "You have a visitor."

I went to the counter.

Joe scowled. "I just wanted to talk to you about that scene out there. Marion has her reasons—"

Little Miss Teenage Counter Help was drinking in the whole conversation. I interrupted Joe. "Come on back."

I ignored the disappointed look on the teenager—I'd just met her the day before, and I couldn't remember her name. I decided the office was a little too close to the front counter, so I led Joe back to the break room. It's more like an old-fashioned dining room, since it's furnished with a heavy oak dining suite, including a tall china cupboard, which had belonged to Aunt Nettie's grandmother, and with several mismatched easy chairs. The floor may be easy-to-clean tile, and the only window may look out on an alley, but the room is bright and cheerful, and even decorated with several watercolors painted by local artists. Aunt Nettie and Uncle Phil used to eat dinner there a lot.

Joe Woodyard frowned. "I guess you and your aunt live here."

It wasn't such an odd thing to say. Nearly all the "downtown" businesses in Warner Pier have apartments upstairs, and some of the merchants do live over their shops.

"No," I said. "But Aunt Nettie's hours are so long she must feel as if she lives here. She comes to work before eight in the morning, and since Uncle Phil died she's been staying until closing a lot of the time." I turned to face Joe. "What did you want to talk to me about?"

"About what happened out at Warner Point." He frowned again. I was beginning to get impatient with Mr. Woodyard. Had he come down to the shop to bawl me out?

"Listen," he said. "I can handle the situation. Don't get any dumb ideas about helping me out. Just keep your mouth shut."

Actually, his remarks made me open my mouth. I was so astonished at what he had said that my jaw dropped like a drawbridge. I was so surprised that I didn't even get mad, at least right away.

"What do you mean?" I said.

"Just because we once knew each other, that doesn't mean you have to cover up for me or anything. Don't let anybody get the idea that we're friends."

What in the world was he talking about? Did he

think that I'd refused to repeat his remarks to Chief Jones because I had a personal interest in him?

Suddenly I was furious. What a jerk!

Joe spoke again. "If Marion heard what I said to Clem, then you must have heard it, too. But you'll be better off if you just say no comment."

"What?"

"I had a legitimate reason for asking Clem for money. I simply don't want—"

By then I knew what I wanted to say, and I said it. "Stop! You keep *your* mouth shut!"

He obeyed so fast his jaws snapped, and I was the one who went on.

"What I said out there had nothing to do with you. If the chief asks me, I'll tell him exactly what I heard. I just didn't want Marion McCoy ordering me around. And frankly, I don't want you ordering me around, either."

"What do you mean? Ordering you around?"

"Why did you come by here to tell me how to handle the situation?"

"The situation? What are you talking about?"

"Chief Jones, of course."

"I don't care about him. Tell him any damn thing you want!"

"Then what are you talking about?"

"I'm trying to warn you about the tabloids."

"Tabloids? I'm not interested in the tabloids."

Joe laughed harshly. "About this time tomorrow you will be."

"What do you mean?"

"After the tabloid reporters hit town, ready to make big bucks from Clementine's death, then you'll care. When you've seen your life displayed for the grocery-store checkout line, you get sort of paranoid."

Maybe I looked surprised, because he laughed again.

"Oh, nobody reads them! Or admits it. But somehow all the people you thought were your friends know what was in the latest issue."

"Why would the tabloids be interested in Clementine Ripley? She was a lawyer, not a movie star."

"True, but she represented a lot of celebrities. When the word got out that we were married—God! It was awful. I was still with Legal Aid, but all of a sudden I couldn't get any work done. I didn't have a staff to insulate me from the reporters the way Clem did. Can you imagine trying to represent some woman whose ex-husband has been using his court-ordered visitation to beat their baby—and you have to do it with a dozen photographers swarming you every time you came out of the courtroom?"

"You may have had problems, but . . ."

Joe didn't hear me. "When we split and I started the boat business, it was worse. For about a month every time I dipped a brush in varnish or sawed a board, a strobe flashed."

"But . . ."

Joe smiled, but he didn't look amused. "I guess I deserved it. Obscure young lawyer walks out on famous wife, chucks law for manual labor," he said, as if quoting a headline. "Defense attorney's toy boy husband flees toy box."

"Stop!" I'd had enough. "Hush up!"

Joe shut up and glared.

I glared back. "Why am I getting this lecture? No reporters will be interested in me."

"Oh, yes, they will. You were a witness. You're involved."

"No, I'm not! And TenHuis Chocolade isn't, either."

"That's the spirit. Just remember that. No matter who calls you—*Time* magazine or the *National Enquirer*—just tell 'em they'll have to talk to the police."

I did my thinking-about-it act for thirty seconds.

"Why do you think you need to tell me this? Do I seem that stupid?"

"No. I'm telling you because you're going to be getting a lot of pressure." He stopped and seemed to consider his next words. "And now I'd better get out of here before the correspondents arrive from Chicago, or you and your aunt are likely to get the full treatment."

"What do you mean?"

"Oh, the tabloids would love our getting together like this, in a quiet back room. Cinderella widower of famed lawyer has tête-à-tête with high school sweetheart."

"That's not true! You and I weren't sweethearts. We barely knew each other."

"The tabloids don't care. They take one little lie and hang a whole string of phony implications on it. Didn't my mom tell me you were in some beauty contest? They'll dig that up. Famed attorney killed by beauty queen's chocolates."

As Joe said the final, bitter word, I heard a loud gasp behind me. For a mad moment I thought the tabloid press had already arrived, and I swung around.

I was relieved for a second. The gasp had come from Aunt Nettie. Then I saw the look on her face.

"Chocolate? The chocolate killed Clementine Ripley? That's just not possible!"

I tried to soothe her. I explained that Gregory Glossop had picked up on the smell of almonds from the chocolates, but that the Amaretto flavoring was a more logical explanation for the aroma.

Joe lost some of his glare when he talked to Aunt Nettie. "Lee jumped right in and told the chief about the flavoring," he said. "Greg Glossop may be an idiot, but his opinion won't count. The medical examiner will be running scientific tests to ascertain the cause of death. And I hope to God it's natural causes."

He gestured. "Is that the alley door? Can I get out that way?"

"Wait," Aunt Nettie said. For the first time I realized that she was holding a TenHuis Chocolade box. "I've got something for you."

Joe took the box, looking perplexed. "Chocolates? Nettie, I don't think this is a good time . . ."

"It's just a sandwich," she said. "A chocolate box was all I had to put it in. A meat loaf sandwich and some carrot sticks. I'm sure you haven't eaten anything. I wish I had something worth giving you."

For a moment Joe stared at her blankly. Then he gave a mocking laugh. "Nettie, you just don't get it," he said. "We can't be friends right now! It will cause too much trouble. Lee, you explain it to her!"

That made me madder than anything else he'd said.

"I won't tell her a thing!" I said. "Aunt Nettie is Aunt Nettie, and if she wants to feed the whole world, it's all right with me."

"I give up," Joe said. "Is that the alley door?"

I opened it without a word, and he went out into the dark. "You two are going to be eaten alive," he said.

I resisted the temptation to slam the door after him. He hadn't even thanked Aunt Nettie for his meat loaf sandwich. But he took it with him.

Chapter 6

Aunt Nettie made me eat a meat loaf sandwich, too. I sat at a stainless-steel worktable in the back of the shop, and she talked to me while I ate.

As she talked she plucked bits of rum-flavored dark chocolate nougat—nougat is what the chocolate maker calls the filling of a truffle—from a plastic dish. This had been mixed earlier and set aside to get firm. Talking a mile a minute, she rolled each piece of nougat into a ball. She made five dozen while I ate my sandwich, her hands working as fast as her mouth. Now and then she stopped to weigh one, to make sure they were all uniform in size, but she didn't once have to start over. Then she took a mixing bowl and drew several cups of dark chocolate from the spigot on the big electric kettle, where a supply is always kept warm and melted. She rolled each nougat ball in the dark chocolate, creating a rum-flavored truffle to die for. And she did it all without looking at her hands. It was a darn impressive performance.

By the time I'd eaten, the counter girls had finished cleaning up the shop. I balanced the cash register, and Aunt Nettie and I went out to the house she and Uncle Phil had shared for thirty-nine of their forty years of marriage. During one year they'd lived in the Netherlands, learning the chocolate business.

I find the house both homey and spooky. It's on the south edge of Warner Pier on Lake Shore Drive. I guess that every town that borders Lake Michigan has a Lake Shore Drive.

We're on the inland side—in other words, we don't have a view of the lake. A lot of well-to-do people have built either summer cottages or year-round homes in the neighborhood, but Aunt Nettie's house is older than most. It was built by my great-grandfather—Uncle Phil's grandfather—in 1904. He was a carpenter in Grand Rapids who put it up as a summer cottage for his wife and kids. One of his sons, my grandfather, opened a gas station in Warner Pier in 1945, and he winterized the family cottage so that he and his family could live there year-round.

So my mother and Uncle Phil grew up in the house. It's a white two-story frame house, with odd bits sticking out here and there for a bathroom and a dining room and a screened porch, which were added on over the years. It's not luxurious; the bathroom has a claw-footed tub that was probably bought secondhand in 1910 and the kitchen sink was new in 1918. It has a "Michigan basement"—cement walls, but a sand floor—which I think must have been ideal for farm families needing a place to store apples and potatoes, but seems kind of odd in the twenty-first century. The decor is authentic country, not decorator "country," and features an accumulation of furniture old enough to be antique, but not valuable enough to be worth selling. As I said, it's homey.

I also find it spooky, because the area is heavily wooded. That makes it beautiful, I suppose, to anybody who wasn't born and raised on the Texas plains. I've read that people raised in wooded areas find plains threatening because the openness makes them feel exposed. But plains people like me find woods threatening because we feel as if some enemy might be hiding among all those trees. I've been spending time in Aunt Nettie's house since I was sixteen, and I'm still a little uneasy about the place.

But I was too tired to feel uneasy that night. I didn't even have nightmares, despite a few vivid pre-sleep flashbacks of Clementine Ripley's body crashing over that railing and landing at my feet.

The next day started off routinely. It was Saturday, the busiest day of the week for a retail business in a resort community at the height of the tourist season.

I got up in time to have a cup of coffee with Aunt Nettie before she went to work at seven-thirty. After she left I turned on a cable news show and caught Duncan Ainsley commenting on the death of Clementine Ripley.

"I'm proud to say she was a friend, as well as a client," he said. "Her death is truly shocking." He seemed quite genuine.

The television newsman said the cause of death was not yet known.

"Well, it's gonna be natural causes," I told him firmly.

I flipped the TV off, washed a load of underwear, and tossed my dry cleaning into the van. I dressed in Warner Pier business casual—clean khaki shorts and chocolate-brown polo shirt with a TenHuis logo. At ten I fixed myself a bowl of local blueberries, lightly sugared, and followed them with bacon, eggs, and toast, a brunch that would last until my six p.m. dinner break. At eleven-thirty, I left. I stopped at the corner where the dry cleaner used to be, only to discover it was now a real estate office. So I left the dry cleaning in the van and went on to TenHuis Chocolade, ready to start my first shift as a supervisor. Which on a Saturday during the busy season was going to include helping out behind the counter—the reason I'd worn the company outfit.

Aunt Nettie, who believes that tourists want to watch chocolates being handmade even on Saturdays, was working with a limited crew—just three hairnet ladies—when I arrived. She kept rolling creamy white chocolate truffles in coconut ("Midori coconut truffles—very creamy all white chocolate truffles, flavored with melon and rolled in coconut.") as she reported on the morning. It had been routine, she said, except for lots of phone calls from her friends as Greg Glossop spread his opinion around town. We were both delighted that neither Chief Jones nor the tabloid press had shown up with questions.

"The longer we wait to hear from Chief Jones," I said, "the more I think Clementine Ripley had a stroke. Or maybe some kind of aneurysm." Aunt Nettie agreed.

Aunt Nettie took a lunch break at one, but worked until four-fifteen, so I was able to ask her some questions before I took over. One of the questions was the name of the counter girl with the stringy ponytail. Her name was Tracy. Her partner that afternoon was a plump girl of similar age, but with better hair, and her name was Stacy. So if I them mixed up, who could tell?

Aunt Nettie obviously wasn't confident about leaving me in charge, but Stacy and Tracy assured her they'd show me the ropes, and we shooed her and the ladies in hairnets out the door.

At four-thirty the phone rang. I didn't exactly jump to answer it, since I expected it to be another of Aunt Nettie's pals wanting to gossip. When I picked it up after the third ring, I was surprised to hear Aunt Nettie herself.

"Lee?" Her voice was all quavery.

"Aunt Nettie? What's wrong?"

"The house is all torn up. We've had a burglar!"

I didn't have to stop and think about that one. "Get out of the house!" I said. "He might still be there. I'll call the cops and be right there."

I called nine-one-one, left Tracy and Stacy on their own, and ran out the back door. I got to the house half a block behind the Warner Pier patrol car.

Aunt Nettie was standing in the drive beside her big Buick. I hugged her, and the two of us waited outside while the deputy checked the four rooms downstairs and the three upstairs. Nobody was there.

When we looked in the door, the house was a wreck. I started inside, ready to begin cleaning up, but I was stopped by the patrolman, a burly young guy whose uniform had been tailored to fit like a second skin. His name tag read CHERRY.

"Let me call in and see what the chief wants to do about this," he said. "He'll probably want photos at least. Maybe fingerprints."

I was surprised. I'd lived in Dallas too long. My mom's apartment there was burglarized, and the cops didn't bother to take fingerprints. She had to wait hours for an investigator to show up at all. I was glad to learn things were still different in a small town.

Aunt Nettie and I were sitting on the porch when another car pulled in, and Chief Jones unfolded his long legs and got out.

I hadn't expected to see him. "What are you doing here?" I said. "Do you do all the investigations?"

"Most of them. Warner Pier has a force of five, and that doesn't include a detective, so I have to do double duty." He looked over the top of his half glasses and grinned his folksy grin. "Besides, when a newcomer to town is involved in two emergency calls in two days, I'd better check it out. What's going on?"

"I don't understand it," Aunt Nettie said. She'd

gotten over being frightened. Now she sounded miffed. "Usually Warner Pier burglars just hit the summer people."

"Guess these guys don't have any hometown spirit," the chief said. He opened the trunk of his car and revealed all sorts of esoteric equipment.

"Oh, you know what I mean," Aunt Nettie said. "It's so much easier to break into a house that's going to be empty for weeks or months. Even that doesn't happen so often since most people have alarm systems. And I don't even have anything worth stealing!"

"You've got a television set, haven't you?"

"Yes, but—"

"A VCR? A stereo?"

"No. Phil and I were at the shop so much that we don't have anything but a TV and a clock radio. All our furniture's old, and none of it's valuable. We don't have silver tea services or jewelry or fine art."

The chief sent Patrolman Cherry off to find out if any of the neighbors had seen anything, and he showed us where the burglar got in, which turned out to be a dining room window. It was an old casement that locked with a latch. Someone had smashed out a pane with a rock, then reached inside and opened the window. He found fingerprints on the window, of course, but I began to have a feeling they were going to belong to Aunt Nettie and me.

As soon as the police allowed us into the house, Aunt Nettie called Handy Hans Home Repair Service to come and fix the window, and then we looked around. I began to think Aunt Nettie's assessment of the situation was right—she and I apparently owned nothing that a burglar was interested in taking. At least I couldn't see any big gaps among our possessions. Things just seemed to be all messed up.

The sheets and towels, which Aunt Nettie kept in a cedar chest at the foot of her bed, had been dumped out onto the floor, and clothes were tossed on the floor of her bedroom downstairs and of mine upstairs. The living room furniture was turned over, but when we put it back in place, nothing seemed to be irreparably damaged. The sofa cushions and the pads in the seats of the rocking chairs had not been ripped open, and the magazines hadn't been shredded. The food stuffs were still in the kitchen cupboards. A couple of bottles of wine—Michigan wine, of course—were still on the shelf in the pantry.

"What about you, young lady?" the chief asked. "Your aunt said she doesn't own any electronic gadgets or jewelry. I hate to quote gossip, but the talk around Warner Pier—among the people who knew you when you worked here before—was that you were married to a wealthy man. Do you have any good jewelry? Diamond watches? What's missing?"

I really didn't want to answer. It's embarrassing to be twenty-eight years old and own nothing worth stealing.

"I don't have anything like that. When I divorced Rich, I left everything behind," I said. "I don't own anything but my clothes and the old van."

He frowned at me. "Nothing valuable?"

"Nothing."

I tried to sound firm, the way I had when I argued with my lawyer. But the chief kept staring at me, and I began to feel that I had to give him some explanation.

"Look," I said. "Money was in the middle of every argument Rich and I ever had. I was sick of it, so I refused a financial sentiment."

Darn, tongue-tied again. "I mean settlement! I refused a financial settlement."

Chief Jones looked unbelieving. "Didn't you at least take the dishes and furniture?"

"I guess you had to be there," I said.

That was all the explanation I could give anybody

for what I did—leave a marriage after five years and wind up poorer than when I said, "I do." But a complete explanation would be a novel, and I didn't feel like writing one.

I called the shop to check on Tracy and Stacy. They were all agog over the emergency, but they said things were going okay. Aunt Nettie and I kept on straightening up. We still didn't find anything gone. Then I heard Aunt Nettie give a gasp.

"What did you find?" the chief said.

"I did have a hundred dollars in my underwear drawer," Aunt Nettie said. "Five twenties. They're gone."

Chief Jones duly noted the missing money.

"I guess the burglars were mad because they didn't find anything else," Aunt Nettie said. "Maybe that's why they messed everything up."

The chief shrugged.

"They could have messed things up a lot more," I said. "A sack of flour and a dozen eggs on the kitchen floor would have kept us busy twice as long as it's taken us to hang up all these clothes. Is this restraint typical of Warner Pier burglars and vandals?"

"I wouldn't say so. Your aunt's right when she says they usually hit the empty summer cottages and clean out the electronic gadgets and other stuff, things that are easy to pawn. Guns—they'll take those. Sometimes they go for antiques. Of course, lots of people are like Mrs. TenHuis and keep a little money in the house, and if a burglar finds it, it's gone." He began to gather up his equipment. Aunt Nettie sat down on the couch and began to sort the magazines our burglar had tossed around.

The chief kept picking up, but he looked at me while he stowed things away. "You know, Ms. McKinney, there could be a connection to what happened at Clementine Ripley's house."

"You don't really think my aunt or I had anything to do with that?"

"I can't rule it out. Or maybe the burglar was looking for something you took away from there."

"What was I going to take? A ladle from the kitchen? A glass from the bar? That house isn't exactly full of stuff that would be easy to steal. There are no doodads on the tables, and the few paintings on the walls are too large to stick in my pocket."

He grinned that Abe Lincoln grin. "I didn't really figure that you stole anything."

"The only things I handled belonged to Herrera Catering. Glasses, linens, sodas, and mixers. Booze. Lemons and limes. And I didn't bring any of them away."

"I sure do hate coincidences."

"You mean the burglary? I agree completely. From my point of view it seems weird to be dealing with the police two days in a row. But coincidences do happen, Chief Jones."

He nodded, but he still looked skeptical.

"Besides," I said, "we still don't know that Clementine Ripley's death was anything but natural."

"Well . . ." The chief seemed to speak reluctantly.

I felt sure he knew something I didn't want to hear. "What's happened?"

"The Grand Rapids office of the state police is going to announce it at six. It seems Greg Glossop was right for once."

"He was right?"

Chief Jones nodded. "Yep. After what he said, the state lab tested the candy for cyanide."

"You don't mean—!"

"Sorry to be the one to break the news. Cyanide had been injected into all the chocolates in the little box your aunt fixed. The cause of death won't be official until the autopsy results are in, and that'll take several days. But Clementine Ripley's death is being investigated as a murder."

All of a sudden the living room was again as topsy-turvy as it had been after the burglars left. I grabbed the back of one of Aunt Nettie's antique rocking chairs to keep from turning upside down myself.

Then I looked at Aunt Nettie. Her face had crumpled like limp lettuce. "Oh, my stars," she said. "*That's* not going to be good for business."

"It certainly isn't," I said.

But all in all Aunt Nettie took the news the way she takes everything—calmly.

"You aren't surprised?"

"Maybe I don't really understand it yet, Lee. At first it seemed impossible. But when a person everybody in the world had some reason to dislike—someone like Clementine Ripley—dies under such odd circumstances . . . Well, maybe it would seem stranger than ever if she'd died of natural causes."

"Mr. Ainsley said he wouldn't have been surprised if somebody shot her," I said. "But poisoning is hard to believe. I was just sure she died of a stroke or something. This is awful."

"It's going to be bad for everybody," Chief Jones said.

"And now I guess you'll need those statements from both of us."

"You'll have to give statements, but I won't be taking them. As soon as we got the report, I called in the state police."

"Oh? Is that standard procedure?"

"It's optional." For the first time Chief Jones sounded short-tempered. "It seemed like the best idea. We'd have to use their lab anyway."

His jaw clenched a couple of times before he went on. "They're sending one of their best men—Detective Lieutenant Alec VanDam. He'll have a team, of course, in a case this high profile. He'll be in touch with you. And I guess I've done about as much as I can around here. Jerry may find a neighbor who saw something."

It took me a minute to realize that Jerry must be the patrolman, the one whose name tag read CHERRY. His name was Jerry Cherry, it seemed. I was too upset to giggle.

The chief was still talking. "Some neighbor may have seen a car, or a stranger. But there's a lot of traffic along Lake Shore Drive, and the trees hide Nettie's house."

Chief Jones went out to his car and began to put his case in the trunk. Patrolman Jerry Cherry came back and told him he hadn't had any luck with the neighbors. "I'll try the mailman," he said. "But I'm afraid he comes in the morning."

When he spoke again he lowered his voice, but I could still hear him through the open door. "Who'd you draw from the state police?"

"Alec VanDam."

"Didn't he work that holdup and shooting over at Perkins Lake?"

"Yeah, he's the one. I was sure they'd send somebody good. High-profile case like this."

"It's still a dirty deal. You woulda done just as good, Chief."

Chief Jones snorted. "It would raise too many questions," he said. He got in his car and drove away.

Dirty deal? What had Jerry Cherry meant by that?

I decided I wanted to know. So I went out on the porch, leaned against the railing, and turned on my Texas accent. "Off-cer Chairy?"

"Yes, Ms. McKinney?"

"We really 'preciate all this attention. I grew up in a small town, in north Texas, and the law enforcement officials were just as kind as you and Chief

Jones have been. In fact, my daddy's garage has the contract for maintenance on the sheriff's cars. But then I moved to Dallas, and it was a dif'rent story in a big city! I'm shore glad to see that the small-town spirit is still alive up here in Michigan."

Cherry straightened his shoulders, just a little. "We try to serve, Ms. McKinney. Chief Jones is real firm about that."

"Chief Jones sure is an interesting man. Is he a native of Warner Pier?"

"Oh, no! He was one of the top detectives in Cincinnati. We're really lucky to have him here."

"From Cincinnati to Warner Pier? The city fathers must have offered him a lot of money!"

Cherry laughed. "He took early retirement from the Cincinnati force, and he and his wife moved up here. That was more than five years ago."

"I see."

"They'd always vacationed in the area—you know, decided they'd like living here. But Mrs. Jones died three years ago."

"That's too bad."

"Yah. It kinda left the chief at loose ends. So when the job of police chief opened, he applied. The council was smart enough to hire him."

I sat on the porch rail. "If he has a lot of experience as a detective—well, I'm a little surprised that he called in the state police to investigate the death of Clementine Ripley. Seems like he would have handled it himself."

I smiled—not flirtatiously, but in a friendly manner. And I looked at Officer Cherry and waited for him to speak.

But he didn't. His jaw clenched just the way the chief's had. I didn't say anything, either.

This game of nonverbal chicken went on for about thirty seconds, I guess, though it seemed like thirty minutes.

Finally Jerry Cherry spoke. "It's up to the chief," he said. "I'd better go. You call in if anything else happens."

He got in his car and drove away, leaving me and my Texas accent flat.

"Lee," I told myself, "you're definitely losing your touch." I'd have to ask somebody else. Maybe Aunt Nettie.

But Aunt Nettie wasn't likely to know. She concentrated on TenHuis Chocolade almost to the exclusion of everything else, and she was too kindhearted to enjoy idle gossip.

So who did I know who would know? Well, all the city officials, the mayor . . .

"Ye gods!" I said. "How lucky! I forgot to go by and give Mike Herrera my Social Security number."

Chapter 7

Mike Herrera's office, Aunt Nettie told me, was down the block from TenHuis Chocolate, above Mike's Sidewalk Café. And, yes, Mr. Herrera did own the café.

"He's bought several Warner Pier restaurants," Aunt Nettie said. "I think he leases most of them, but Mike's and the main restaurant, Herrera's—down on the water—he operates himself."

I went down the street—past T-Shirt Alley, with silly sayings in the window; Leathers, which displayed expensive handbags and luggage; and the Old Time Antique Shop, whose window was packed with stuff Aunt Nettie and I used at home every day. I crossed the street and climbed the stairs to the office of Herrera enterprises. A middle-aged woman who identified herself as the bookkeeper gave me the proper forms to fill out so I could get paid for the few hours of work I'd done. There was no sign of Mayor Mike Herrera.

"I need to talk to Mr. Herrera," I said. "Is he here?"

"I think he's over at city hall," the bookkeeper said. "But he'll be back soon. He always checks on things before the evening dinner crowd shows up at Mike's."

Mike's was new since my high school days, and I had noticed it seemed to be packed at every meal. It wasn't quite your standard sidewalk café. Yes, it had tables on the sidewalk, inside a little railing, but it really got its name from its decor. The floors of both the outside dining area and the inside room were covered with graffiti—they looked like children had been writing on a sidewalk. I'd figured out that this was actually paint, since the waitresses ran back and forth all the time and the chalk never wore off.

The aisles between the tables were delineated by hopscotch games, and the walls were decorated with jump ropes, jacks, and other children's toys and games. There was a big black slate wall, too, where customers were invited to write their own graffiti.

Kids loved the place, obviously, but after five p.m. children were only served in one section and by ten p.m. or so, I'd noticed, Mike's turned into a date bar. It seemed as if Mr. Herrera had covered all the bases at Mike's—Aunt Nettie had even remarked that the food was pretty good, high praise from her.

When I came down the steps and looked into Mike's, it was nearly six p.m. and the place was filling up. Mike Herrera was at the back of the restaurant, headed into the kitchen. I went inside and called out. "Mr. Herrera! Can I talk to you a minute?"

He stole a glance at his watch before he motioned me to a stool at the end of the bar and stood beside me. His beaming smile contrasted with his earlier look at his watch. "Miss Lee. A pleasure."

I decided a frontal attack was going to be the best plan for a busy man. "I'm here with a nosy question," I said quietly, "but I have an excuse. I heard that cyanide was found in Clementine Ripley's chocolates, and I'm determined to stay on top of this situation because of my aunt."

Mike Herrera looked concerned. "The situation is

truly shocking, but I'm sure the lovely Mrs. Nettie has nothing to do with the events."

"I'm sure of that, too, but her chocolates were apparently used as a murder weapon. So she—and I—are involved whether we like it or not."

"So what was your question?"

"I'm trying to understand why the state police have been called in when I hear that Chief Jones is himself an experienced detective. Can you explain?"

"Eet is a motter of routine," Herrera said.

Hmmm. His Spanish accent had abruptly reappeared. Did that mean my question had made him nervous?

"The choice was up to Chief Jones heemself," he said. "The officials of Warner Pier weesh to cooperate fully in the death of thees prominent woman, to make sure that all channels of investigation are fully explored. Chief Jones—indeed, all the city employees—weel work with the state detectives en any way we can."

I felt that I'd just given him a chance to practice for a press conference. But I hadn't gotten any kind of an answer.

"I'm sorry to be a pain in the neck," I said. "It's just that so much gossip goes around a small town. I'd much rather get the story from an authoritative source—such as the mayor himself—rather than relying on Glossop. I mean, relying on gossip!"

I couldn't believe I'd done that. I'd actually threatened to ask Greg Glossop, the bigmouthed pharmacist, and I had pretended the threat was a slip of the tongue. I waited for Mike Herrera's reply.

He stared at the floor for a moment, then leaned close and gave me a smile that told me I was about to receive a confidence. "I'm sure you've been told that Chief Jones and Ms. Ripley had a history."

A history? I raised my eyebrows, but I kept my mouth shut.

"In his previous job in Cincinnati, our chief was a witness in a case Ms. Ripley defended. I do not think this is a pleasant memory for the chief. I hope that as the press descends to cover Ms. Ripley's death—well, we all hope that they will not make this factor of too much importance." He shook my hand solemnly. "Now I mush check on the kitchen. Jason! Please give Ms. McKinney a drink on the house."

He turned and almost ran into the kitchen. I looked around to see my ponytailed cohort from the Ripley party grinning at me from behind the bar. "Hi, Lee," Jason said. "What can I get you?"

"Nothing, thanks. I've got to get back to work. I hope I didn't upset Mr. Herrera."

"Oh, the first reporters have arrived. That's what upset him."

"I didn't help. But I really feel I need some background, or I might put my foot wrong. Do you know what the situation was between Chief Jones and Clementine Ripley?"

"I know Mike doesn't want the reporters to figure it out, but . . ."

I waited without saying anything while Jason polished a glass. His hair and his big dark eyes made him look like an eighteenth-century pirate.

Finally he grimaced and spoke again. "There's no way to keep it a secret. But so far none of the reporters have tumbled to the fact that Chief Jones used to be Detective J. H. Jones—the guy who lost the Montgomery case for the Cincinnati Police Department."

"Oh? I have only a vague memory of the details . . ."

"He was the chief investigating officer. The only way the Ripper could keep Thomas Montgomery out of jail was to make the police look incompetent. So she did it. It ruined Hogan Jones's career." He leaned across the bar. "You didn't hear it from me."

I nodded, thanked Jason, and headed back to the chocolate shop, mulling over what he had told me. So Clementine Ripley had ruined Chief Jones's career. The guy must have felt haunted by her. First she ran him out of Cincinnati, so he retired and moved to Warner Pier. He became police chief here. Then she showed up and built a showplace weekend home.

Yikes! That alone was motive for murder. It's as if she had deliberately had it in for him.

Yes, Chief Jones definitely needed to step aside and let someone else investigate her murder. He might not want her murderer caught at all.

He would even be a suspect. After all, he'd been out at the Ripley estate before the party—he'd been going in as I left after delivering the chocolates.

And the state police's top detective had been assigned to the case. I shoved the door to the shop open. I felt sure I'd get to meet this Alec VanDam from the Michigan State Police—and his team—quite soon.

When I got inside, Aunt Nettie was in the workroom.

"What are you doing here?" I said.

"Some detective called the house and asked me to come in. He wants to talk to both of us."

She didn't look at all afraid. And suddenly I loved her so dearly that I could have cried. When I was an obnoxious teenager upset about my parents' divorce, she'd taken me in—given me someone who would listen, who taught me to work hard and be proud of what I did, who was always there for me. Now, twelve years later, my own marriage had fallen apart, and she had taken me in again. She was simply good through and through, and she saw only goodness in others.

The only exception to this had been Clementine Ripley. Aunt Nettie had adored Uncle Phil, and she had blamed Clementine Ripley for his death, as lots of people had known. And now a chocolate Aunt Nettie had handled and packaged might be linked to Clementine Ripley's death. Aunt Nettie might be accused of killing her.

Did she even see her own danger? She might not. She was such an innocent that she might walk right into some sort of trap, incriminate herself.

But she wasn't alone. She had me. And I was going to make sure her innocence wasn't used against her.

I gulped and got ready to face down that detective.

At least he hadn't come to take either of us away. We didn't seem to be threatened with arrest. I toyed with the idea of recommending that Aunt Nettie call her lawyer. But wouldn't that make it seem as if she was guilty? Besides, Aunt Nettie's lawyer would be some local guy who drew up wills and checked land titles. Would he be any real help in a murder investigation?

And the state police's request to see us obviously centered on the chocolate shop. If not, they would have come out to the house, or asked the two of us to meet them on their own turf. This was perfectly logical; the investigators would have to understand how the suspect chocolates had been handled—where they'd been made, stored, packaged.

Anyway, I didn't mention calling a lawyer.

Warner Pier's traffic was typical for a Saturday night, of course—awful. Half the tourists in western Michigan were circling through the business district looking for parking places, and two tour buses were in town, so the sidewalks were packed as well. It was twenty more minutes before two men in suits came in the front door and showed their badges.

Detective Lieutenant Alec VanDam looked as Dutch as his name. He had the face of a Van Gogh peasant, a plodding gait suitable for wooden clogs, and a shock of hair of such a bright gold it would have looked natural on one of those Dutch boy dolls they sell up in Holland, Michigan. He introduced his companion—his subordinate, obviously—as Detective Sergeant Larry Underwood. Underwood was younger than VanDam, maybe around thirty, with a blocky build and blunt features. He wore a buzz cut that left only an inch or so of black hair standing on top of his head. Neither of the detectives was quite as tall as I am.

"Please wait a few minutes, Ms. McKinney," VanDam said. "Then we'll go over the events of yesterday afternoon with you. Right now we're simply trying to understand what happened and the order it happened in, and we'd like to talk to Mrs. TenHuis first."

Aunt Nettie took them back to the break room, and I worked with Tracy and Stacy. They'd had to cut their dinner breaks short, but they were so excited that neither of them complained. I stood behind the counter with them while I waited for the detectives.

I was nervous about the interview, of course. I reminded myself to stand quietly and pretend to be poised—a lesson I was taught during my semisuccessful career on the beauty pageant circuit. Don't twitch your hands, I'd been told. Don't fool with your hair or jewelry. Don't bounce your foot or pick at your nails.

Don't twist your tongue—that wasn't on the list, but it was the one I had the most trouble with. As I loaded boxes with chocolates and made change I tried to prepare answers for every question the detectives might ask, all the time knowing that was probably the worst thing I could do. But I was willing to look dumb—I had to be ready to fight for Aunt Nettie, even with my malapropish tongue.

I stayed in the shop, but I saw Aunt Nettie lead the detectives out of the break room. She showed them the workroom and the storage area, where racks on wheels held stacks of twenty-five trays of chocolates at a time. No doubt she described the routine of the middle-aged ladies who made the candy, the ones who had gone home at four p.m. She wheeled out a rack that held storage trays, then pulled out the tray on which the Amaretto truffles were stored. She pointed out the white chocolate that covered them and the accent stripes of milk chocolate that identified the Amaretto truffles. Then she took an Amaretto truffle from the tray, gave the detectives a rather defiant look, and ate it in two bites.

Of course, I was way ahead of the detectives in one way. They were still checking how the chocolate had been handled here at TenHuis Chocolade. I was sure those truffles had been pure, unadulterated yummy when Aunt Nettie gave them to me. If one of them had been used to poison Clementine Ripley, it had been given the cyanide treatment after I left it at the big, cold house on the point.

When my turn came, I went over the same material. I described how I had watched Aunt Nettie arrange the chocolates and dipped fruits on the silver trays that Clementine Ripley had sent us and how I had tasted an Amaretto truffle. How they'd gone into the van. How I'd left the van locked while I walked around to the house to pick up a check. How Clementine Ripley had taken a chocolate cat, gulped it down in two bites, then instructed Marion McCoy to take the box up to her room.

I was careful to include the exchange we'd overheard between Joe Woodyard and his ex—"I want my money." Frankly, VanDam and Underwood didn't seem too interested. I guess they'd already heard about that, maybe from Joe.

Then I explained why I happened to go back that night as a waitress.

"You can ask Lindy Herrera," I said. "She suggested it."

"We'll talk to her," VanDam said. "Did you see the little box of chocolates after you went back?"

"No."

"And you stayed in the kitchen, the dining room, and the reception room?"

"Except when I went down to the office."

"You went down to the office? That room back by the garage?"

"I didn't see a garage, but there was a utility room across the hall. It's at the east end of the house."

"And why did you go back there?"

"The cat, Junker. I mean, Yonkers! Champion Yonkers. Ms. McCoy was trying to find him. She said they planned to lock him in the office. After she'd gone, he showed up out in the main party room—jumped onto the bartender from the balcony, then tried to eat a bowl of olives. I grabbed him and took him back to the office."

"How did you know where it was?"

"I figured it was the same one she'd taken me to that afternoon, so I kept going east until I found a familiar landlord. I mean, landmark! When I saw the utility room, I turned left."

"You didn't see the chocolates in the office?"

"Not then. They should have been upstairs with Clementine Ripley by then."

He didn't ask me what I did see in the office, and I wasn't about to volunteer any information. We went over the rest of the events—my walk back down the peristyle and past the kitchen and dining room, and my arrival in the main reception room just in time to see Clementine Ripley tumble over the balcony and land on the polished wooden floor.

At that point VanDam and Underwood seemed to be about to close their notebooks and leave. So I felt called upon to make a statement.

"Lieutenant VanDam," I said, "I'm sure of one thing."

"Yes, Ms. McKinney?"

"Those truffles—well, they weren't poisoned here!"

A slight smile flashed over VanDam's serious Dutch face.

I went on. "I wouldn't even have any idea of how to get hold of cyanide, and I'm sure my aunt doesn't either."

"Actually," VanDam said, "getting hold of cyanide is not a big problem in this part of Michigan. Not in the summertime."

"What do you mean?"

"Peach pits contain it."

"Peach pits!"

He nodded. "Also cherry pits. I understand the process of brewing a little isn't too hard."

"That may be true. But after meeting my aunt Nettie, you can see that she'd never—well, it's not possible for her to have any connection with any action that would harm anyone. She's—she's just good clear through."

VanDam smiled at that. "Right now we're just trying to understand how the chocolates were handled," he said. He flipped his notebook closed and stood up. Detective Underwood imitated his actions almost exactly.

"We need to find out who had an opportunity to tamper with them," VanDam said. He grinned. "Like you, Ms. McKinney."

"Me!"

"You were alone with them for quite a while," he said. Then he headed for the front of the shop, and my stomach went into a knot no Boy Scout could have tied.

I followed the detectives. I didn't know what to say or do. VanDam's comment wasn't exactly news, of course. Both Aunt Nettie and I had had access to the chocolates. In theory I could have spiked them with cyanide.

So should I maintain my innocence? Point out that I had no reason for killing Clementine Ripley? Deny that I had ready access to cyanide? Yell? Scream? Beat my breast?

I decided that a dignified silence would be best. I pretended I was Miss America taking her final trip down the runway as I escorted the two state detectives to the front door. I even offered them a sample chocolate from the front counter. They declined.

I opened the door for them. "Good-bye, Lieutenant VanDam," I said. "Good-bye, Sergeant Underling."

I had closed the door before I heard VanDam laugh and realized what I'd said. I went back to the break room ready to cut my tongue out. It seemed determined to betray me.

Aunt Nettie had taken her interrogation calmly. The detectives had been polite, she said. They'd wanted to know how things were handled in the workroom at TenHuis Chocolade and specifically how the chocolates she'd sent to Clementine Ripley were selected.

"I just told them the truth," she said. "I knew her favorites, because she always buys Amaretto truffles—I mean she always bought them. Sometimes she'd buy a whole pound of nothing but Amaretto truffles. I knew she had quite a sweet tooth, and I didn't want her to mess up the display trays before they were served. But those specific truffles were taken right from our regular stock. And I do not believe that one of my ladies had poisoned some Amaretto truffles at random, and that Clementine Ripley just happened to get them."

"I agree," I said. "That would be too hard to swallow."

She looked at me narrowly, then laughed. "Oh, Lee, you're so funny!"

Then we had a big discussion on whether she

should gc home. I was still nervous about the burglar.

"Handy Hans called to say the window is fixed," Aunt Nettie said firmly. "The house is as safe as it's been for the past hundred years, and I've been living there for forty of those years. I'm not leaving my home."

"That house may be inside the city limits, but it's still awfully remote."

"I have wonderful neighbors."

"I know! But you also have an acre of ground. The neighbors aren't close enough to hear you holler, and they can't see the house for all those trees."

Aunt Nettie sighed. "I guess you have a point. And if you're nervous about staying out there . . ."

"You're not staying alone!"

We never made any progress beyond that. She wasn't leaving her home, and I wasn't leaving her. I did call the nonemergency number for the Warner Pier Police Department and request a few extra patrols of our area. The dispatcher—or whomever I talked to—assured me that Chief Jones had already laid that on.

"So if you see a police car in your drive," the dispatcher said, "don't worry."

We left it at that. We were spending the night in our own beds.

Aunt Nettie left the shop around eight-thirty p.m. At eight-forty p.m. I started cleaning the big front window. At eight-forty-five p.m. a car stopped in front of the shop and a man wearing a funny mesh vest with lots of pockets got out. He leaned back inside his car and pulled out a camera.

I yanked the shade down on the window and turned to Tracy and Stacy.

"Let's close up early," I said.

I pulled the shade on the other big display window, then locked the front door. I stood by it while Tracy and Stacy finished up with the last two customers. The man with the camera came to the door and rapped, but I ignored him.

I opened the door just a slit for the customers. They had barely squeezed through when a second man draped with photographic equipment came running down the sidewalk.

"Hey!" he said. "Did the fatal chocolates come from here?"

CHOCOLATE CHAT

ORIGINS

- The first chocoholics believed that the cocoa bean was the gift of a god. The god was Quetzalcoatl, a benign deity of the sometimes blood-thirsty Aztecs. According to legend, Quetzalcoatl stole the cocoa plant from the "sons of the Sun" and gave it to the Aztecs. They made the beans of the tree into a drink seasoned with pimento, pepper and other spices. They called it tchocolatl.

- Quetzalcoatl may have done the Aztecs a favor in giving them chocolate, but their belief in him helped end their empire. When the conquistador Cortez arrived in Mexico in 1519, he came in wooden sailing ships unlike any the Aztecs had ever seen. The Aztecs thought Quetzalcoatl had returned and greeted Cortez with open arms—and gifts of chocolate. Cortez—obviously not a man who went for spicy, bitter drinks—traded the chocolate for gold, and the Aztec empire began to fade away. The Spanish took chocolate to Europe.

- The myth of chocolate is echoed in its scientific name—Theobroma Cacao—which translates as "food of the gods."

Chapter 8

Stacy and Tracy were staring at me.

"Let's clean up fast and skedaddle," I said. "And you girls may get tomorrow off. I'll call you if it looks as if we'll be open."

They were still staring, so I went on. "And you'll get tomorrow off with pay if you don't talk to those reporters outside."

That seemed to suit them, and the three of us did the final cleanup—sweeping out, scrubbing down the counter, and restocking the showcase—in record time. We ignored repeated knocks on the front door; the crowd seemed to be growing. I scooped the cash from the register and left it unbalanced, although that almost crushed my accountant's soul. I stuck the money in a bank sack and put the bank sack in my purse. Tracy and Stacy waited at the door to the alley while I turned out all the lights but the security light behind the counter. Then I made my way to the back of the shop.

Tracy's eyes were big, and her hair looked stringier than ever. "Do you think they'll be waiting in the alley?"

"I hope not," I said. "I'll go out first, and I'll take you girls home."

They both assured me this wasn't necessary, but I

insisted. I didn't want them waylaid; they were just high school kids, no match for the tabloid press. I was afraid the reporters were lurking in the alley, lying in wait like lionesses at a waterhole.

Which turned out to be almost the case.

The business district of Warner Pier is quaint enough to make the back entrances hard for strangers to figure out, but the first reporters found the alley just as we reached the van. I guess it was lucky Tracy and Stacy were teenagers; the hairnet ladies would never have been agile enough to jump into the van fast enough for us to make our escape.

As it was I had to drive through a half dozen reporters and photographers. Strobe lights were flashing, and people were yelling, but I kept edging the van down the alley toward Peach Street.

"Hey! Let us tell your side!" That was one of the yells.

"Is it true your aunt's been arrested?" That was another.

"Is it true you're having an affair with Clementine Ripley's husband? Is it true you were Miss Texas?"

I tried not to even look at them, just kept moving slowly forward. When I got to the street, I whipped the van left and pressed down on the accelerator. "Look back," I said. "See if they follow us."

"There are a couple of cars," Stacy said. "But it's hard to tell just who's who."

I cut through the alley on the next block.

"One car followed us," Stacy said. "Why don't you head down Lake Shore Drive?"

"I don't want to lead them to Aunt Nettie's. Her house is hard to find, so maybe they won't find it tonight. If I go somewhere else—"

"I mean the north shore end," Stacy said, "and I can tell you how to lose them!" Tracy (stringy hair) was being real quiet, but Stacy (plump) was enjoying the whole thing. "Head for the old Root Beer Barrel," she said. "Circle around it, and there's a drive at the back, kinda hidden by bushes. The guys do it all the time."

"The Root Beer Barrel? It's still there?"

"Yes, we can get away that way."

"You're sure?"

"I guarantee it!"

I started north on the Lake Shore Drive. In that part of Warner Pier, the road runs right along the lake, and the lake side has been eaten away. The road is only about one and a half lanes wide, and there's no shoulder at all, only a guardrail. On the other side of the guardrail there's a steep drop, almost a cliff, about forty feet down to a narrow beach. When I see an article about Great Lakes erosion, I think of that spot. Years ago it used to be a stretch of road with businesses facing the lake, between Lake Shore Drive and the beach. Now the buildings have collapsed into the lake, half the road is gone, and the section is supposed to carry only local traffic.

The old Root Beer Barrel had been a landmark. The drive-in has been closed for years, since the state highway was moved, but now I saw that the giant barrel was still there. And, I noticed, there was a streetlight at the entrance to what was once the drive-in's parking lot. The lot was now a mess of broken asphalt and sand.

The car that was following us wasn't staying too close; the guy must have been hoping to follow me home and find Aunt Nettie. I drove as fast as I dared when I got near the barrel, then whipped into the drive. I cut my lights as soon as I was off the street, but I'd seen the tracks in the sand. "You're right, Stacy," I said. "Lots of cars have been using this lot."

"Yeah, the guys do doughnuts in here. Go around on the left side of the barrel, then make a sharp right."

I followed directions, coasting to slow down without hitting the brakes, since I didn't want our pursuer to see the lights. Once I was behind the barrel, I faced a solid wall of green, and the streetlight was a long way off.

"Go straight through," Stacy said. "See the tracks?"

Now I saw them. A faint, two-rut driveway led into the bushes, and I followed it. Branches and leaves hit the windshield and the sides of the van.

Magically, I came out into the clear almost immediately. And I was in the back of the parking lot of Warner Pier's one supermarket.

"I can't believe this!" I said. "I had no idea that the Superette was that close to the Lake Shore Drive."

"You can drop us here," Tracy said. "I'm supposed to call my mom for a ride anyway."

"I'll park over there where the other cars are and wait until your mom comes," I said.

Tracy and Stacy agreed to that. They went to the pay phone, then came back to the van. It was a warm night, so I rolled the windows down.

"I'm sorry y'all had such a scary ride," I said. "But I appreciate your help in getting away from that bunch."

The two of them looked at each other. Then Stacy took a deep breath and spoke. "Is it true?"

I decided I'd better be careful about what question I was answering. "Is what true, Stacy?"

"Were you really Miss Texas?"

I laughed out loud. "That one's easy. No."

"Oh." Stacy's face fell.

"Sorry if you're disappointed. I was in the Miss Texas Pageant once, along with about a million other girls, but I did not place in the top ten."

"What about Joe Woodyard?"

"I don't think he placed in the top ten either." I tried to keep the sharpness out of my voice. "When I was your age, Joe was a lifeguard at Warner Pier

Beach. I knew who he was. I don't recall ever having a conversation with him. I hadn't even heard anything about him again until yesterday when I ran into him out at the Ripley house."

"You didn't date him?"

"Not when we were in high school. Not recently. Not anytime in between." And Rich's private detectives would back me up on that, I thought. Rich had had them investigate every aspect of my life.

"Oh." This time both girls looked really disappointed.

I laughed again. "Sorry if I've let y'all down. I lead a very dull life."

Tracy spoke then. "My mom says she hates to see such a smart guy throw his chances away, and my dad says Joe's turned into a gigolo."

She pronounced "gigolo" Gig-alow. Tracy was my kind of girl, stringy hair and all. I hid a laugh, but I decided I'd be better off not joining in Warner Pier's gossip sessions during my first week back in town, even if I wasn't impressed with Mr. Woodyard.

"I guess I'll let Joe handle his own life," I said.

"He doesn't seem to know how to handle it, according to my mom," Tracy said. She dropped her voice and spoke confidingly. "He quit being a lawyer and—"

I tried to cut her off by interrupting. "What kind of car does your mom drive?"

"Ford Fiesta. Joe got all kinds of scholarships, see, and he did real well at Ann Arbor. Then he went to law school."

"Good for Joe," I said desperately. "What color is your mom's car?"

"It's red. Then he got mixed up with that Clementine Ripley, and he blew it all. That's what my dad says. He says Joe's really got a chip on his shoulder."

She paused for a breath, and I decided I was going to have to be blunt.

"Listen, Tracy, Joe has plenty of friends in Warner Pier, and I'm sure they've all been interested in what's happening in his life. But Clementine Ripley has been murdered, and you saw all those reporters that have shown up, nosing around. Now is the time that Joe's going to need all the friends he's got. And the first thing he needs from those friends is silence."

Tracy looked big-eyed. "But—"

"I mean it, Tracy. I already asked you not to talk to the reporters about my aunt and the chocolate company. Now I'm asking you not to talk about Joe Woodyard. That kind of speculation is exactly what he doesn't need right now."

"But if you're not friends with him—"

"Joe and I are not enemies," I said. "We just don't know each other."

"Then why . . . ?" Tracy sounded completely bewildered. "Then why is he here?"

"Here?"

I heard a sardonic laugh behind me, and I whirled around so fast that I nearly got a crick in my neck.

Joe Woodyard was standing right outside my window.

I could have killed the jerk. "You nearly gave me a heart attack!"

"Sorry." He didn't sound sorry.

"What are you doing here?"

"I saw that the reporters had laid siege to the chocolate shop, and I toyed with the idea of creating a diversion. But you didn't need me."

"There was only one car after us. Stacy told me how to escape."

"Actually, there were two cars. I was the second one." Joe leaned down and looked in the van window. "That swing around the old Root Beer Barrel was slick, Stacy. I drove over here the long way round. I thought you might stop in the parking lot, and I wanted to make sure everything was okay."

He was still treating me as if I were incompetent. "Thanks, but you don't have to help out," I said.

He gave me a dirty look, then turned his attention to Stacy and Tracy. I could see both of them perk up. Even with anger bubbling just beneath the surface, Joe still had the pizzazz that had made the girls at the beach stand around the lifeguard's perch drooling. Luckily, my drooling days were over.

"I appreciate you girls helping Ms. McKinney escape," he said. "Now could one of you help me out?"

"Sure." They answered in unison. He could have asked them to blast the tabloid reporters with a bazooka, and they'd have simply asked where the ON switch was.

"I need a bottle of Tylenol, but the Superette drug department is the last place I want to go tonight."

Stacy laughed, and Tracy spoke. "Mr. Gossip."

"I didn't say anything," Joe said. "But if I gave you girls a ten, would you run in and buy me a bottle of Extra-Strength Tylenol Gelcaps?"

"Sure!" They were delighted. They climbed out quickly. "We'll be right back!"

"I won't be here," Joe said. "It's not smart for me to hang around with Ms. McKinney. I'll go back to my truck. The blue one over on the next row."

They scampered off across the parking lot, toward the door of the Superette. Joe turned away and looked after them.

He still sounded gruff when he spoke again. "Thanks for the kind words."

"Kind words?"

"The antigossip advice. When I walked up here."

"That was more to do with Aunt Nettie and me than with you." I gripped the steering wheel. "Tracy and Stacy are nice girls. They're just young. They don't know yet how much harm talk can do."

"Sounds like you've learned."

"I've had a few opportunities to find out." Like when your ex-husband's first wife calls and says she heard at the beauty shop that you're dating a Dallas Cowboy and she wants to know which one, and you've never even met a Dallas Cowboy in your life, much less gone out with one, and all you can think is that your ex-husband started the rumor himself.

"Anyway," Joe said, "thanks." He turned away.

Suddenly he looked incredibly lonely. Just the way he had out at the Ripley house, when he'd moved the chair to sit beside his ex-wife's body. Maybe he wasn't such a jerk as I'd thought.

"Joe," I said, "did you see the state detective? VanDam?"

"Oh, yeah. After today we're well acquainted."

"What did you think of him?"

"He's polite."

"That's one of the things I found scariest about him."

"You've got a point. But I called a law school buddy who's now in the Detroit prosecutor's office. He says VanDam is about the best Michigan has."

"I'm worried about Aunt Nettie. She simply lives for TenHuis Chocolade. She's afraid that the company will be damaged."

"That could happen."

"I'm terrified that she'll even be a suspect." I thought back to the warning I'd had from Inspector VanDam. "I guess we will all be suspects."

Joe gave a humorless laugh. "Yeah. The ex is always the prime suspect. VanDam didn't seem impressed when I told him I didn't gain a thing from Clemmie's death. In fact, we had a business deal, and now . . . Anyway, her death leaves me in deep water with the bottom of the boat stove in. And I've got nothing to bail with."

Joe and I looked at each other for a long moment. Then he turned and walked away.

A small red Ford cruised slowly through the parking lot, and in a minute Tracy and Stacy came out of the Superette and flagged it down. The car waited while they took a small sack over to Joe's blue pickup. Then they waved in my direction and left.

One responsibility out of the way, I started the van and headed home, using back streets only a little less obscure than the escape hatch behind the Root Beer Barrel. I had to cross the bridge over the Warner River, but apparently the out-of-town reporters hadn't figured out that that would be the best place to watch for a gray van with Texas tags.

I wished I could do something about those Texas tags, but I was stuck with them until Monday at least. Besides, I didn't have the money to buy Michigan car tags. For the moment I was financially dependent on Aunt Nettie.

Aunt Nettie's house was in a semirural area; in fact, it had been outside the city limits of Warner Pier until two or three years before. As I mentioned, there were a lot of bushes and trees between the house and the road. And the drive was just one lane of sand; it didn't really look like a driveway. It would be hard for the reporters to find in the dark. But I stopped on the Lake Shore Drive, where the mailbox was located, and tossed a rag over the nameplate on top of the mailbox. As a final touch, I parked the notorious minivan with Texas tags behind the garage of the next house down the road. The Baileys lived there, and Aunt Nettie had mentioned that they were out of town.

I walked along the path that led through the woods from the Baileys' house to Aunt Nettie's. Her big Buick—she insisted a big car was best for the Michigan winters—wasn't in the drive. That surprised me for a minute, but then I saw her moving in the kitchen, and I realized that she'd been cautious enough to take the unusual step of putting her car in the garage, a remote little building that during the summer was usually reserved for garbage cans and snow shovels. She had locked the back door, too, and I had to knock. She even called out, "Lee?" before she let me in.

Aunt Nettie had finished straightening up the mess the burglar left. So much had happened since the burglary—interviews with detectives, the invasion of the tabloids—that it was hard to remember we ought to be nervous about staying in a house where there had been a break-in. So we weren't.

The phone rang, but we unplugged it and rehashed the events of the day. Aunt Nettie found my wild chase around the old Root Beer Barrel quite entertaining. And she agreed, sadly, that we'd probably better plan on closing TenHuis Chocolade Sunday.

"Sundays aren't as busy as Saturdays," she said, "but I sure hate to miss a single day during the season."

We went to bed around eleven. I read until I dropped off, and I was deeply asleep at three o'clock when Aunt Nettie shook me awake.

"Lee! Wake up!" she said. "Somebody's trying to break in!"

Chapter 9

I sat up and listened. I didn't hear a thing. Maybe I didn't want to hear a thing. I listened some more. For at least thirty seconds I sat there with my ears perked up like a German shepherd, trying to convince myself that Aunt Nettie was just nervous. Heaven knows she had every reason to be.

Aunt Nettie didn't move, but she finally whispered, "He's around behind the house."

Then I heard the sound, a sort of thump. Aunt Nettie clutched my hand, but she didn't speak.

"Sounds like the back porch," I said. "Maybe it's a raccoon."

I threw back the covers, got out of bed, and stuck my feet into my slippers. The night was cool, and Aunt Nettie turns her heating system off between Memorial Day and Labor Day, so I was wearing flannel pajama pants and a T-shirt. I didn't fumble around for a robe. I tiptoed out of my room, across the hall, and into the back bedroom, the one with the window overlooking the back porch. Unfortunately the window was closed, and I was afraid opening it would make noise. I pressed my head against the glass, but the porch roof blocked most of my view.

Then I heard something again, and that something

was fumbling around with some small metal trash cans Aunt Nettie keeps on the back porch as raccoon-proof storage. As I watched, a large black blob moved close to the porch rail, then again disappeared under the roof.

If that was a raccoon, it was the biggest sucker in Michigan.

I turned around and found myself nose to nose with Aunt Nettie. I jumped so high my T-shirt nearly turned into a parachute as I came down.

Luckily, I didn't scream. "You scared me," I whispered. "I thought you'd stayed in the other room. Have you called the police?"

"The phone won't work."

We'd unplugged it. Aunt Nettie had forgotten that, I decided. I crept across the hall and down the narrow stairs—there are doors at the top and the bottom so Aunt Nettie can compartmentalize the Michigan winter cold—with her close behind me. The stairs end in the corner of the living room, and I peeked around the door at the bottom before I came out. I saw nothing, but once again I heard that noise.

I walked into the kitchen as quietly as I could and found the phone cord where I'd draped it across the back of the kitchen stool. I ran my hand along the cord, feeling for the funny little plug that would fit into the bottom of the telephone. And my hand ran right up the cord to the telephone.

The phone was already plugged in.

I picked up the receiver and put it to my ear, but it was just a gesture. If that phone was plugged in, then Aunt Nettie was right. The phone wasn't working.

It was time to panic.

I was stuck in a house well out of earshot of any neighbor and surrounded by bushes and trees. There was an intruder on the back porch. He or she had disabled the telephone. And I felt responsible for my aunt—who was a perfectly capable sixty-year-old woman, although she might not be much help in a fight.

But if that black blob on the back porch got into the house—again?—fighting might be our best option.

I put my lips close to Aunt Nettie's ear. "Think of some kind of a weapon," I said.

She whispered back, "I don't own a gun."

"I know! But this house should be full of blunt instruments."

"I'll grab Grandma TenHuis's big iron skillet."

"Good! Just don't hit *me* with it. I'll go get the fireplace poker."

I tiptoed into the living room. I was feeling for the poker when I heard a crash from the kitchen, and I nearly jumped out of my T-shirt again.

Aunt Nettie spoke, sounding perfectly calm. "I dropped the skillets," she said.

There was no more point in trying to be quiet. I grabbed the poker and sent the tongs and shovel flying onto the brick hearth, then ran back toward the kitchen. "Turn on the porch light!"

I heard a terrific clamor on the back porch.

I flew to the window of the dining room, which stuck out at an angle to the main house and had a clear view of the back porch. I got there just as the porch light came on, and I looked out on a scene of complete slapstick. Aunt Nettie's porch chair was ricocheting off the railing. A hanging pot was swinging wildly, the petunias in it bouncing. Tin trash cans were rolling everywhere, and the lid of one of them flew away and crashed into the back door like a badly tossed Frisbee. Unfortunately it had covered the can filled with sunflower seed for the bird feeders, and the slick black seeds poured down the back steps like lava.

And in the middle of it all, a black figure was falling off the porch.

It had arms and legs this time, and I tried to get a good look at it. But it was still just a faceless blob, and the darn blob wouldn't hold still. It rolled around with the tin cans, got up to its knees, slipped on the birdseed and fell down again, got up once more and staggered off around the corner of the house.

I ran to the living room window, on the side of the house, parted the curtains, and looked out. All I could see was a flashlight beam, moving rapidly toward the drive.

I turned to run to the front door and look out, and I had another one of those moments of sheer terror when I bumped into Aunt Nettie. Again.

"Auntie! Make some noise!" I pushed past her and ran to switch on the front porch light and look out the window that faced the road. Aunt Nettie was right behind me. But we were too late to get any kind of look at the intruder. The black figure had disappeared into the trees, and all we could see was the bouncing beam of the flashlight. Aunt Nettie and I stood there holding the skillet and the poker and watched the light disappear when it reached the Lake Shore Drive.

"Whew!" I said. "I'm sure glad you heard that noise."

"I'm not," Aunt Nettie said. Her lips were pursed angrily. "That burglar apparently didn't want to get into the house this time. If I'd just kept quiet, maybe we could have had an uninterrupted night's sleep."

At that point our sleep had definitely been interrupted. I went upstairs, turned on the dim bedside lamp—somehow that seemed safer—and started getting dressed in black jeans, a dark sweatshirt, and an old pair of dark-colored sneakers.

Aunt Nettie came to the door. "What are you doing?"

"The phone's out. I've got to go call the police."

"No! You're not leaving this house!"

"What if he comes back?"

"Then we'll scare him off again."

"Aunt Nettie, he might bring weapons next time. Or reenactors. I mean, reinforcements."

"What if the reinforcements are already here? What if he wasn't alone? What if someone else is hidden outside?"

Well, that had already crossed my mind. But we couldn't simply sit in that house and wait until daylight. So I clenched my jaw, hoping that would keep my teeth from chattering. "I don't think that's too likely," I said. "I'll run along the path to the Baileys' house and call the police."

"The Baileys aren't home."

"Don't you have a key? Anyway, my van's parked over there. If I can't get in the house, I can drive down to the all-night station."

Then I stopped and considered Aunt Nettie. I wasn't sure I wanted to leave her alone. "Maybe you'd better come, too."

"No! Neither of us is stepping out that door."

We were still at an impasse when I tied my last sneaker string and went down the stairs. I was determined to go, and Aunt Nettie was determined that I wasn't leaving the house. The argument had almost reached the "Are not!" "Am too!" stage by the time we got to the living room.

That was when somebody knocked at the front door.

Of all the things that had happened, that one was the scariest. I do believe my heart stopped dead right inside my rib cage.

Aunt Nettie and I clutched each other.

"Mrs. TenHuis?" a deep voice said. "It's the police. Are you all right?"

We did have the sense to look out the window and check to make sure the vehicle in the drive had a light bar on top before we opened the door. Then we yanked a young blond patrolman inside so quick he almost got a knot in his nightstick.

"I saw the lights on," he said. "Is anything wrong?"

We poured out our tale, and he pulled his radio off his shoulder and told the dispatcher to send him some backup and to contact Chief Jones. Then he looked at the back porch.

"We might get some footprints," he said. "Not out here, but around at the side of the house."

"Well, when you find the guy," I said, "he's going to have bruises up and down his shins and shoes full of sunflower seeds."

"Oh, dear," Aunt Nettie said, "the birds are going to be all over the porch tomorrow morning."

She was wrong. By morning the porch was so thick with reporters and photographers that the birds couldn't get near it.

Both front and back porches were thick. We found out later that the just-out-of-journalism-school editor of the *Warner Pier Weekly Press* listened to the scanner on his way back from a party in Kalamazoo, and he apparently let out the news that two witnesses in the Ripley killing had been threatened by an intruder. He probably did it to curry favor with the big city reporters. I guess it worked for him; he left for a new job the next week, before TenHuis Chocolade could yank its advertising.

Thanks to his efforts, by sunup we were under siege. And I don't mean sunup as when the sun hit the house. I mean sunup as when it came up over the horizon way over there behind all those trees and bushes that were habitat for deer and turkeys and which kept Aunt Nettie's house gloomy until after eight o'clock on July mornings.

We didn't answer the door, once we saw who was out there, but it sure wasn't like a relaxing Sunday morning. And we didn't even have a working telephone. The phone company had told the police they couldn't get a repair crew out until Monday.

"Maybe we should go down to the shop," Aunt Nettie said. "We could hide in the break room."

"But how will we get there? We'd have to fight our way through."

Rescue came in a truly surprising form.

First we heard a siren coming down Lake Shore Drive. It grew louder and louder. Then it seemed to be right at the end of our drive, not moving. I peeked out around the shade on the upstairs window, and I saw the Warner Pier rescue truck edging through the crowd of press.

"Good heavens!" Aunt Nettie said. "I hope none of those reporters has had a heart attack or anything."

"I'm not as charitable as you," I said. "I wouldn't mind if the whole bunch dropped dead."

As we watched, the rescue truck drew up right in front of the front door, and Greg Glossop got out and strutted up onto the porch. He pounded on the door.

Aunt Nettie gave a deep and disgusted sigh. "Well, I can't ignore him," she said.

"I can."

But she was already on the way downstairs.

"Don't open the door," I said. I followed her.

Aunt Nettie went into her bedroom, which had a window that opened onto the porch. She moved a chair, pushed the curtain back a few inches, then opened the casement window a crack. A roar went up from the reporters, and Glossop moved over to the window.

"Chief Jones sent us to get you out," he said. His light-colored eyes were dancing with excitement, and his plump face was self-important.

"Why?"

Glossop bounced on his toes, and his round belly looked like a basketball being dribbled. "Don't you want to get away from these reporters?"

"Yes, but why does the police chief care?"

"That state detective wants to talk to you."

"Then why doesn't he come and get us himself?"

Glossop's belly jiggled again. "The chief talked him out of that. He says if they come in here with a police car it'll look like you're being arrested."

"But neither of us needs an ambulance."

"We're calling it a practice run."

"Oh."

Aunt Nettie closed the window and turned to me. "Should we go, Lee?"

"We can hardly refuse. If the state detective wants to talk to us, and if the chief doesn't want to cause more commotion . . ." I shrugged.

Aunt Nettie cracked the window again. "Give us ten minutes to get ready."

Glossop nodded, then crossed to the front door and stood there, arms folded, on guard. He didn't look quite as intimidating as Hugh, Clementine Ripley's goonlike security guard.

Aunt Nettie put on blue chambray pants and a coordinating tunic, and I put on a plaid flannel shirt over my jeans and T-shirt. Then Glossop and the other two members of his crew formed a protective arc around us and escorted us across the porch and into the back of the ambulance. We ignored the yells. "Who's sick?" "Where are you going?" "Did you poison the chocolates?" "Who tried to break in?"

Once we were inside, the driver turned on the siren and edged through the crowd and onto Lake Shore Drive. Looking out the back window, I saw reporters and photographers running for their cars, and I sighed. They were obviously going to chase us, and then everyone would know that we'd been taken in for more questioning.

But after about a block, the driver suddenly sped up, and I saw a Warner Pier police car pull out into the road behind us with lights flashing. Then another pulled out. The two of them blocked the road, and we drove off—figuratively giving the press the finger. It was a great moment.

As soon as we were around the curve and out of sight, the driver cut the siren.

"Oh, my," Aunt Nettie said. "That was fun."

Glossop preened. "The chief and I worked that maneuver out. Now we'll have you at the Ripley house in a few minutes."

"The Ripley house!" I almost yelped out the words.

"Yes, that's where they've set up a sort of command post. It's easy to control access there, you see. And there's lots of space."

"I guess so." Yes, access to Clementine Ripley's house was controlled.

"Of course, you and Nettie are going to see the top-dog detectives. They sent another team over to the police station. They're interrogating the catering staff." Glossop shrugged off the importance of the catering staff.

Huh, I thought. The catering staff was all over that house. Any of them could have poisoned those chocolates. I was somewhat comforted to learn that we weren't the only people being questioned.

"I can understand why you wouldn't want to go back to the Ripley estate," Glossop said.

"Oh, I don't mind."

"Well, I mind going! I don't even want to think about that terrible woman."

"No one seemed to like her."

"Well, I certainly didn't! She caused me a lot of

problems—and only because I insisted on performing my duty." Greg Glossop reached under his seat and produced a can of Diet Coke. He took a drink, then leaned back against the side of the ambulance, looking self-righteous.

I found myself madly curious. Glossop had obviously had a run-in with Clementine Ripley, but he was such a notorious and obnoxious gossip that I didn't want to encourage him to talk—about anything. I leaned against the other side of the ambulance and closed my eyes. I'd find out some other way, I told myself.

Aunt Nettie chatted easily with the other EMT, but neither Glossop nor I had anything more to say on the way to the Ripley house. More reporters were stationed there, and I ducked instinctively when we turned into the drive. And I admit that my stomach knotted up again as the big iron gate shut behind us. It was too much like being led into jail.

The ambulance drew up in just the same spot where I had stopped to unload the chocolates two days earlier. The back doors opened, and I started to climb out.

To my surprise the person who stretched out a hand to help me step down was Duncan Ainsley.

"Mr. Ainsley!" I said. "I thought you were going back to Chicago."

"I haven't been allowed to leave. Stuck here like a coon up a tree."

"We all have to cooperate, I guess. And perhaps they like having someone with some business connection to Clementine Ripley on the scene."

"They don't need me," Ainsley said. "They have the new owner of the property here to lend authority to their investigation."

"The new owner? Oh. I wondered who Ms. Ripley's heir would be."

"Clementine may be astonished at the way things have turned out. At this very moment she may well be standin' at the Pearly Gates gapin' in surprise."

"Surprise?"

Ainsley grinned sardonically. "Yes, even the heir appears to be amazed."

"The heir?"

"It seems Clementine never got around to signing her will. Joe Woodyard gets everything."

Chapter 10

That was a shocker. Just twelve hours earlier Joe had told me he would suffer financially because of his ex-wife's death, that he faced ruin because she had promised him money for a business deal and hadn't come through before she died. Now it seemed he scooped the pot.

I wondered, wickedly, if Marion McCoy had known this all along. Was that the reason she'd been so mad at Joe after she learned that Clementine Ripley was dead? And I wondered how she was taking the news.

I didn't expect Ms. McCoy to be happy, but I was still surprised by what happened when a uniformed state trooper opened the front door of the Ripley mansion.

Marion McCoy rushed toward me, shrieking, "Get him! Get him!"

For a moment I thought she wanted us to join her attack on Joe Woodyard. Then I realized a large white-and-brown dust bunny was slithering past my shinbone.

"Stop him! Don't let him get out!"

Champion Yonkers was sneaking out the front door, headed for freedom.

Duncan Ainsley made a valiant grab. He caught

Yonkers and wrestled him up. There were a loud yowl and a flurry of brown feet. Duncan cursed and dropped the cat. Blood oozed from his hand, and the cat ran under a shrub beside the flagstone steps.

Marion came to the door with an expression more lethal than poison gas. "Duncan, you fool! You know he hates men."

The bush in which Yonkers had taken refuge was a fairly bushy bush, with branches close to the ground. Marion knelt and looked under it. Then she looked at me. "You! Go around on the other side. Make sure he doesn't get out that way. You!" That was directed to Gregory Glossop. "You stand in front. Be ready to grab him. And, Duncan, you go to the cat cupboard and bring out his can of treats and his catnip mouse."

Her fury was so great that I didn't even consider not obeying. I scurried around to the other side of the bush, which looked like some sort of holly, and Greg Glossop covered the front. We had the cat surrounded, but I couldn't see that it was doing us any good. Our perimeter was full of gaps.

Duncan Ainsley gave an exasperated sigh, but he went into the house, as ordered. Marion began to coo at Champion Yonkers. "Here, Yonkers. Here, kitty. Nice kitty." It didn't sound sincere.

The forgotten person in all this was Aunt Nettie. Now she appeared at my shoulder. "Here, Lee," she said.

She handed me the Diet Coke can Greg Glossop had been drinking from in the ambulance. I stared at her in amazement. "That's Greg Glossop's," I said.

"Rattle it," Aunt Nettie said firmly.

I moved it halfheartedly, and I nearly jumped out of my skin when it made a noise.

"I put some pebbles in it," Aunt Nettie said. "Rattle it. Some cats like that."

I looked back at Champion Yonkers, huddled

under his bush. "Here, Yonkers," I said. "Come and see this toy." And I rattled the can.

Miraculously, Yonkers crept toward me.

Greg Glossop moved, but Marion McCoy stopped him with an imperious gesture. Aunt Nettie knelt next to me, maybe four feet away. I rattled the can and spoke coaxingly again. "Here, Yonkers. Come and see what I've got. Come and get the can. You're such a handsome fellow."

Flattery will get them every time. Yonkers crept closer to the edge of the bush. I rolled the can back and forth, then moved it toward him, keeping it within my reach. Then I rolled it to Aunt Nettie. She rolled it back to me. We all held our breath.

And Yonkers pounced on the can. He batted it back and forth idly, not far from Aunt Nettie. She reached out and petted his head, managing to tuck a thumb under his collar. Then I slid my hand around his body, and we had him, Coke can and all.

I scooped him up. "You are a naughty cat," I said. "You scared Ms. McCoy." She was looming over me, and I handed him to her.

"Thank you," she said. She glared. The look wasn't for me or for Champion Yonkers, but for some target behind me. "He's a valuable animal, and I certainly wouldn't want to fail in my responsibilities to his new owner."

With that, Ms. McCoy turned and marched back into the house. I heard a snort—maybe it was a growl—and I turned to see Joe Woodyard approaching from the path that ran around the house. Ms. McCoy's glare had apparently been aimed at him.

Joe didn't acknowledge my presence, and I didn't speak either. I was still withholding my opinion on Mr. Woodyard. A uniformed state policeman motioned, and I followed Aunt Nettie toward the door of the Ripley mansion.

Joe Woodyard had disappeared, but Duncan Ainsley reappeared with cat toys, holding a tissue to his scratched hand. He was all attention to both Aunt Nettie and me. Chief Jones materialized—from behind the bushes, I guess—and headed off Greg Glossop, keeping him outside.

We entered through a massive door and found ourselves in a large foyer. Although the decor was as severe as that in the house's main reception room, on that day it seemed suitable. It formed a quiet background for masses of flowers and plants. At least Clementine Ripley's demise had been a windfall for the florists of Warner Pier. Probably for the florists of every town in western Michigan.

Detective Underwood met us in the foyer and motioned for Aunt Nettie and me to go into that big reception room. It, too, was full of flowers and plants, but its atmosphere was still cold. But Marion McCoy was mad enough to heat things up. She spoke sternly to Underwood.

"I'm going to have to leave the cat in here, since the detectives won't allow me to use my office, and that's the spot we ordinarily use if we have to coop him up." She put him down on the floor, and he immediately made for the stairs to the balcony. Once up them, Yonkers disappeared behind a large white ceramic pot.

Marion spoke again. "I would appreciate everyone taking care not to let him out. *Again.*"

She glared around at all of us, as if we'd conspired to let the cat reach the dangerous outdoors. For the first time I noticed that Marion was wearing what appeared to be deep mourning—calf-length black skirt, black turtlenecked T-shirt, black loafers—even opaque black stockings. Her skin looked washed out, and there were deep shadows under her eyes.

"Perhaps if we *try*, we can handle this situation with a modicum of efficiency," she said.

Underwood was plainly annoyed at her dressing down, but I could see that he was in a bad position. His superiors would obviously have adopted a policy of politeness for this group, given the intense press scrutiny the crime was getting, and apparently some representative of the state police had been responsible for the cat getting in a position to slip out the front door. But Marion McCoy wasn't in charge there; the state police were. Underwood could hardly allow her to give the orders.

I was relieved when Duncan Ainsley smoothed the situation over, speaking quietly and in his most folksy tones. "Marion, I know you feel like you've been pulled through a knothole, but you and the investigating officers will need to work together if y'all are goin' to get all your coons up one tree."

Marion McCoy laughed. It wasn't a pleasant sound. "I'm going to my suite," she said. "Duncan, I leave you in charge of the cat."

It wasn't much of a curtain line, but she exited on it.

Duncan Ainsley left, too, murmuring something about finding a Band-Aid. Underwood seated Aunt Nettie and me on the couch in front of the stern stone fireplace. Then he disappeared, and Lindy Herrera appeared.

She came from the kitchen, neatly dressed in black slacks and a white jacket. She winked at me and said, "Could I get you a cup of coffee?"

"Lindy!" I struggled up from the couch, which turned out to be just as hard to get out of as I'd anticipated it would be.

Aunt Nettie spoke to her without getting up. "What are you doing here?"

"Joe decided he needed somebody around to keep things picked up and to feed the two houseguests."

"Houseguests?"

"Ms. McCoy and Mr. Ainsley."

"Oh. Mike sent you over?"

"No, Joe called me himself. He knew we could use the money, with Tony laid off. I'll just be here from ten until four for a few days, and my mother said she could watch the kids some, if Handy Hans calls Tony to work. So I came. All I really have to do is fix lunch and then leave something that Ms. McCoy can heat up for dinner. But I've been keeping a pot of coffee on. Do you want a cup? Or a soda?"

Aunt Nettie and I both declined. Lindy went back to the kitchen, and I looked around, assessing the situation before I sank into the couch again. That was how I happened to witness the next Yonkers attack.

Chief Jones came into the room from the foyer, an entrance that required him to walk under the balcony from which Clementine Ripley had fallen. Just as he reached exactly the right spot, there was a flurry of white and brown, and the chief gave a loud yelp. Yonkers bounced off his shoulders and onto the bar—almost exactly as he had the night of the party.

It was just as funny as it had been when Yonkers gave Jason the treatment. I stood there and tried to keep a straight face.

The uniformed state policeman, however, didn't try. He hooted with laughter. "Gotcha, Chief," he said. "Now I'm not the only one."

The chief looked at me, and I belatedly tried to look sympathetic. "I'll carry an umbrella when I walk under that balcony," I said.

"Ms. McCoy says you're safe," Chief Jones said. "She says the cat only does that to men."

"I thought you had taken yourself off the case," Aunt Nettie said.

"I'm just a gofer," the chief replied. "Just coordinating between the local force and the state police. They took over my office, so I came out here to get under their feet." He went out the door onto the terrace.

I sank back into the soft leather cushions. I'd barely hit bottom when something furry brushed against my leg, and I looked down to see that I'd been joined by Champion Yonkers.

I offered him my hand. "Hi, Champ. You'd better behave yourself."

Yonkers narrowed his blue eyes, twisted his milk-chocolate snout into a sneer, then scooted under the couch, turned around, and poked his head back out between Aunt Nettie's feet and mine.

Aunt Nettie leaned over and looked at him. "He certainly looks like his picture."

"Looks like his chocolate copy, too. I was a little surprised when I saw him wandering around Friday. I thought champion cats would be raised in cages and wouldn't be allowed the run of the house."

"It's called raised underfoot," a deep voice said. "It helps what they call socialization."

I looked up and saw Joe Woodyard coming in one of the doors from the terrace. He left the door open, but pulled a sliding screen door across it.

"Are you into showing cats, too?" Aunt Nettie said.

"No. But Yonk and I got along."

"Does he jump on you, too?"

"Hasn't so far." Joe pulled one of the spindly chairs over and sat down near the fireplace. Yonkers immediately came out from under the couch and wound himself around Joe's feet, mewing and rubbing his fluffy side and tail around Joe's jeans.

"He's beautiful," Aunt Nettie said.

"Do you want him?"

"Heavens, no! I have no place for a pet. Are you looking for a home for him?"

Joe nodded. "I can't have him around the boat shop. He mostly lives at the Chicago apartment, and that'll be gone pronto."

"This place . . ."

"Will also go on the market."

"Oh. Yonkers ought to be worth a lot of money."

"I suppose so. Maybe he'd be happier with a breeder, at that." Joe reached down and scratched Yonkers under the chin. The cat arched his neck and lifted his head, indicating the exact spot he wanted to receive attention.

Joe grinned at the cat. "Yonkers would probably love having a large harem."

"I can picture him lying on a silk cushion," I said, "watching his ladyfriends do the cat equivalent of a belly dance. He'd just loll around like a Persian pasha."

"Uh-oh!" Joe reached down and covered Yonkers's ears. "Don't use the word 'Persian' around Yonkers. Birmans are not Persians, and some of the breeders are very touchy about that. It's an old controversy."

I bowed to the cat. "I do apologize, Champ. I had no idea."

Yonkers gave a sassy meow, and disappeared under the couch with a haughty flick of his chocolate-tipped tail. Aunt Nettie, Joe, and I all laughed.

Interesting. Joe had been nothing but rude to me, but he had no trouble being friendly with a cat.

Joe started to speak to Aunt Nettie, but before he had more than a few words out—"Thanks for the sandwich. It"—we heard a bang behind us.

Joe jumped to his feet. "Bad cat!" He moved toward the sound. I looked over the back of the couch and saw that Yonkers had knocked over a wastebasket that had been under a spindly little writing table. "You still have your bad habits," Joe told the cat.

He set the wastebasket upright again, but Yonkers had captured a wadded-up piece of paper and was batting it around the polished floor. Joe let him keep it.

"I guess that's his favorite trick," I said. "He

knocked the office wastebasket over Friday, then batted the trash around."

I saw movement out of the corner of my eye, and Duncan Ainsley came in, walking rapidly, reappearing out of the hall where Marion McCoy had disappeared a few minutes earlier. "Joe, have you got a minute?"

"Sure," Joe said. He frowned at something behind me. I followed the frown and discovered the uniformed state policeman sitting quietly against the wall, taking in our whole conversation. "I'm waiting to see VanDam."

Ainsley took him aside and spoke quietly. However, I could hear what he said, and I'm sure the state policeman could, too. He was making a pitch, asking to keep Joe as an investment client after he assumed control of his ex-wife's estate.

Joe frowned. "It's all very much up in the air, Duncan."

"Who's the executor?"

"Apparently I am."

"Oh?"

"I was surprised Clemmie left it that way," Joe said. "Anyway, the first thing I need is a report on just what Clemmie's investments are."

"Certainly." Ainsley's voice was enthusiastic. "I'll E-mail my assistant this afternoon, and she'll have the report for you tomorrow morning."

"Let it wait, at least for a few days. I may not have time to look at it that quickly."

"It's just a matter of pressing a few buttons. We can get you a report anytime."

Just then a new voice was heard. "Mr. Woodyard!"

It was Detective Underwood. He had entered from the hall. "Please come back and talk to Lieutenant VanDam."

"That's what I've been waiting to do," Joe said. He followed Underwood.

Aunt Nettie pulled a notebook from her purse and began to write in it. I settled back on the uncomfortable couch and folded my arms. This was worse than the dentist's office. At least the dentist provided magazines. I was toying with the idea of lying down on the couch, pretending to be relaxed, when Duncan Ainsley pulled up a chair and sat down beside me.

"I wanted to talk to you," he said.

I recalled his phone call Friday night. "If it's local information, you'd be better off asking Aunt Nettie."

"No." He smiled his most winning smile. "I wanted to know more about you."

"Me? Why?"

"Humor me. Did you say you're an accountant?"

"I have a bachelor's degree in accounting."

"Where did you graduate?"

"University of Texas, Dallas. Finally."

"Finally? You went to several colleges?"

"No, I did it all there, but it took me a long time. I was what they call a nontraditional student. My parents couldn't help me, and I was determined to get through without a load of debt."

I didn't explain why I had a horror of debt. Growing up with bill collectors pounding at the door will produce that effect, and so will seeing money problems wreck your parents' marriage.

"I worked and took a few courses every semester. Then I got married, and I didn't work at all for five years, but that didn't help me get through college any faster. I still just took one or two courses a semester." I decided not to explain that either. How can you tell a stranger your husband actively obstructed your efforts to get a degree? Or that he was furious when you made the dean's list?

"So it took me a long time to graduate," I said. "Why do you ask?"

He gave me a direct look. If we'd met at a party,

I'd have thought he was coming on to me. "What's your particular field of interest?"

"In accounting? I know I'm not interested in taxes. It may depend on what sort of opportunities open up."

"Then you're not wedded to the chocolate business?"

"Not permanently. Right now Aunt Nettie needs me, and I need her."

"Lee, you should have a great business career. If you ever decide to leave Warner Pier, let me know."

I could feel my jaw drop.

Ainsley laughed. "You look astonished."

I didn't answer.

"Do you have any interest in investments?" he said.

"Not in picking them."

"Good! There are too many of us trying to do that already. But you'd be great at client presentations."

"Oh, I can't do oval—I mean . . ." I stopped, formed the words in my mind, and said them slowly. "Oral presentations. I can add like crazy, and I know an asset from a debit. But I don't talk well."

Ainsley looked quizzical. "But according to this morning's *Chicago Tribune,* you've done the beauty pageant circuit, so you didn't just fall off a turnip wagon. I judged a few pageants, some years past. They require a lot of poise."

"If the reporters get around to checking my pageant scores, they'll reveal that I did okay in bathing suit and evening gown and so-so in talent. But I completely bombed the interviews." I decided it was time to change the subject. "Now your career has been really remarkable, Mr. Ainsley. Why were you drawn to investments?"

"Just like to be around money, I guess." He grinned. "You're like all the other girls. Just interested in me because I know . . ." He mentioned a famous movie actor.

"I admit I'd love to know what he's really like," I said.

For the next fifteen minutes, Duncan entertained Aunt Nettie and me. He told me the in-stuff about that actor, about a certain rock star, about a well-known author of trash novels, about a soap opera star I had idolized as a teenager. It was amusing and just slightly wicked. I enjoyed it thoroughly. At the same time, I had the feeling I was watching a well-rehearsed and carefully developed stand-up act. He'd told those stories a lot of times, and he knew just when to pause for a laugh.

But it was still a pleasant interlude, and I hadn't had many of those lately. I was almost sorry when Chief Jones came in.

"Ms. McKinney," he said, "it seems the Warner Pier Police Department has assumed the duties of your social secretary. I have a phone message for you."

"A phone message? Oh, with the phone at the house out of order . . ."

"Right. The caller couldn't get through. Since the call seemed to be of a personal nature and the dispatcher said the party was pretty concerned about you, I said I'd hand it along."

"Thank you, Chief Jones." He handed me a pink message slip. "It's a Dallas number," I told Aunt Nettie. "It must be Mom. I thought she was in the Caymans. She must have read about all this mess in the newspaper."

"You'd better call her."

Lindy showed me a telephone in the kitchen. I found my credit card and dialed the number. The phone was picked up on the first ring.

"Lee?"

It wasn't my mother. It was Rich Godfrey, my ex.

"Rich? Why are you calling?"

"Honey, I just heard about this situation up there. I'm getting on the first plane to Detroit."

"Detroit?"

"I'll rent a car and be there by this afternoon."

"Why?"

"Lee honey, you're going to need money—money for attorneys, for public relations consultants. You don't have to face this alone."

"I see."

And I did see. It was more of the stupid Lee syndrome. It works this way: A. Lee is attractive. B. Lee has a problem with saying the wrong word. So she's stupid.

Rich thought I was too stupid to handle the situation. And maybe Lieutenant VanDam thought I was stupid enough and Aunt Nettie was naive enough that one of us would incriminate herself and admit we had poisoned Clementine Ripley's chocolates.

I'd been trying to protect Aunt Nettie by taking an active interest in what was going on, but now I saw that "active" wasn't going to be good enough. I needed to move up to "aggressive."

But first I had to take care of Rich.

"Rich," I said, "if I need help, I'll call on someone who knows Lake Michigan from Lake Erie."

"Huh?"

"You said you were going to fly to Detroit. Warner Pier is on Lake Michigan and Detroit is closer to Lake Erie—a couple of hundred miles from Warner Pier. And if you show up here, I'll throw you to the tabloid press. Get out of my life! And take your money with you!"

I hung up and took two deep breaths.

Lindy laughed. "Right on!" she said.

I pumped my fist at her and headed back into the reception room.

"Aunt Nettie!"

I must have sounded different, because her eyes were wide when she swung around to look at me. "What's wrong?"

"What's wrong is that I'm tired of people pushing us around. Burglars. State police. Cops and robbers. It's time we stood up for ourselves."

Aunt Nettie smiled. "What do you suggest?"

"I suggest we ask Lieutenant VanDam to step down here and then we insist he assign his best officers to search the chocolate shop and the house. Right now!"

Chapter 11

Aunt Nettie beamed at me. "Lee, that's a wonderful idea!"

But Duncan Ainsley jumped to his feet, looking horrified. "Lee! Mrs. TenHeist! What are y'all thinking of?"

Ainsley almost squeaked out the words, including the "t" he put at the end of Aunt Nettie's name.

"Ask any lawyer!" he said. "The authorities should get a warrant."

"What on earth for?" Aunt Nettie said.

"You can't just allow the police into your home."

"I've begged them to come twice in the last two days, thanks to our burglar," she said. "A piece of chocolate from my business contained poison. I know it didn't get poisoned at the shop, but the police don't. So the authorities are going to have to search the shop sometime. Besides, if somebody's put something poisonous in my house or my shop or my car, I want to know about it. I want the police to look in every nook and cranny. I want them to test every bottle on the flavoring shelf, check out every bar of chocolate in the storage room, look under every chocolate mold, behind every pot and in every pan."

I was glad she saw it the same way I did. I knew that Aunt Nettie and I hadn't poisoned the chocolates. I felt sure none of the hairnet ladies or the teenage counter girls had done it. And the police knew we'd had two break-ins—or one break-in and an attempted break-in. If they found evidence in the garbage can full of birdseed on the back porch at Aunt Nettie's house or in the plastic bin of cherry filling in the shop's storeroom or in a shoe box in my closet, good enough. I wanted them to have it.

But Ainsley was still arguing. "Ask your lawyer," he said. "He'd be ready to cut his suspenders and go straight up!"

Aunt Nettie waved his objections away. "Don't be silly. If our break-ins are related to a poisoning, we need to search the whole house anyway, just to make sure the burglar didn't leave any surprises for Lee and me. If the state police are willing to do it for us—and to check out the shop at the same time—well, I hope it's a complete waste of public funds, but I appreciate their doing it."

Joe came out of the hall right then, and Ainsley appealed to him. "Joe, you're a lawyer. Tell this nice lady she shouldn't encourage a search of her premises."

"I'm not a lawyer anymore," Joe said. But he did react in a lawyerly fashion, I guess. At least he asked Aunt Nettie to explain her side before he expressed an opinion.

"Clem would have gone for the search warrant," he said. "But I don't think you need to insist on one." He turned to look back toward the hall, and I saw VanDam standing there looking at us. "After all," Joe said, "the police are fully aware that you've had a break-in at the house. It's possible that something was planted. You need to know."

"Exactly." Aunt Nettie beamed. She struggled up from the couch. "Let's go on and get started. I've got a lot of work I need to do at the shop, and I can't do it until we get this over with."

"Ahem!" I said loudly. "And I have another suggestion. Aunt Nettie and I need to stop avoiding the press."

Duncan Ainsley frowned, Joe glared, and Aunt Nettie looked dubious.

But I went on. "We need to write a statement pointing out that the reputation and the business of TenHuis Chocolade are threatened by this investigation, demanding that the police proceed as quickly as possible, and telling the world we're asking the authorities to make a complete search of our premises."

Aunt Nettie smiled. "That's an excellent idea, Lee. And we'll both wear TenHuis shirts, and we'll insist on getting the shop's logo in every photograph."

Joe laughed. "Maybe you've got something. If they don't kill you."

I ignored him. "We'll meet them on the sidewalk in front of the shop, where they can't miss the sign in the window. We'll pass out chocolates, if Lieutenant VanDam will allow it, and we'll include copies of that fact sheet on all the different varieties of chocolate."

"And a price list," Aunt Nettie said happily.

"Sure," I said. "We'll even offer to answer questions, but no matter what they ask, we'll talk about chocolate."

Even VanDam grinned at that, but Joe still looked unconvinced.

"That's a good plan," Aunt Nettie said. "Can we start the search of the premises now?"

Chief Jones, who had been a silent spectator to all this, joined the conversation at that point. "How about it, Alec? Can I ask a favor for one of my Warner Pier merchants?"

VanDam shook his head. "Well, I guess the lady is right. We do need to search the place. Might as well do it now. But when you face the press, no talk about the case, okay?"

"Of course not," Aunt Nettie said. "That's your business. It has nothing to do with TenHuis Chocolade. Can we leave now? We've got a lot of work to do."

Of course, it wasn't that simple. We couldn't get into the shop to start work until the state police crew was out. They did agree to start on the office, so that we'd be able to get in there as soon as possible. Aunt Nettie went over to the shop with Underwood, and Chief Jones took me out to the house to get Aunt Nettie's car. I still didn't want to drive that conspicuous Texas tag around town, so I left my van behind the Baileys' garage for the moment.

"Okay, Chief," I said as we drove away from the Ripley house. "Are we doing the right thing?"

"Yeah, I think so. Us coppers get real suspicious of people who insist on search warrants. Normally an innocent person reacts like your aunt; they see the necessity for the search and want to get it over with. The only time people are likely to stand on their rights is if they're involved, or if they are afraid some member of their family is involved."

"What about talking to the press?"

"That's probably a good idea, too. But my relations with the press were so bad at one time—I'm not the one to ask."

He glanced over at me. "When it comes to motive, VanDam knows I belong at the top of the list."

"I heard that you tangled with Clementine Ripley on the witness stand."

"If I'd known she was going to move to Warner Pier, I'd have retired someplace in Wisconsin."

He spoke with his usual easygoing drawl, but his hands were clutching the steering wheel tightly. As if he were strangling it.

I decided to ask one more nosy question, concealing it as well as I could. "You might have a motive, but you didn't have opportunity, did you?"

"Yes, I did. Clementine Ripley summoned me out to the house Friday afternoon. She wanted to tell me how she wanted my boys to handle the extra traffic for the benefit. We talked in that office back by the garage, and I had to wait for her for a while. And I think that box of candy was sitting on the desk the whole time. Now I'm told it had her name on it, a big hint that it was for her exclusive consumption."

So Chief Jones wasn't kidding when he said he was a suspect. Maybe that would work to Aunt Nettie's advantage.

The press had deserted the house. I grabbed a khaki skirt and a chocolate-brown shirt with a TenHuis logo from Aunt Nettie's closet and a TenHuis shirt and khaki slacks from mine, then headed back. By the time I got to the shop Aunt Nettie and I were allowed to begin working in the office, so I booted up the computer and wrote a simple news release. I never had a class in public relations, but I took several business communications courses, so I just wrote a letter and left off the salutation. It might not be slickly professional, but we wanted to look like a folksy small-town business. I also called the *Grand Rapids Press*, the Grand Rapids office of the Associated Press, and a couple of the television stations to tell them about our "press conference." I refused to answer any questions, but told them we'd have a statement at two p.m. at the shop.

While I did that, Aunt Nettie cut up a large white cardboard box and used a marker to write PRESS CONFERENCE 2 P.M. in big black letters. She wrote, HERE, in slightly smaller letters just underneath. She offered to add something about door prizes, but we decided that was a little too silly. We wanted to look like mid-America, not Hicksville.

She stuck the sign in the window, and almost immediately it got attention. A crowd gathered out front, and some people knocked at the street door, but we didn't answer, and the search team didn't either. They were using the back door to go in and out.

I was running off twenty-five copies of the statement I'd written when a member of the search team stuck her head into the office. "There's a guy in the alley who wants to see you, Mrs. TenHuis. He says he's the mayor."

"Mike Herrera?" I said.

"I'll talk to him," Aunt Nettie said. I went with her.

Herrera had switched from his black-and-white caterer outfit to navy-blue shorts and a polo shirt.

"Mike!" Aunt Nettie said. "What can I do for you?"

"Tell me what you're up to," Herrera said. "This town has gone loco. I'm having to neglect my restaurants to hang around city hall all day. That never has happened before!"

"Come in, quick," Aunt Nettie said.

We got Mike inside and took him into the office. Then Aunt Nettie gleefully explained that we were going to try negative psychology on the press. Instead of running from them, we were going to demand their attention.

Herrera shook his head sadly. "I've been answering questions from those guys all day."

"Oh, Mike! I'm sorry," Aunt Nettie said. "I've been so worried about my own problems that I didn't think about your position."

"Yah," he said. "My whole crew is being questioned, since we were on the scene. But I never saw those chocolates, and I don't think any of my people did either."

He patted his well-gelled hair. "But maybe you got the best idea about how to deal with those reporters," he said. "You could borrow the little sound system from city hall."

"Oh, Mike! That would be such a help."

Herrera grinned. "You need something to stand on, too. A platform. I'll call the park superintendent. We'll see what we can come up with."

Aunt Nettie sighed admiringly. I had no idea she could be so flirtatious. "I'd be happy to pay a rental fee."

"That won't be necessary." Herrera leaned over, and only Aunt Nettie and I heard him whisper. "If you killed her, you could submit a bill, and the city council would pay it without discussion." He closed his eyes. "That woman, she went back on her word. Made me look stupid." His eyes opened again. "I thought I was tellin' the council the truth—but she changed her mind. She made me a liar. It was a matter of honor. I hated her."

Aunt Nettie patted his hand. "I did, too," she said softly. "I thought of killing her a million times."

"Shut up!" I whispered, too, but I was emphatic. "Both of you! Yecch!"

Aunt Nettie giggled and whispered, "Oh, Lee, everybody knows neither Mike nor I would actually do anything to hurt anyone."

"You're wrong, Aunt Nettie. Not everyone knows that. We're surrounded by a whole group of people who don't know it and who could testify about your jokes."

Honestly! Sometimes I thought Aunt Nettie had chocolate for brains. But Mike Herrera should be a little more sophisticated, if he was going to be a politician.

At least he offered to bring us a sandwich from Mike's Sidewalk Café. We accepted. "Business is good down there," he said. "Humans is crazy people. They act like they doan have good sense. Act bad. And it's just curiosity."

His comment made me remember my own curiosity. "Okay, y'all," I said. "I've got my own problem with curiosity, and you can just help me figure something out."

Aunt Nettie looked politely interested, and Mike Herrera frowned. I told them about what Greg Glossop had said during the ride to the Ripley house.

"He definitely had it in for her," I said. "It was more than just a general dislike. Do either of you know anything about this?"

Mike frowned. "I haven't heard anything about that. Seems like Clementine Ripley left trouble everywhere she went." He looked at his watch. "I'll get your sandwiches."

The state police had almost finished their search by the time two p.m. came, and we were ready to face the press. Chief Jones sent Patrolman Jerry Cherry down with some crime scene tape to mark off an area for the reporters, keeping the hordes of tourists outside the area. Prime viewing space became the broad windows of the Upstairs Club, right across the street from us. If everybody who was pressed up against the screens over there bought lunch, the "upstairs" must have had a big blip on their profit chart. Whoever lived in the apartment next door to the upstairs must have cashed in, too. They removed their screens and rented their windows to two different TV crews.

Mike Herrera, now wearing long pants and a dignified stance, opened the event with a few remarks about the many attractions of Warner Pier as a vacation paradise and citing what a valuable asset TenHuis Chocolade was to the community. Tracy and Stacy had showed up, mainly to see what was going on, and they handed out samples of chocolate. ("It's a Bailey's Irish Cream bonbon," I heard Tracy say to one reporter. "It has a classic cream liquor interior." I made a mental note to talk to her about how to pronounce "liqueur.")

Most of the reporters were brave enough to dip

into a box. The two girls also handed out the press releases. We'd stapled each release to a sheet describing all the varieties of bonbons and truffles produced and sold by TenHuis Chocolade and to a price list, including an order blank. As we'd hoped, our flagrantly commercial ploy seemed to cool the press's interest in us more than anything else had.

Aunt Nettie opened by saying, "We don't make fudge." That got a laugh; fudge is the saltwater taffy of western Michigan—on sale everywhere. Then Aunt Nettie talked about how hard she worked to make her chocolates of the highest quality, about how she and my uncle had gone to the Netherlands for a year to learn how to make chocolates, and how proud she was of her employees.

"If I find out who has damaged the reputation of my business—well, if that person has a penny left after he's convicted of murder, then he'll also face a serious lawsuit from me," she said. "My husband and I worked for thirty years to build this business, and I'm not going to sit on my hands and see it destroyed."

"When will you reopen?" some reporter on the back row asked.

"Tomorrow. Unless the state police want me to stay closed. We're cooperating in every way."

She handled the whole thing very well. She was completely natural. Completely Aunt Nettie. I was proud of her.

The reporters and photographers seemed to love her. The bulbs flashed; the tape recorders were out. I saw that this cute little old gray-haired chocolate-maker was going to be good copy.

For a few minutes I thought I was going to escape without having to say anything. But then somebody yelled my name. "Hey, Ms. McKinney! Is it true that Ripley's ex was your high school sweetheart?"

Aunt Nettie looked at me, handing the question off just like the straight man handing off the joke for a punch line.

Think, Lee, I told myself. "If you mean Joe Woodyard," I said, "the answer is a firm no. For one thing, I didn't even go to high school in Warner Pier. For another, I never exchanged two words with him until day before yesterday."

A woman reporter on the front row spoke up. "But you were here summers, working for your aunt."

"Three summers."

"Did you know Woodyard then?"

"I knew who he was, because the girls I ran around with knew him. I don't recall ever having the nerve to speak to him."

"Why would speaking to Joe Woodyard have required nerve?"

I'd gotten myself into a mess. *Don't say anything else stupid,* I told myself. I took a deep breath. "Joe was a college guy! He scared me spitless! Weren't you ever sixteen?"

Evidently she had been, because she laughed, and most of the other reporters joined in. The moment passed, and I relaxed. Too soon. The next question nearly got me.

It came from the same reporter, the woman in the front row.

"Still, I imagine you joined most of the people in Warner Pier in thinking Joe Woodyard had made a foolish marriage?"

I just stared at her. I couldn't believe what she had said.

So she spoke again. "At least, that's the gossip I've picked up around here. People don't seem to feel that he behaved very sensibly."

I saw what she was trying to do, of course. They couldn't get me to say anything nice about Joe, so this reporter had decided to settle for getting me to say something naughty about him. It was infuriating.

"That's none of my busybody," I said.

The whole front row of reporters looked confused, and I knew immediately that I'd botched up. "Business," I said. "It's none of my business."

I took Aunt Nettie's arm and we got off the little platform that the park superintendent had improvised out of forklift pallets and plywood. We went back into the shop with as much dignity as we could gather around us, considering that twenty reporters were yelling out more questions.

Aunt Nettie locked the door and smiled. "That went about as well as we could expect," she said.

"Until the end, when I tied my tongue in a knot," I said.

I became aware then that one of VanDam's technicians had walked up to us. "The lieutenant wants to see you," she said.

We followed the woman into the break room, where VanDam and Underwood were looking at something in a small paper sack. VanDam hastily put the sack down before he spoke. "Is either of you ladies diabetic?"

"No, thank heavens!" Aunt Nettie said. "That would make it difficult to handle the chocolate business."

"Does either of you use injections of any sort?"

"Drugs? Of course not!" I said.

"Injections are not necessarily illegal, Ms. McKinney. Lots of medications are injected."

"Not by me. Not by Aunt Nettie. I take nothing but vitamin capsules."

"And I take nothing but Premarin, calcium, vitamins, and the occasional Tylenol. All by mouth," Aunt Nettie said. "Why do you ask?"

VanDam lifted the paper sack. "Can either of you

identify this?" He dumped a plastic bag containing a few pieces of plastic out onto the table.

I stared at the sack. Somehow its contents seemed familiar. But the memory eluded me.

"I don't know anything about them," Aunt Nettie said.

"It's a broken syringe," VanDam said. "We found it in the Dumpster out in the alley."

CHOCOLATE CHAT

TYPES

- Bitter chocolate is the simplest form of processed chocolate—basically cooking chocolate. It contains no sugar and must be from fifty percent to fifty-eight percent cocoa butter. The remaining content is chocolate liquor.

- Bittersweet chocolate contains sugar, but is not as sweet as sweet chocolate. In the United States it must be at least thirty-five percent cocoa butter.

- Sweet chocolate is similar to bittersweet, except that it contains more sugar. Since it contains more other ingredients—sugar, cocoa butter, perhaps a slight amount of milk—it contains less chocolate liquor.

- Milk chocolate contains less chocolate and more milk, sugar and flavorings. Because it contains less cocoa, only the beans with the strongest flavor are used in milk chocolate.

- Cocoa is basically chocolate liquor with almost all the cocoa butter pressed out. It then becomes a dry cake that can be made crumbly. But cocoa does usually contain some cocoa butter. Most brands contain between fourteen percent and twenty-five percent.

- White chocolate contains no chocolate liquor, but it does contain cocoa butter.

Chapter 12

"Anybody could have put that there." I spoke quickly, but my voice sounded weak. Just about as weak as my stomach felt.

VanDam nodded. "Right. That alley obviously gets a lot of use."

"So the syringe doesn't prove anything," Aunt Nettie said. "Some drug user might have walked through there and tossed it in the trash."

"Right," VanDam said. "It will have to go to the lab for testing."

I spoke again, and I tried to make my voice a little stronger. "Even if it was used to poison the truffles, the only thing that would prove is that somebody is trying to make sure my aunt and I are the prime suspects. After all, our Dumpster is plainly marked with TenHuis Chocolade."

VanDam kept his face deadpan, but Underwood looked skeptical. I could understand why. The broken syringe was circumstantial evidence, of course, and it could easily have been planted. But it was right at our back door, so it pointed to us. Though it was hard to visualize either Aunt Nettie or me being dumb enough to put the broken syringe in our own Dumpster, then demand that the state police search our business.

Any of the numerous suspects in the murder of Clementine Ripley could have gotten hold of a syringe. Greg Glossop sold them. Chief Jones probably had an evidence locker full of them. Any of the rest of us—Mike Herrera and his crew; the inmates of the Ripley house, Marion McCoy and Duncan Ainsley; Joe Woodyard; even Aunt Nettie and me—any of us could have stolen one from a diabetic friend or gone behind the counter at the Superette pharmacy or pocketed one from the cabinet in a doctor's office. This was a small town, after all.

Any one of us was smart enough to go to the library in a large city—like Grand Rapids, less than a hundred miles away—quietly take a book on poisons from the shelf, look up how to make cyanide, get hold of either peach or cherry pits and follow the recipe, fill our stolen syringe, then go to Clementine Ripley's house prepared to kill her by injecting the poison into some sort of food. The appearance of the chocolates in a box particularly set aside for her would have been—what's the word?—serendipitous.

Greg Glossop did have the edge in one regard. As a pharmacist he ought to know how to manufacture cyanide from cherry or peach pits without looking it up. He could have injected cyanide directly into Clementine Ripley's body, then also injected cyanide into the chocolates, which were still around after he got there. Hard to do, but not impossible. In fact, he might have even doctored some prescription he'd filled for her, causing her to fall ill. As an EMT he'd know he would be called in if she collapsed.

Actually, as far as I was concerned, Glossop was the leading suspect. Maybe that was simply because I didn't like him. I wasn't even sure he had a motive. But I was willing to bet that he'd had some unusual run-in with Clementine Ripley.

Who would know for sure? The answer, of course, was Marion McCoy. But how could I ask her?

Why not try plain English?

The answer was so simple that it made me shake all over. Did I have the nerve to seek out the intimidating Marion McCoy and ask her a question about Greg Glossop and Clementine Ripley?

But even more terrifying was the thought that Aunt Nettie might be a suspect in Clementine Ripley's murder. Compared to that, bearding Marion McCoy would be a snap.

I'd do it. But how could I get hold of Marion privately? If I went out to the Ripley estate, she'd probably tell the security guard to send me away. How could I get in?

If Joe Woodyard inherited, he'd actually have the say-so on who came in and out of "his" house. I could call him.

No. Joe and I hadn't had friendly relations. I didn't want to ask him for any favors. So how could I do it?

By then the search team was leaving. They were going to take a short break, the team leader told us, then head out to Aunt Nettie's house to search there. I agreed to meet them in forty-five minutes.

I was so downhearted that I didn't have much energy, but Aunt Nettie immediately went to the refrigerator and took out ten pounds of butter and two half gallons of heavy whipping cream. She paused and looked at me. "You'll be here to help me lift the copper kettle, won't you?"

"For half an hour. What are you going to make?"

"Crème de Menthe bonbons. We're nearly out. Nancy Burton came in Friday and bought six dozen."

"Who's Nancy Burton and why on earth did she need that many Crème de Menthe bonbons?"

"Nancy manages the Deer Forest B-and-B. She puts our bonbons on the pillows when she turns the beds down, so she uses several dozen a week. Usually she warns us when she runs low, but Friday she got caught short. So we got caught short. We got the *bojkie* made yesterday, but I need to get them filled and ready to go into the enrober tomorrow."

I thought I knew what she was talking about. The *bojkie,* a Dutch word pronounced "bokkie," is the chocolate shell that holds the filling for a bonbon. The "enrober" is a key piece of equipment in making bonbons. As its name implies, the enrober coats—or "enrobes"—the filled bojkie to produce the finished bonbon.

The enrober is the reason that very good truffles can be made at home, but making good bonbons in a typical kitchen is a lot harder. Truffles are little balls of filling that are rolled by hand in melted chocolate, but bonbons are made by filling little cups molded from chocolate. The whole bonbon is then put through a sort of shower-bath of chocolate in this special machine, the enrober. Aunt Nettie explains the difference by saying truffles are made from the inside out and bonbons from the outside in.

A small chocolate shop like TenHuis Chocolade enrobes once or twice a week; the Brach's Chocolate Cherry plant probably enrobes twenty-four hours a day. Our enrober is four feet long; theirs probably covers a city block. The theory is the same, but our chocolate doesn't contain preservatives, and we think it tastes a lot better.

Aunt Nettie usually runs the enrober on Monday, which is usually her slowest day.

"Call me when you need me," I said. I went into the office and began to balance out the cash register receipts from Saturday night, finishing up the chore I'd left undone when Tracy, Stacy, and I fled the reporters. As I counted nickles, quarters, dollars, and fives, I worried about how to get through to Marion McCoy.

When I glanced through the big window that overlooked the kitchen, I could see Aunt Nettie lighting the gas fire for the big copper kettle. That kettle is a beautiful object, but it's made for use, not admiration. It has its own freestanding gas burner, about the size of a small charcoal cooker. Copper is used for the kettle because it heats more evenly, and Aunt Nettie always uses this particular kettle to make the "base"—the mix of butter, sugar, and cream that is then flavored and turned into all the different fillings for bonbons and truffles.

Aunt Nettie added sugar and lifted the kettle onto the gas burner—the kettle isn't hard to lift when it's not hot—and began to stir.

I had balanced the register and prepared my deposit, and steam was rising from the copper kettle when I suddenly knew how to get into the Ripley estate.

"Lindy," I said. "Lindy will be there until four o'clock."

I glanced at my watch. It was already three o'clock, and I couldn't leave for a few minutes—until I'd helped Aunt Nettie with the kettle.

I shoved the deposit into a drawer, locked my desk, and went out to the workroom. "How quickly will the base be ready?"

"Maybe ten minutes. Why?"

"I thought of an errand I need to get done before I meet the search team. And I need to make a phone call."

For once my accountant's methodical mind was useful. When I had used my credit card to call Rich, I had written down the number I was calling from. It was the kitchen phone in the Ripley estate, and Lindy had told me it was a separate line. I found the number deep in my purse and called it. Lindy answered.

"It's Lee. I need a favor."

"Sure."

"I need to talk to Marion McCoy. Can you tell the security guard to let me in?"

"Well . . . I guess so. I could tell him you're bringing me a pound of coffee or something."

"Great! What kind of coffee do you want?"

Lindy laughed. "I really could use some. They usually use the special blend from Valhalla Coffee and Tea. Drip grind."

"I knew it wouldn't be Folgers. Valhalla's right down the block, so it'll be easy to get some. Please don't leave until I get here."

I whipped down the block to Valhalla ("Coffee fit for the Gods"), one of Warner Pier's three specialty coffeehouses, and picked up the coffee, getting back just in time to help Aunt Nettie lift the heavy kettle onto a metal worktable.

"Please call the police station and pass the word along that I may be a little late meeting the state police," I said.

Aunt Nettie nodded. She was already in the storeroom looking for her Crème de Menthe. "Whatever you say, Lee. Oh, dear, they did move the flavorings around when they searched!"

I headed for the Ripley estate. After I identified myself as a coffee deliverer, the massive gate slid back, and I drove in. I circled the house and parked near the kitchen, in the gravel area where the catering vans had been two days before.

Lindy was looking out the kitchen door. I handed her the coffee.

"Now," she said, "what's this all about?"

"I need to talk to Marion McCoy. I hope I don't get you fired."

"Oh, this job's only going to be for two or three days anyhow. And Joe's the boss, not Marion. He won't fire me if she gets annoyed. They can't stand each other."

"Do you know where Marion is?"

"In the office back by the garage. The cops finally left, and she went right in there and started working on the computer. Mr. Ainsley was in there, too. But he went out for a walk. Listen! Why don't I make Marion a cup of tea? You can take it in to her."

Lindy said the kettle was already boiling, so I agreed. Lindy made the tea in a china pot and put it, along with a cup and saucer, sterling silver teaspoon and little sugar bowl, on a tray.

"I hope she doesn't get so mad at me she throws the teapot," I said.

"Oh, that wouldn't be 'being responsible for the estate,' " Lindy said.

Actually, I nearly broke the teapot when Champion Yonkers decided to walk under my feet as I started out of the kitchen.

"You come over here, cat," Lindy said. "Stay out of the way. Come on. I'll give you a plastic cup to bat around on the floor."

"I'm just glad he didn't jump on me," I said. "Well, here goes."

I walked quickly down the peristyle, trying not to lose my nerve. I really don't like unpleasant scenes, but the thought of Aunt Nettie in jail gave me courage. I gulped only once before I rapped on the office door.

Marion's "Come in!" sounded exasperated. She frowned when she saw who was disturbing her. "What are you doing here?"

"I ran an errand for Lindy. She sent you some tea. But I wanted to ask you a question."

I placed the tea on the credenza behind her desk, and I went on talking before she could call the security guard.

"Did Ms. Ripley have some problem with the pharmacist at the Superette?"

"That Glossop? She didn't have the problem. He did. Did he tell you about it?"

"No. In fact, he wouldn't say much—and that's what made me feel they'd had trouble. He talks a lot about everything else. But he wouldn't say anything about her."

"He's an officious ass."

"No argument there. But was there some specific problem between them?"

"He refused to fill a perfectly legitimate prescription."

"How could he do that?"

"It was marked no refills. Normally, a druggist would be satisfied with calling the prescribing doctor for an okay. But not Glossop! He refused to refill it at all until Clementine had seen her doctor again. And of course, he did all this on a Saturday afternoon, so it was difficult to get hold of the doctor. It caused a lot of inconvenience. Clementine was planning to file a complaint with the State Board of Pharmacy."

Marion frowned. "Why are you asking about this?"

"My aunt and I both handled the chocolates that held the cyanide. So I feel that I must learn all I can about the whole situation."

Marion stared at me. Abruptly, without changing her expression, she began to guffaw.

Her laughter was more hysterical than hilarious. It was more frightening than if she'd shouted in anger.

Almost immediately—as if someone had been waiting for an unusual sound—the door behind me opened. The security guard, Hugh, rushed in.

"Marion!" he almost shouted. "Calm down!"

Her laughter diminished. "Oh, Hugh! This stupid girl thinks Greg Glossop killed Clementine!"

Hugh looked from Marion to me and back again. "Well, I guess he could have," he said.

"Glossop! That milksop! His tongue may be poisonous, but he's too cowardly to give anybody cyanide." Marion turned to me. "No, you little fool. You're completely on the wrong track."

She stood up and glared at me. Oddly enough, what struck me was that she was as tall as I am. When you're almost six feet tall, it's unusual to look another woman in the eye.

Hugh went around the desk and patted her shoulder. "Now, Marion, you've got to calm down," he said. "We're not through this yet. Just hang on a few more days."

Marion shoved him away. She kept glaring at me. "You idiot. Glossop didn't have anything to do with Clementine's death. Surely any fool can see that Joe Woodyard killed her."

This conversation wasn't going anyplace. Which doesn't mean that silence fell.

Marion kept raving. "I tried to tell Clementine he was no good. He was just after what he could get—connections, money, a reflection of her status. But no! He had a hold over her no friend or associate could break. She used to look at him just the way she looked at your aunt's chocolates! It was embarrassing to see her. She'd stand any humiliation from him."

"Marion, Marion!" Hugh yelled, but he couldn't stop her tongue. I didn't even try.

"She turned her back on all her friends, on the people who loved her best, the ones who did everything for her, because of Joe Woodyard! We wanted her success. But Joe—as soon as he got into her life, he started trying to change her. Take that case, Clem. Don't defend that man, Clem—he's actually guilty!" She slapped the top of the desk. "You'd think a lawyer would know that even the guilty deserve a defense.

"Then he had the nerve to walk out on her! Thought she'd come running after him, I guess." She smiled wickedly. "But that didn't work. And now he tells the state police he didn't know he inherited. That's a lie! He and Clementine talked for half an hour Friday. I'm sure—I'm positive!—she told him she hadn't signed her new will. I feel certain of it. He had to act fast or he wouldn't inherit. He's a murderer!"

She pounded on the desk again. "God! I'm going to go insane if I can't get out of this house! If I can just last till tomorrow when I can fly away forever!"

Hugh had been trying to get a word in, trying to soothe her, and now she turned on him. "And you! You're as big an idiot as this girl is. Get out! Get out of my sight!"

I looked at Hugh, and he looked at me. He came around the desk and motioned. The two of us went into the hall. He closed the door behind us. Marion was still screaming and sobbing.

"I hate to leave her alone," I said.

Hugh nodded. "I guess I'd better ask Joe to call a doctor. Or the state police. Or somebody."

We stood there. Obviously, Hugh was as reluctant to make a decision as I was. Then a door opened behind us, and I looked around. Duncan Ainsley had come in through the utility room.

"What's going on?" he said. "Who's yelling?"

Hugh, still looking worried, explained.

Duncan gave an exasperated sigh. "Marion's been a half bubble off plumb all day," he said. "I'm hoping the state police will let her go back to Chicago tomorrow."

"She seems to be counting on it," I said. "I'm so sorry I pushed her into this, this—crisis."

"Don't you feel responsible. You were just walking by when the accident happened. I think it's time she went to bed with a hypo as big as Dallas. Is there a doctor in this town?"

"There used to be. Lindy will know."

"If she doesn't, Joe will. He was upstairs in Clementine's office." He gestured. "Would you see if you can find one of them?"

I turned and ran down the peristyle, feeling panicky. Seeing a person as strong as Marion McCoy melt down was shattering. I was still running when I reached the dining room and pivoted toward the kitchen.

And I careened right into Joe Woodyard.

Chapter 13

In a life full of humiliating experiences, nothing I ever do will match that moment. Except maybe stepping on my hem and ripping the skirt off my costume during the opening number of the Miss North Dallas pageant.

I will say a head-on collision with a six-foot-tall woman seemed to startle Joe as much as colliding with him did me. At least he jumped as high as I did, and he came down yelling, "What the hell!" Behind him, Lindy gave a little yelp.

I came down dithering. "I didn't mean to cause a commotion! I'll apologize later! Is there a doctor in Warner Pier?"

Joe grabbed me by the arms. "A doctor? What's happened?"

"It's Marian McCoy! She's hysterical."

"Thank God." Joe looked relieved. "I was afraid somebody else was dead!"

"She's screaming. Hugh couldn't calm her down. Mr. Ainsley thinks we should call a doctor."

"If Duncan or Hugh can't calm her, yeah, we'd better call somebody."

"I'll go see if I can help," Lindy said. She headed back the way I'd come.

"I'll see if I can get hold of Dr. Schiller," Joe said.

"I'm an interloper here," I said. "I'll get out."

"No!" Joe's voice was as brusque as usual. "Stick around. I want to talk to you." He headed toward the reception room, and in a minute I could hear his tennis shoes thumping as he ran up the stairway to the balcony.

I didn't know what to do. I was supposed to be out at Aunt Nettie's house, letting the state police's technical team in to search the place. But after I'd been rude enough to invade a house that now apparently belonged to Joe Woodyard, it would be even ruder to run off without giving him an explanation—feeble as my explanation might be. I did not want to face him, but I'd feel like a coward if I didn't.

In desperation, I did what I've done before. I turned to Aunt Nettie. I picked up the kitchen phone and called the chocolate shop.

The phone rang four times, and then I got a recording. "Darn!" I said. I waited until the beep, then yelled, "Aunt Nettie! It's me! Lee! Please pick up the phone!"

It took a few seconds, but she did. "Lee? What's wrong?"

"What's wrong is that I'm stuck out at the Ripley house and I'm missing my date with the technical team. Is there any way you can get out there to let them in?"

"Oh, dear. I guess I shouldn't have started these Crème de Menthe bonbons. I'm spouting."

Aunt Nettie didn't mean she was blowing her top. She meant she was using a funnel to fill square, dark chocolate shells with the Crème de Menthe flavored filling she'd made earlier. She manipulates the little stick as a plug and exactly the right amount of filling comes out the end of the funnel, filling one by one the dozens of little chocolate shells—the *bojkie*—set up on a tray. The filling has to be exactly the right temperature for this to work.

"I'll just have to leave here," I said.

"No," Aunt Nettie said. "I'll call Inez Deacon. She has a key to the house."

"Mrs. Deacon! Is she still patrolling the beach?" Mrs. Deacon and I had shared some dangerous times a dozen years earlier, when I was sixteen. She was one of Aunt Nettie's closest neighbors.

Aunt Nettie laughed. "Inez doesn't miss a day at the beach. She'll be glad to get in on the excitement. What's the number there? If she's not home, I'll call back."

I waited five minutes—timing it by the kitchen clock—then called the shop again. This time Aunt Nettie picked up on the first ring. She assured me that Mrs. Deacon had readily agreed to let the search team in and to tell them that one of us would be there as soon as possible.

With that taken care of, I got a glass of water, leaned against the kitchen cabinet, and assessed my position.

My try at active detection had certainly been a fiasco. My goal had been to find out why Greg Glossop had it in for Clementine Ripley. And I'd found the answer. He'd refused to fill a prescription, and she'd been planning to report him to the State Board of Pharmacy.

Did that matter? I couldn't believe that the picky Greg Glossop wouldn't have some legalistic defense. He was so insufferably egotistical that I felt sure he'd believe he could beat a complaint, no matter who it came from.

But that issue had paled beside the importance of the other two things I'd learned. First, Marion McCoy was telling the state police—and anyone else who would listen—that Joe Woodyard killed Clementine Ripley. Second, Marion was close to the breaking point. If she hadn't already broken. I was sorry about that, but I decided it wasn't my problem.

My problem was giving some explanation to Joe Woodyard. How should I handle this? Sitting in the kitchen like a kid waiting outside the principal's office did not appeal to me. I decided I'd better take the initiative and go to him, upstairs in Clementine's office.

I marched resolutely through the dining room and reception room and mounted the stairs. When I was halfway up, Joe came out onto the balcony.

"Were you able to reach the doctor?" I said.

"It took threats, pleading, and bribery, but he agreed to make a house call. He said he'd be here in half an hour."

"I apologize—"

Joe cut me off and pointed to the door he'd come out of. "I want to talk to you. Wait in here while I go tell Duncan and Hugh the doctor's on the way."

"Joe!" He ignored me, going down the stairs past me and turning toward the peristyle.

I stood looking after him, tempted simply to leave the premises. But that would seem cowardly. Finally I went on through the door Joe had pointed to. At least I'd get to see a little more of the house.

The room I entered was obviously the office, and it looked like someone actually worked there. The desk was enormous and held nothing but a computer, giving the maximum work space. The desk chair was the kind that can be adjusted to do anything but somersaults, and the lighting was topnotch. Bookshelves lined one wall, and they were stuffed with books, not doodads or gimcracks or even art objects. A second wall held built-in filing cabinets, flanked by decorative paneling.

The walls were painted white, just like the walls in the reception area, but they weren't blank, as the walls downstairs were. At least fifteen pictures—oils, watercolors, and woodblock prints—were hung in an arrangement behind the desk. The pictures weren't ones I'd have selected, but they were distinctive and obviously reflected the taste of a real person.

I walked over beside the desk to take a closer look at them. That was when I saw that the computer was on. Joe had been working on it, or maybe playing solitaire, when Marion's crisis arose.

I couldn't resist, of course. I looked at the computer screen to see what he'd been doing.

He'd been checking Clementine Ripley's Visa bill.

That was definitely none of my business. So naturally, I couldn't stand not taking a peek. Feeling curious—and guilty about my curiosity—I sat down in the desk chair to look at the computer screen. Then something rubbed against my leg, and I jumped up again.

Champion Yonkers walked out from under the desk.

"You again? What are you up to now?"

He yowled at me, in his usual haughty manner, then went around the desk and climbed into one of the two armchairs. He leaped from there to a shelf over the filing cabinets. He settled down there and surveyed the world with such aplomb that I deduced that it was his regular spot.

"I guess you won't rat on me," I said to him, turning back to the Visa bill.

And one item caught my eye immediately.

"Cheuy's! That's in Dallas."

I leaned close to the screen. Cheuy's is not a usual name for a restaurant, and I was sure there wasn't more than one. Sure enough—the charge was marked with DALLAS. I read on down. Neiman's. Well, nobody goes to Dallas without checking out Neiman's. And Clementine Ripley had succumbed to their goods, too. In fact, she'd spent a couple of thousand there.

I was looking on down the list of items when something clicked behind me. I jumped up guiltily, sure Joe had caught me checking out his—or his ex-wife's—private business.

But there was no one there. Then a section of the wall near the filing cabinets moved, and I jumped again. I moved from behind the desk and discovered the culprit.

"Yonkers!" I said. "You scared me."

The cat was using one white paw to open a door. The paneling on each end of the bank of filing cabinets camouflaged a closet.

"You know, Yonk, I expect they don't want you in there," I said.

I hauled him out, despite his angry yowls. I closed the door and made sure that it was latched.

Just then I heard tennis shoes thumping on the stairs. I moved away from the closet and the desk and tried to look innocent when Joe came in the door.

"I apologize for coming out here without an invitation and for stirring up Ms. McCoy," I said.

"Forget it," Joe said. "She loved having a new audience for her tale of how unworthy I was to touch the hem of Clem's gown."

"She doesn't seem to be a Joe Woodyard fan, true."

"Clem relied on her for everything—and I mean everything. Marion paid the bills, balanced the checkbook, ordered the meals, took the phone calls, told Clem when to go to the doctor and when to get her hair done. My presence interfered with all that. It's natural that she didn't like me. So she thinks I killed Clem."

So Joe knew Marion thought he'd killed his ex-wife. "Did she live with you?"

"She has a private suite here, but she has her own apartment in Chicago. And she always thought I was the intruder! But that's not what I wanted to talk to you about." He gestured at the computer screen. "You've lived in Dallas, haven't you? I don't understand these."

"Oh?"

"Clem's Visa bills. Marion is refusing to turn any financial records over until she has a court order, but I accessed the account on the Web."

He motioned, and I went around the desk and sat down in the fancy chair. I looked the list over. "This looks like a standard Visa bill to me."

"I don't understand why the balance is so high. Marion always claimed that she paid it off every month."

I studied the listing of charged items. "All of these charges were made in Dallas."

"Yes. These cover a period when Clem was trying the Romero case. She was in Dallas for two weeks. That's the reason I thought you might see something in them I don't."

"Neiman's. Stanley Korshak. Pretty upscale stuff."

"Clem liked to live well."

And Joe liked the simple life—fooling around with boats and wearing work clothes. I told myself to mind my own business. Then my fingernail tapped on an interesting item.

"Dr. Rockwell Stone!"

"I guess Clem had a cold or something."

"Maybe so, but I doubt she would have gone to Dr. Rockwell Stone for the sniffles. He's one of Dallas's leading plastic surgeons."

"Plastic surgeon?" Joe's voice was incredulous. I didn't reply, just looked at the computer screen and let him take it in.

"I can't believe Clem had plastic surgery," he said.

"This could have been simply a consultation. Except . . . well, it's quite a lot of money." Yes, the figure listed would have sent my Visa to a heart surgeon.

Joe leaned over to take a closer look. "Even a high-priced Dallas plastic surgeon should give you more than an opinion for that amount of money," he said. "I can call his office tomorrow. But there's another interesting item right under that one. A cash advance."

"Why is that interesting?"

"If Clem needed money, she wrote a check."

"Well, the rest of the charges look pretty standard. I mean, they were at exclusive stores, stores where I'd expect Clementine Ripley to shop. This makeup, for example—"

"Makeup? She bought makeup?"

"Several hundred dollars' worth."

"Impossible!"

"Joe, a purchase like that isn't unusual. Those little jars and bottles cost the earth when you go to a shop like Vivienne Rose, where they blend everything personally for each customer."

"I can believe that; Clem used to pay a bunch for that kind of gunk. But she'd never have bought it in Dallas."

"Why not?"

"Because she has a close friend in Chicago who sells that stuff. A consultant. All she had to do was call, and Jane sent over a batch. Besides, she was in Dallas to work." Joe's gesture dismissed the entire bill. "Clem was all business in court. The restaurants—maybe. Even Clem had to eat, and she entertained clients and other attorneys a lot. But she'd never have stopped in the middle of a trial and gone shopping, bought new makeup, talked to a plastic surgeon. This whole thing stinks!"

"Then who did charge these things? Do you think her credit card was stolen?"

"Not exactly."

"Then what?"

"Like I say, the only person who handled Clem's credit cards was Marion McCoy."

"Oh."

Joe stared grimly at the wall for a moment. "I guess I just wanted confirmation of my feeling that there was something funny about this bill," he said. "I never trusted Marion, but she was down on me from the time Clem and I hit it off. So I never knew if I was right about her or just reacting to her open dislike of me."

"I don't understand all this."

"You don't understand how Marion could resist my charm?"

"Oh, you're charming as all get out. But how could Ms. Ripley stand this situation? I hadn't been out at this house for ten minutes on Friday when I realized everybody was at everybody else's throat. I was glad to hand over my chocolates and get away."

"I got away, too." Joe's voice was bitter.

"I'm sorry," I said. "It's none of my affair, and I should have kept my mouth shut."

Joe went on, still speaking bitterly. "Clem had her life arranged just the way she wanted it. It suited her. She thrived on all that discord. She deliberately stirred it up. Any efforts I made to make her life smooth and happy were not welcome."

He stood up. "Maybe she only married me to make Marion mad. Anyway, thanks for taking a look at this."

"What do you intend to do?"

"Call in the accountants."

"Are you going to tell the state police?"

"I hope it won't mean filing charges."

"But doesn't this give Marion a real motive for killing Ms. Ripley?"

Joe paused. "I can't believe she did it. Her problem was that she adored Clem. I can't picture her doing anything to harm her."

"She appears to have harmed her financially. Joe, I'm sure the state police have accountants. It'll be better if you tell VanDam about this yourself than to let them find it out and have to say, 'Oh, yeah. That. Well, I was hoping not to have to file charges.' "

Joe frowned. "Accusing Marion would look so stupid. Tit for tat. She's accusing me, so I'm accusing her. I'll think about it until tomorrow."

Tomorrow. There was something about the word . . . My memory clicked into gear, and I gasped.

"Rats! Joe, tomorrow may be too late!"

"I don't think VanDam is going to arrest anybody today."

"No, it was something Marion McCoy said! When she was hysterical she yelled out that she could barely wait until tomorrow so she could get out of here. Duncan Ainsley thinks she's going to go back to Chicago then. Except . . ."

"Except what?"

"She didn't say she was going to 'go' tomorrow. She said she was going to 'fly' tomorrow."

Joe and I stared at each other. "It's possible to fly to Chicago," he said.

"Sure. Lots of people drive an hour to Grand Rapids so they can sit in the airport two hours, then fly forty-five minutes to Chicago. That would take a total of three hours in and forty-five minutes. I guess some people would rather do that than drive two and a half hours the other direction and get to Chicago faster."

Joe just frowned.

"It may be silly," I said, "but it sounds to me as if Marion is planning to go someplace besides Chicago."

"It doesn't sound good. Maybe I'd better call VanDam." Joe sighed. "I can see that this estate is going to be a mess. I'll have to cash in some investments if I'm going to get the money Clem owed me."

I decided not to comment on that, though I was

dying to know just why Clementine Ripley owed Joe money. "If you sell the house . . ."

"It's mortgaged to the hilt. That's the way Clem ran things. On credit. The Chicago apartment is mortgaged, too. Even the apartment building we still owned jointly is mortgaged, and Clem's promise to buy me out isn't much good now."

"Oh!" I heard myself say. That must be what Joe and Clementine had been talking about Friday. I felt quite relieved, then surprised at myself. Joe's finances were no concern of mine, were they?

"Is there anything else I can do here?" I said. "I'm supposed to be out at Aunt Nettie's, meeting with the state police technical team."

"Then you'd better get going. I'm sorry I held you up."

"It's okay."

We headed for the stairs. "I'm sorry if you're having problems getting your business going," I said.

"Wooden boats are a specialized field," Joe said. "My granddad worked on them, and I always liked fooling around in the shop with him. Now I'm trying to buy six boats—one's a cruiser built in 1928—from a guy who's retiring. It's a once-in-a-lifetime chance, and it could really set me up. But even in the shape these boats are in, and they all need complete restoration, it calls for a lot of money. If I can't get my money out of the apartment house . . . Well, I told the guy I wanted them, so it's going to be embarrassing if I have to back out."

"Do you have a contract for sale?"

"Just a handshake deal. But we're talking about the world of wooden boats. There are just a couple of hundred people doing this. Contracts aren't as important as keeping your word."

We walked on down the stairs without talking. But the atmosphere had changed. For the first time I didn't feel that my presence—my mere existence—made Joe angry. Suddenly we were almost friends.

He led me to the kitchen, then stopped. "Listen," he said. "You kept trying to apologize, but I'm the one who should be saying I'm sorry."

"Why?"

"I haven't been very polite."

"You've been under a lot of stress."

"Which is a cliché excuse for rudeness."

"You seem to be the only person who really cared for Ms. Ripley and who was genuinely sorry she died."

"I don't know if I'm sorry or annoyed. I was so angry when we first split up—it's taken me two years to get my head halfway straight, to get to the point when I'd pretty well put her behind me and begun to move on. Then she's murdered! And I can't ignore it. I'm a suspect. And her heir. Even if I don't get arrested, I'm going to have to settle her estate. It's thrown me back into some kind of emotional limbo."

I didn't know what to say. I fell back on a platitude. "It's not going to be easy, but I'm sure you'll handle it."

"I hope. . . ."

He went on to the outside door, opened it, and stepped back to let me out. Or I thought he was going to let me out. I stepped forward, and he stepped sideways, and we bumped into each other again. Suddenly we were standing in the doorway, nose to nose. This time neither of us moved. We stood just there.

The moment would have passed if either one of us had reacted normally. Or maybe we did react normally.

It was a heck of a kiss.

Not that it involved a lot of action. We didn't even put our arms around each other. Just stood there in a lip lock. For a long time.

Then I heard a loud, piercing noise. A siren.

Joe and I jumped apart like a couple of teenagers when Daddy flipped the porch light on.

We both ran out into the back driveway just as an ambulance came around the corner of the house and skidded to a stop. Greg Glossop jumped out of the passenger door.

He yelled, "Where is she?"

We spoke at the same time. "Who?"

"Marion McCoy! That Hugh called and said she needed an ambulance."

"Did Dr. Schiller think she needed hospitalization?" Joe said.

"I don't know what Schiller thought! All I know is Hugh said she wasn't breathing."

Joe and I both turned and ran, with Glossop on our heels and the other EMT close behind him. We ran back through the kitchen and dining room and down the peristyle toward the office.

Hugh was standing in the hall. "Hurry! Hurry!" he said.

Glossop and his teammate rushed in. Marion was lying on the couch.

"I managed to get her up on the couch to make her a little more comfortable," Hugh said.

We all held our breath while Glossop yanked her shirt up to her armpits, then used his stethoscope. He touched the skin of her face.

"We'll try," he said, "but it looks like another cyanide death to me."

I forced myself to look away from Marion's flushed face. And when I looked away, I saw the teapot.

It was still sitting on the credenza behind Marion's desk. Right where I had put it down a half hour earlier. But the teacup Lindy had sent was now on the desk, half full of tea.

Chapter 14

For the second time in three days, someone had died after eating or drinking something I had handed her.

My first impulse was to throw myself down and kick and scream. But Joe spoke, and he sounded calm, so I decided to pretend to be calm, too.

"Are the state police on the way?" Joe said.

In response, we heard another siren.

"Hugh, Lee—everybody except the EMTs had better go into the big living room," Joe said. "Where's Duncan?"

"He went back to the guest house," Hugh said. "I can go get him."

Joe and I were a somber pair as we walked back to the main part of the house. We stood before the fireplace until Hugh and Duncan came in, almost running down the long hall toward us. The mood was not lightened when Yonkers jumped off the balcony onto Duncan Ainsley's shoulders, using him as a springboard to bounce onto the bar. Duncan lost his Texas folksiness over that; the words he said were basic Anglo-Saxon. But neither Hugh, Joe nor I took any notice of his language, and Yonkers had the sense to make himself scarce. He jumped down behind the bar and peeked around its end.

Joe let two uniformed state police in the front door. Then he, Duncan, Hugh, and I sat in the big black-and-white reception room. The beautiful views from the banks of windows failed to soften the cold effect, and the flower arrangements made it worse. In a few minutes I glimpsed VanDam and Underwood arriving, followed almost immediately by the technical team—including a couple of the people who had searched the chocolate shop. Then Chief Jones came in. Each group went back toward the office, leaving a uniformed officer in the front hall.

We just sat there. Joe spoke once. "I'm glad I told Lindy to go home," he said. "We're going to be here all night."

But it was only half an hour later when Chief Jones came in and joined us. He sat down in one of the spindly chairs and looked at us over the top of his glasses.

"Lieutenant VanDam has allowed me to have the honor of telling all of you that you can go home."

The three of us inhaled so sharply that the air pressure in the room dropped fifty percent. Then we all talked at once.

"What about statements?" Joe said.

"Why? What's happened?" Duncan said.

"But I gave her the tea!" That was me. "And she's dead, and she looked like Clementine Ripley. . . ."

"Yes, that's true." The chief paused—I'm sure for dramatic effect—before he spoke again. "But Clementine Ripley didn't leave a suicide note."

I almost collapsed, but Joe spoke. "Did Marion confess?"

"Said something about, 'I loved Clementine. I never meant to hurt her.' Like that."

A huge load seemed to lift off my shoulders. "It was the Visa bill," I said.

The chief frowned, and Joe made a succinct report of the questions he had about Clementine Ripley's

Visa bill. "I guess she knew that was going to come out," he said.

"Sounds likely," Duncan said. "Clementine must have found out that her Visa bill was crazy as a steer on locoweed. Marion would have seen disaster on the horizon, so she killed Clementine. Then she was sorry."

"It was the chocolates," I said.

The chief frowned again. "Well, Marion apparently injected cyanide into the chocolates, but—"

"No! I mean it was the charge for the chocolates. The Visa bill. Clementine Ripley ordered over two thousand dollars' worth of chocolates from us. She wanted to put it on her Visa, but Visa wouldn't accept the charge. So I called and told Marion McCoy we'd have to have a check. When I delivered the chocolates, Clementine Ripley found out that Visa had refused her charge." I gestured at Joe. "Joe was there. He heard her. She made me tell her just what had happened. Then she told Marion to give me a check, and she said something like, 'We'll discuss this later.' So it looks as if the charge for the chocolates must have tipped her off."

"That sounds likely," Chief Jones said.

We asked for details, and he told us Marion had apparently heavily sweetened the hot tea I'd carried into the office, then spiked it with cyanide. Underwood found the suicide note propped up on Marion's dresser. The envelope was marked FOR THE POLICE, and it was sitting on top of a bottle the lab was going to test as possibly containing cyanide.

The detectives believed the note had been printed out on the ink-jet printer in Marion's office, and the original message had been found saved in her computer. The message was in memo form, printed out neatly on Clementine Ripley's letterhead, signed, folded in thirds, and sealed in a white business envelope.

Anyway, an hour after Joe and I stood in the

kitchen door kissing each other, the crisis about the murder of Clementine Ripley seemed to be over. I rushed back to the shop and told Aunt Nettie what had happened, of course. Then the phone began to ring.

Nancy Burton, the customer who had taken all our Crème de Menthe bonbons for her B-and-B, called and told Aunt Nettie that only that morning she'd rented her last two rooms to reporters, and within an hour of Marion McCoy's death they'd both checked out and gone back to Chicago. So we figured that the press had gotten the word. We found out later that CNN put an item on right away, being careful not actually to say that Marion had confessed.

A steady stream of cars must have been leaving town, each with a PRESS decal on the windshield, because we saw no more of the press—tabloid or otherwise—after Marion's death.

The chief did come by the shop to give us one other interesting bit of information. "You said the burglar you had last night fell off your porch, didn't you?" he said.

"Yes," Aunt Nettie said. "He fell down the steps."

"Try she, not he."

"Marion McCoy?"

"We may never figure it out for sure, but when the EMTs got that long-sleeved black thing off of her, her arms were covered with bruises. Like she'd had a fall. So VanDam had them check her legs before they took her away. They were bruised, too."

"But why did she do that?" Aunt Nettie said. "Did her note explain that?"

"Nope. We may never know the answer to that one. But I guess she did it." He ducked his head and looked like a tall, skinny elf. "Another thing—when they got that turtleneck shirt all the way off—well, they found scars. She'd had surgery." His lips twitched. "Pretty recent. A boob job."

I gasped. "So that's what she saw the plastic surgeon about in Dallas!"

"I guess so. Anyway, I've learned a lot during the past couple of days. I've never been a suspect before, and it sure gave me a new outlook on law enforcement."

"I guess you're glad it's over," Aunt Nettie said. "Has Lieutenant VanDam left?"

"Oh, no. He'll hang around a couple of days, or Underwood will, making sure the lab work gets done."

"Then they're still investigating?"

The chief's manner became evasive. "They have to tie up all the loose ends. Check the fingerprints. Wait for the autopsy results."

I started to ask the chief if Joe had told him or VanDam about my idea that Marion might have been about to go on the lam, to "fly" away. But the phone rang, and by the time I got it answered, the chief had left. So I didn't mention it to Aunt Nettie.

In fact, I told myself, the whole idea had probably been wrong. If Marion was planning to kill herself, she wouldn't be worrying about flying anywhere.

But one more question did cross my mind: What had Marion hoped to gain by killing Clementine Ripley? Even if Clementine were dead, somebody was going to check that Visa bill. Then I remembered that Marion had been surprised to learn Clementine had not signed her new will, the one cutting Joe out of the estate and naming someone else executor. She'd probably thought she'd be named executor herself.

But it seemed sort of fishy. And Joe had agreed with me, had seemed to think my interpretation of Marion's ravings could well be correct. When I thought about the whole thing, my relief turned to unease.

Chief Jones might have left, but we still had visitors. First Mike Herrera knocked at the street door and came in to exult over Clementine Ripley's murder turning out to involve "outsiders."

"Now Warner Pier can get back to normal," he said. "I suppose this might even improve business this season. You know, lotsa people will have read about Warner Pier in the newspapers and seen our beautiful city on the television news."

This inspired one of the few tart answers I heard from Aunt Nettie. "I certainly hope we didn't go through all this just as a tourist promotion."

Mike seemed a little embarrassed. "Oh, nice lady! I didn't mean I'm glad it happened! I just want us to make the best of what we're stuck with."

Aunt Nettie let him off the hook. "I know what you mean, Mike. But this has surely been a strain. I just hope it really is over."

As Mike went out the front door, a new caller showed up—Greg Glossop. Since we had the door open, it was impossible not to let him in.

He was enjoying the situation thoroughly. "You can't believe the silly gossip that's already started," he said. "Someone asked me if it was true that Clementine Ripley's secretary made a run for it and drove her car into a bridge abutment down by South Haven." He preened. "Luckily, I could tell her that was a complete fabrication."

We had to hash over the whole affair before he was satisfied. And the phone kept ringing. The word was spreading like the great fire of 1871, which left half of Warner Pier in ashes. All of Aunt Nettie's friends called.

The result was that I thought we'd never get rid of Greg Glossop. In fact, he was still there when I got a call. From Joe.

Luckily, I answered the telephone that time.

"Hi," Joe said. "Your line's been busy for thirty minutes."

"I know. All of Warner Pier's called up to tell us

how glad they are that we're not going to be tried for murder."

"People around here are really nice, aren't they?" Joe's deadpan tones emphasized the sarcasm in his remark.

I laughed. "Oh, people are pretty much the same everywhere, I guess. You should have heard the strange questions the Texans asked when I left my ex. Are the detectives through out there?"

"No. They're still at it. Working in the office. I'm on the kitchen line. I wanted to talk to you."

"Oh?" Was he going to bring up that kiss?

He didn't say anything for a long time. I didn't say anything either. Finally, we both spoke at the same time.

"Listen . . ." I said.

"I hope . . ." Joe said.

We both shut up again, and there was another silence. Then Joe spoke.

"Back there as you were leaving . . . I was way out of line. I owe you an apology."

His comment struck me funny. "That's not very complimentary," I said.

"I don't mean I didn't enjoy it!"

I laughed, and in a few seconds, I heard a chuckle from the other end of the line.

"As long as you're not mad," Joe said.

"No, I obviously enjoyed it, too. But . . . listen, let's forget the whole thing, okay?"

"Forget it? That's a tall order."

"I mean—well, we've both had some bad experiences, and I think . . . I think both of us need to get out more!"

There was another long silence. Then Joe spoke seriously. "You don't want my class ring?"

"No, but I'd be tempted by the letter jacket."

We both laughed. It was such a relief to be able to

joke. But I couldn't forget my unease about Marion's plan to fly away.

"Joe, I had one thing I wanted to talk to you about."

"I gotta go," Joe said. "VanDam's waving at me. Can I call you later, when things calm down?"

"I may call you."

We both hung up, and I looked up to see Aunt Nettie standing in the office doorway. "Lee, do you think we could go home now?"

"Did Greg Glossop leave?"

"Finally."

The phone rang again, but this time I let the answering machine catch it.

"We're not here," I said, turning off the sound. "In fact, we're no longer murder suspects, and we're going to go out on a toot to celebrate."

"And just what kind of a toot did you have in mind?"

"I have enough room left on *my* Visa card to treat us to a pizza. How does that sound?"

"Wonderful. I definitely don't want to cook."

"Come on then. There's no cloud hanging over our heads, and we're gonna howl!"

I stuffed my doubts about the details of Marion's crime under a mental rock and led Aunt Nettie out the door to the alley.

Chapter 15

Peach Street was still crowded with tourist traffic as we drove out of the alley. The most interesting thing I noticed was a black Mercedes convertible parked in front of Downtown Drugs. There was no sign of Duncan Ainsley, however.

"Is the Dock Street still the best place for pizza?" I said.

"Well, I think they have really good sauce—and plenty of it. And they've become a sort of social center, too."

"You mean the tourists discovered it?"

"No, I mean it's a center for us locals. I understand that if a couple is seen together in the Dock Street it's practically an announcement that they're going steady. And they've put in a dining room since your day."

"A dining room? Do you want to eat there?" I nudged her. "Everybody already knows we're related."

"Sure. If we can get a table."

The Dock Street Pizza Place has been a Warner Pier institution for a long time. It's the best kind of pizza place—long on spices, cheese, and toppings and short on ambiance. I was pleased to see that we still ordered by walking up to a counter and that the "dining room" consisted of a dozen tables in what had been a garage off the alley back when I went there as a teenager. And it still smelled like garlic, tomatoes, pepperoni, and hot bread.

Aunt Nettie and I snagged a table for two in a corner, and I went up to the counter and ordered a medium Italian sausage and mushroom pizza, two side salads, and two glasses of red wine from our local winery.

I took the salads and wine back to the table. I was sitting with my back to the counter, and I was so tired that I was ignoring the social side of dinner at the Dock Street. So I was surprised when Aunt Nettie looked behind me and her eyes grew wide. "That Mr. Ainsley is coming over here," she said softly.

Amazed, I turned around. Duncan Ainsley was the last person I'd have expected to see in the Dock Street. "Duncan!"

"Lee." He smiled and patted my shoulder. Then he turned to Aunt Nettie. "And Nettie TenHuis, the famous chocolatier. I sure am glad to run into y'all. May I join you?"

"Of course," Aunt Nettie said. There was no way to refuse. Plus, I was rather honored that a man as well known as Duncan Ainsley wanted to sit with us. The *Business Week* article had described him as a "bachelor who likes to be seen with a beautiful woman on his arm." That night "beautiful" hardly applied to either Aunt Nettie or me. Duncan, however, was as suave as usual. Not a hair in that beautiful head of gray was out of place.

"I thought Lindy was fixing dinner for you," I said.

"She left something to heat up, but—thank the Lord!—I was finally allowed to get out of that house," Duncan said. "So I got."

"Are you going back to Chicago tonight?"

He shook his head. "No, I'll wait and go in the

morning. There's no point in fighting Sunday evening traffic. I was able to check into a B-and-B."

"How did you find the Dock Street?" Aunt Nettie asked. "I thought only us locals knew about it."

"I asked somebody where to get some good Italian food." Duncan smiled broadly. "Pizza sounded good. And the company's a lot better than out at the Ripley house."

"Is Joe the only other person there?"

"Except for the security guard. And Joe may well be a fine fellow, but I heard too much about him from Marion."

"I know you must have known her well."

"Marion and I had an odd relationship. Sometimes it was such a headache that I was sorry Clementine Ripley had become a client. Oh, I made money on the deal, but I rarely saw Clementine, and Joe refused to have anything to do with her business affairs, even before their divorce. That left all the details to Marion. And her relationship with Clementine . . ." He wiggled his eyebrows. "You'll have figured out that it was kinda peculiar." He turned to Aunt Nettie. "Will y'all be leaving Warner Pier next winter?"

"Maybe for a vacation," she said. "Why?"

"Then you don't spend the winter in Florida, the way some of the resort shopkeepers do?"

"Oh, no," Aunt Nettie said.

I spoke then. "TenHuis Chocolade is quite busy year-round. We do a lot of mail-order business."

"I had no notion."

"I think Aunt Nettie should expand, but she wants to keep a close eye on just how TenHuis chocolates are made."

"You have to watch every detail," Aunt Nettie said.

Duncan frowned. "But I've been in the shop. You're obviously not making all the chocolates yourself. Lee, do you help?"

"Nope. I keep my hands strictly out of the chocolate and into the business side. TenHuis has about thirty-five ladies who make the chocolates."

"Thirty-five! That's a much larger business than I realized, Mrs. TenHuis." He turned to me again. "Then you don't put on hairnets and gloves and dig into the marshmallow cream?"

I laughed at the horrified expression that the notion of marshmallow cream inspired in Aunt Nettie. "We use neither marshmallow cream nor plastic gloves," I said.

"No? I thought health department rules said food handlers had to use them."

"Not always," Aunt Nettie said, "but we have what the health department calls an alternate policy. Our employees are specially trained in hand washing and food handling, so they don't have to wear gloves." She leaned over and spoke confidingly. "McDonalds's has the same kind of deal. My ladies do wear hairnets. But it would be extremely hard to do some of the detail work we do while wearing gloves."

"I can see that you're as busy as three windmills in a tornado."

At that point the counter girl called my name, and I went up to collect our pizza. Duncan shared our sausage and mushroom until his arrived, and we had quite a companionable time, with Duncan entertaining us with more stories about his famous clients.

At the end of the meal Aunt Nettie excused herself to speak to a friend across the room. Duncan and I stood up, and I extended my hand. "This has been most enjoyable," I said. "I hope everything is calm for a while. I don't think I can stand any more incitement—I mean, excitement!"

Duncan stood up, too. He smiled, gave me a lot of eye contact, and made shaking my hand more than a polite gesture.

"I hope you get to leave tomorrow," I said.

"I plan to be off as soon as I have breakfast. Have a nice evening, Lee, and a nice life. If you ever want to try the big city, let me know. I hate to see a young woman as personable and intelligent as you stagnating in a little town—even a cute little one."

"The big city life doesn't appeal to everyone. Look at Joe."

Duncan raised his eyebrows. "Of course, Joe may change his mind about the big city now that his situation has changed."

"You mean because big-city life is more fun with money?"

"No, I mean that he might decide to go back into law practice. Now that Clementine isn't around to pressure him to stay out of it."

I must have looked amazed, because Duncan laughed. "Hadn't you heard that particular piece of gossip? Marion was spreading it so busily that I thought it would be all over Warner Pier."

"Clementine Ripley pressured Joe to stop practicing law?"

"According to Marion, that was part of their divorce settlement."

"But how could she do that?"

"Supposedly she had the goods on him—threatened to get him disbarred. But she gave him the out of voluntarily leaving the practice of law."

I was stunned. "Then why did Clementine leave Joe as her heir? Why didn't she sign her new will?"

"Thought she'd live forever, just like the rest of us do, I guess." Duncan shrugged. "Ask your aunt about it. She may have heard something. Anyway, if you decide to leave Warner Pier for the big city, to trade in the historic farmhouse for a high-rise condo, let me know."

I tried to swallow my amazement and keep our

good-bye light. "Ah, but a condo wouldn't have a Michigan basement."

"Is that what that sand-floored cellar is called? I learn something new all the time."

Duncan smiled as Aunt Nettie reappeared. He left a lavish tip on the table—not strictly necessary in a place where you get your own food from the counter—and escorted us to the old Buick, settling Aunt Nettie in the driver's seat as gallantly as if she'd been driving a Rolls. He gave me one of his business cards and even waved as we drove away.

I could barely wait to ask Aunt Nettie if she'd heard the gossip Duncan had passed along, the news that Clementine Ripley had threatened to get Joe disbarred.

"No, I hadn't heard that," she said, "and I'm sure his mother hasn't heard it either. She was furious with Joe for quitting law and did a lot of moaning about his lack of ambition. She certainly didn't act as if he was being forced to get out of the profession."

I liked Joe. I had even kissed him. But that had just been my hormones telling me he was an attractive man. It didn't give me any insight into his character.

I reminded myself that my past record on judging people wasn't too good. I had thought Rich was one of the good guys. Now I knew that I'd never marry another divorced man without finding out more about why his first marriage broke up.

We discussed the ramifications of Duncan's revelation all the way home. Once inside, we checked out the house. The state police search team had been much neater than the burglar. Mrs. Deacon had left a note saying some of the searchers left at four o'clock—that would have been when Marion's death was reported—and the others at five-thirty.

"I guess I don't need to hide the van any longer," I said. "I'll go over to the Baileys' and get it."

"Oh, dear!" Aunt Nettie frowned. "I just remembered—I forgot to stop for gas. I'd better go back to town."

"You put your feet up. I'll take the Buick and get gas."

I don't have any excuse for what I did next. In fact, I wasn't aware that I was doing it until after I'd done it. My brain apparently went into cruise control, and my subconscious handled the whole thing.

I drove straight to the Ripley estate.

I had pulled up at the security gate before I realized where I was going.

As soon as I saw where I was, I put the car in reverse and started to leave. But it was too late. The security guard was already speaking to me electronically. I knew he could see me on his closed circuit camera. I was trapped by my own subconscious. I decided to act as if I'd come on purpose.

"Lee McKinney to see Joe Woodyard."

"Is he expecting you?"

Actually, I did have some vague memory of telling Joe I wanted to talk to him again that evening. I tried to sound confident. "I believe so."

The guard decided to believe me. "Drive on around the circle," he said. The gate slid open.

Once again I headed up the long drive that led through the trees. An elaborate system of hidden lights illuminated the driveway. Why wasn't I surprised by that?

When I pulled up in front of the flagstone steps, Hugh was waiting for me. "Mr. Woodyard's down at the boathouse," he said. "You can wait for him inside."

He opened the front door, and I went into the big foyer, still packed with flowers, then walked on into the reception room. I heard a meow over my head and looked up to see Yonkers, again hiding behind the huge white ceramic pot.

"Are you going to jump on me?" I said.

"No," Yonkers said. Actually, I suppose it was more like *naow* but he certainly responded. Then he turned and trotted along the balcony to a door that opened into a lighted room I realized was the office. I was moving toward the big, soft white couch when I heard a loud clang from upstairs.

"Yonk, did you knock over the wastebasket?" I decided I'd better see what the cat was up to, since Joe was not in the house to keep an eye on him. I ran up the stairs and went along the balcony to the office.

When I looked inside, the wastebasket was still upright, and Yonkers was nowhere in sight. "Yonk! Here, kitty!" I looked behind the desk, noting that the computer was off this time, and under the chairs.

"Where did you go, you pesky cat?"

I got a clue when the paneled door moved, just as it had that afternoon. Yonkers had once more opened the closet. But this time he was inside.

I opened the door. The closet was apparently an afterthought, maybe put in just in case Clementine Ripley or some future owner ever decided to make the office room over into a bedroom. For the moment, however, it was lined with shelves and stocked with paper, boxes of paper clips, and other office necessities. All very businesslike.

Except for the filmy black nightgown that hung on a hook on the inside of the door.

CHOCOLATE CHAT

ROMANCE

- Chocolate has long been associated with romance, but it's hard to tell how much of this was based on fact and how much on marketing. When chocolate was introduced to Germany during the 1600s, for example, the sellers whispered of its value as an aphrodisiac. Ladies were urged to offer a cup to their husbands.

- The Aztec emperor Montezuma reportedly drank chocolate before visiting his harem.

- The Spanish kept chocolate a secret for nearly a hundred years, but in 1615 Princess Maria Teresa gave her finacé, Louis XIV of France, a gift of chocolate and the secret was out.

- Casanova was quoted as saying chocolate was more useful in seduction than champagne.

- After chocolate candy was developed, luscious, creamy bonbons and truffles came to be known as a ideal romantic gift. This developed into the heart-shaped box of chocolates—the Valentine's Day gift every teenage girl longs for—and into luxury chocolates for more sophisticated lovers.

- Still, the physical effects of eating chocolate—stimulating the heart muscle, providing extra energy, and maybe even acting as a mood booster—are a lot like falling in love!

Chapter 16

A black lace nightgown?

It was the last thing I expected to find in an office closet. Two more things were hung on top of it—a lightweight sweater, the kind you might keep around in case you got cold while finishing up a report, and a man's flannel shirt. The shirt and sweater were on wooden hangers, but I could see that a fancy padded hanger held the nightgown. Its hanger was scented, too, or something in the closet was.

Yonkers seemed as interested in the gown as I was. He began to exercise his claws on the fragile skirt.

"Bad cat!" I said. I tried to lift the skirt of the gown up, out of his reach, and it slipped off its fancy satin hanger.

"Rats," I said. I wrestled the gown away from Yonkers, tossing it onto the desk. "You're going to ruin it, you naughty thing." I clapped my hands at him. "Get up on your perch and let this alone."

Yonkers went to his perch on the shelf with a sneer, making sure I understood he was doing it because he wanted to, not in response to my order. I picked the gown up, ready to hang it on the closet door again, but first I held it up to myself, admiring its beautiful lace and delicate embroidery.

This was the moment, of course, that Joe walked into the office.

We stared at each other. Then Joe spoke. "Why did you bring *that*?"

I fell back on my say-nothing habit and merely stood there. Then I caught the implication; he thought I had come out to see him, uninvited, and had brought a sexy black nightgown along.

I gasped. "I didn't bring it!"

Joe blushed.

And I got the giggles.

Joe blushed more brightly. "I guess that wasn't a cool thing to say."

I spoke again. "I didn't bring it out here. I was trying to research it. I mean, rescue! I took the gown away from Yonkers."

"Yonkers?" Joe's color was fading, but he looked confused.

"Yes. I heard a crash, and I thought Yonkers had knocked the wastebasket over. So I came upstairs to see if he was tearing things up. He'd gotten the closet door open and was inside. I had to haul him out. When I did, I saw this gown on a hanger on the back of the door, and Yonkers began to claw at it. So I took it away from him. I was just admiring it before I hung it back up."

Joe looked more confused than ever. "The thing was here?"

"Yes. It was inside that closet."

He opened the closet door and looked inside. "In here?"

"See? The hanger's still there."

Joe lifted the scented hanger down, still frowning. "What was it doing here?"

I took the hanger. "I suppose it belonged to Ms. Ripley."

"No."

"It's obviously something she got recently."

"Clem would never have worn a thing like that."

"Maybe it was a gift." I sighed. "Joe, you and Ms. Ripley had been separated for two years. She was a very attractive woman. Frankly, it's the kind of thing a guy would give his girlfriend."

Joe shook his head. "I'd be delighted to find out that Clem had a new man in her life. But if he knew her well enough to give her a sexy thing like that, he ought to have known her well enough to see that she'd never have worn it."

"Maybe she would have—if it were a special request."

"Clem never wore anything. Like that." Joe was slightly red again. "I mean—not for sleeping. Besides, she wouldn't have kept something like a nightgown out here in the office supply closet. She had a big dressing room."

I ducked my head to look at the skirt of the gown, then took hold of it and fanned it out to examine it more closely. The skirt was of sheer nylon, practically transparent. A vision of Joe drooling as I modeled it for him flashed through my mind. I thought of the flannel sleep pants and T-shirt I wore for Michigan nights, and I almost sighed.

"Well, it's beautiful, of course," I said. "Some women do wear this sort of very feminine thing just for their own pleasure. But I'd really expect it to be worn to please a husband or a lover."

"No, Clem would never have worn something like this for any reason."

"Then I don't understand. Have the police seen it?"

"Probably. They went over this section of the house pretty thoroughly."

"But they might not have seen anything unusual about it," I said.

We both stared at the filmy black gown. I reached for the hanger again. "It's a beautiful garment. You can always give it to the National Association of Former Good Girls."

As I held it up, I caught a glimpse of the label. It was a brand I'd never heard of, since I've never been a particular fan of expensive nightgowns. Rich never bought me clothes; he gave me money or jewelry. But beneath that label was another smaller label that said 10.

Size ten? The gown was a size ten? I held the straps against my shoulders and let the skirt of the gown drift down. The hem reached past the cuff of my khaki slacks.

But Clementine Ripley had been on the short side.

I mused aloud. "I wonder what size Ms. Ripley wore?"

"Twelve petite. I asked Marion the first Christmas Clem and I were married. She said the 'petite' was important. Why?"

"This gown would never have fit her. It's way too long, for one thing. It would have trailed on the floor. And for another thing, it's too small through the bodice. I don't think Ms. Ripley could have gotten into it. And if she did, it's designed to enhance the bust, to make it look larger."

"Clem would never have worn something that would have made her look bigger."

"So even if somebody gave it to her, it wouldn't have been her favorite gift."

Joe and I looked at each other for a moment. Then he spoke. "I hope somebody did care about her. Somebody besides Marion."

I hung the gown up.

"But I still can't see any reason it would be in the closet off her office," Joe said.

"Maybe she was going to return it. Exchange it."

"Or give it to the National Association of Former Good Girls."

We both smiled, and I turned around. "I don't suppose she would have given clothes to Marion McCoy. It would have fit Marion great."

Joe's jaw dropped.

"She was tall enough to wear it," I said, "and she was thin—Oh, my gosh!"

"Marion," Joe said.

"Marion," I said. "She'd bought all those clothes in Dallas. She'd had a boob job. I'm willing to bet that gown was hers. And what's the most logical reason for all that?"

"She had a boyfriend."

"But she certainly wasn't wearing any of those new clothes when I saw her Friday, Joe. Or Saturday. Or today. She looked really dowdy. Yet she'd actually stolen—stolen!—money to buy clothes. Why would she do that?"

"She didn't want anybody to know about the boyfriend."

"I think you're right. She was keeping the boyfriend a secret even from Clementine."

"Maybe especially from Clementine."

"Why?"

Joe didn't have an answer for that, and neither did I.

The conversation was at an impasse. For the first time I looked down and saw that Joe was in his stocking feet.

"My shoes were wet," he said, "so I left them outside. The sign of being raised by a mother who hated cleaning house."

"That's why I didn't hear you coming up the stairs." I shook my head. "Actually, I didn't come here to discuss black lingerie. I wanted to know if you told Lieutenant VanDam about that flying comment Marion made."

"Yes, I did. He didn't seem too impressed."

I moved toward the door. "I just wanted to know if you'd told him. I'd better get home now." Joe followed me out onto the balcony and down the stairs.

"Apparently everybody thinks that Marion's suicide solves Clementine Ripley's murder," I said.

"That seems to be the general attitude."

"You don't sound convinced."

"I'd like to be. I'd like it to be settled for once and for all."

"How about the state police? Did VanDam talk as if he considered the case closed?"

"He seems to be keeping his options open. I know he kept the mobile lab people here overnight—or in Holland maybe. I don't think they could get rooms here."

"Duncan found one. Aunt Nettie and I ran into him at the Dock Street and he said he'd checked into a B-and-B."

"Is he still around? He left here so fast I thought he was headed back to Chicago. I'm going home in an hour or so. I'm only staying out here until I can find somebody to take care of the cat for a while tomorrow."

"A cat-sitter?"

"Yeah. A breeder from Grand Rapids is going to board him for a while, but she can't pick him up until eleven. And one of the attorneys from Clem's firm called to say he thinks we can get started on the Michigan end of the estate if we appear at the Warner County Courthouse at nine. So I need a place to leave the cat."

"That's just a couple of hours. I could keep him."

"That would be asking a lot."

"I don't go to work until noon. I could go a little early and meet the breeder at the shop."

Joe made appreciative noises, and we went on down the stairs.

"You said you intend to sell the house," I said. "Will Yonkers mind finding a new home?"

"He's more at home at the Chicago apartment. The housekeeper there is the primary person who takes care of him." Joe gestured at the imposing reception room. "I've always hated this place. The weird part is that in a way Clem built this house for me."

"I'd wondered if she came here because it was your hometown, or if you met her because she came here."

"Oh, she was here first, but she used to rent a beach house—the old Lally place, on Lake Shore."

"That's right near Aunt Nettie's."

Joe nodded. "I was with Legal Aid in Detroit then, and we had a case that was a doozy. We really needed some help with it. Something that would draw some public interest. I came home for the weekend. My mom mentioned that she'd heard Clem was in town. I decided I didn't have anything to lose by approaching her. So I went out to the Lally place, talked my way past a part-time security guy—I'd never have gotten past Marion, if she'd been there. Clem and I clicked. She helped us with the case; the rest is history." He opened the front door for me.

"How did Ms. Ripley come to build the house?"

"She already owned this property. I mentioned that I'd always wanted a place on the lake where I could have a private boathouse. The next thing I knew the architects were hard at work." Joe reached for the handle of the Buick's front door. "The plans were drawn before I knew anything about it. I got to comment on the plans for the boathouse."

I saw a chance to check out the rumor Duncan had passed on. "Do you ever think about going back to practicing law?" I kept my voice real innocent as I slid into the driver's seat.

"No. I've been approached by a couple of guys I

was in law school with—but, no. I guess I'm permanently soured on law. Boat owners don't argue like legal clients do." He grinned. "I'll just keep being a disappointment to my mother."

He leaned closer, and a kiss seemed possible. Then I chickened out and looked away, and the moment passed.

He watched as I drove off. Was it my imagination, or did he look lonely? For a moment I wondered if I should have offered to make him a sandwich. But no, that would have been what my Texas grandmother called forward. I decided that after that kiss and now the mix-up over the nightgown, I'd better not even invite Joe Woodyard to church to hear a sermon on chastity. I shouldn't have gone near him. I still wasn't quite sure why I had gone.

I wasn't interested in him, I told myself, ignoring the signals my innards were sending, but he sure could get the wrong idea easily. He might even get the idea I was interested in the money he inherited from his ex-wife. Worse and worse. I took a few deep breaths and thought about a cold shower.

I had to tell Aunt Nettie I'd stopped at the Ripley estate because I had to prepare her for Joe to bring the cat by the next morning. She looked at me narrowly, but she didn't make any comment except "We can't have a cat in the shop."

"He'll be in his carrying case. Maybe I can leave him in the van."

"If he's in a case, he can probably wait in the break room."

A few minutes later a car pulled past the house and into the drive. We both ran to the window and looked out to see a Warner Pier patrol car in the driveway.

"What now?" I asked.

"It's Chief Jones," Aunt Nettie said.

The chief came in the door holding out a cell

phone. "It occurred to me that you two ladies were out here with no telephone," he said.

"Don't you need it?" Aunt Nettie said.

"I can let you have it for a few days. It's an extra. Used to be my wife's."

Aunt Nettie laughed. "If you'd brought it before we stopped for pizza, we could have called the dispatcher and asked her to pass the order along. Would you like a leftover slice?"

"No, but I would like a look around the house."

"We checked under all the beds after the state police left," I said.

"I know, I know," Chief Jones said. "But humor me."

I made a pot of coffee, while Aunt Nettie followed the chief around the house. They started by going into the Michigan basement. Then they came back up and went through the kitchen and into the living room. Next I could hear them chatting in the bedroom, then on the stairs and upstairs. I don't know what the chief was looking for, but he didn't yell, "Aha!" at any point during the tour.

When they were back in the living room I offered the coffee. I knew Aunt Nettie would say yes; the chief did, too, so I got out a tray, napkins, and the whole schmeer. The chief took two spoonsful of sugar, and he seemed to relish the real cream, which Aunt Nettie snitches from the shop, taking a half cup at a time out of the half-gallon cartons she buys it in. "Ah," he said. "Great stuff."

"Lee, I think there are a few Jamaican rum truffles ("The ultimate dark chocolate truffle.") in a box in the pantry." Aunt Nettie was going all out.

I put the truffles on a plate and brought them back to the living room. "Did you find anything when you looked around the house?" I asked.

"No. Not even an idea."

"An idea? Is that what you were looking for?"

"I guess so. I hate loose ends, and I just don't understand that burglar."

"Wasn't it Marion McCoy?"

"It probably was, but what was she looking for?"

"If she took it away, we may never know."

"I don't think she found anything. After the first burglary, Saturday afternoon, you and Nettie said you looked all over and couldn't find anything missing."

"Except my grocery money," Aunt Nettie said. "Lee had to put the pizza on her credit card tonight because we haven't had a chance to get to the bank."

"True." The chief sipped his coffee. "But I wondered if that wasn't just a cover-up. Because the burglar—Marion—came back that night."

"Yes," I said. "Apparently she thought we'd hidden valuables in the birdseed."

"In the birdseed?"

"Yes. That's all that was touched really. Just those tin trash cans on the back porch. The ones Aunt Nettie uses to store seed for the bird feeder."

"Tin trash cans." The chief's voice was thoughtful. "Of course, the burglar might not have known that Nettie stores her birdseed in trash cans. She might have thought that they actually contained trash."

"You mean Marion might have been looking for something she thought we might have thrown away?"

"Why else would she have gone for those trash cans?"

"Maybe she wanted to lure some birds in for Champion Yonkers to jump on. Or maybe she wanted to plant something—like that syringe we found in the Dumpster. Sorry, Chief Jones, I just don't understand. What could we have that was so unimportant to Aunt Nettie and me that we'd be likely to throw it out, but was so important to Marion that she'd break into the house once and try to break in again looking for it?"

"I don't know." He turned to Aunt Nettie. "Did she break into your car?"

"I don't think so. Saturday afternoon the car wasn't even here. Last night it was in the garage, and the garage was locked. The garage was still locked this morning, and the Buick looked just the same."

"Oh!" I said. "I wonder if the searchers found my van."

"Your van?"

"Yeah. It's been hidden at the Baileys' house since Saturday night."

The chief choked on his coffee, and after he got his breath back I realized he was laughing. "You hid your van? That's rich."

"Why? I didn't do it on purpose."

"I don't know if you fooled your burglar or not, but you sure did fool Alec VanDam. His lab team didn't search your van."

"I didn't mean to mislead them. I thought I'd be here while they were searching, but then Marion died, and I had to stay out at the Ripley house. After that, I wasn't even sure they were going to finish the search of the house anyway."

The chief put his coffee cup back on the tray and stood up. "Maybe we ought to take a look. The van is the one thing you and your aunt own that hasn't been searched by either that burglar or the state police."

We got flashlights and jackets and hiked the two hundred feet or so along the path that led through the woods to the Baileys' house. I led the way around behind the garage and unlocked the van.

"The van's probably a mess," I said, "though I try not to leave too much junk in it."

"It looks pretty good," the chief said. "You wouldn't believe the way Jerry leaves his patrol car. I get on him all the time."

He looked in the glove box and under the front seats, using his flashlight to augment the interior lights. Then he opened the van's side door and slid it back. "What's this back here?"

"It's clothes for the cleaners. I was going to take them to Al's, but I couldn't find it."

"Al's closed," the chief said. He picked the garments up. "When did you wear these?"

"Oh, the dress I wore to work the last week I was in Dallas. The coat—well, I never got around to getting it cleaned last spring. Now the slacks—those I wore out to Clementine Ripley's house the night I worked for Herrera Catering."

The chief looked through the rest of the van, but he didn't seem to find anything else very interesting.

"I will take those slacks, the ones you wore out to Warner Point," he said.

"They're my best."

"You should have them back pretty quick."

I decided just to leave the van at the Baileys' until morning. The chief saw Aunt Nettie and me into the house, scolding us because we'd left the back door open when we went over to the Baileys'. He urged us to lock all the doors and keep the 911 phone handy that night. Then he left, Aunt Nettie curled up with a PBS special, and I eventually got in the shower.

The shower felt great. I luxuriated in the hot water for a long time and put the whole nightmare of the past three days out of my mind. So I wasn't happy when I turned off the water and heard the chief's rumbling voice. Why had he come back?

I didn't hurry out. I dried off, applied some baby powder, put on my glamorous baggy flannel sleep pants, blew my hair dry—well, half dry. I could still hear the chief's voice, and I was becoming really curious about why he was there.

I slipped into my terry robe—this outfit was certainly different from the filmy black number Yonkers had found in the closet—and went out to the living room.

"I thought you left," I said.

Then I realized that Aunt Nettie and the chief weren't the only people in the living room. Alec VanDam was also there, with his pal Jack Underwood.

"What's going on?"

"Sorry to bother you, Lee," the chief said. "But those slacks . . ."

"What about them?"

"I think Alex wants to ask you about the gloves in the pocket."

"Gloves? What gloves?"

VanDam cleared his throat and reassumed direction of his investigation.

"The food-service gloves," he said. "The lab people were still in town, so they took a preliminary look at them. The gloves may have traces of cyanide on them."

Chapter 17

"Sinus?" I said. Or later I realized that was what I said. After I'd calmed down a little.

But at the moment all I realized was that VanDam was scowling harder than ever. "Cyanide," he said again. "We need to know what you handled with those gloves."

"Food-service gloves?"

"Yes. The gloves in the pocket of those slacks."

"I didn't know there were any gloves in the pocket of those slacks. I wouldn't normally put anything in that pocket. Those pants are too tight to begin with. If I put anything in the pocket, it looks like I've got a big lump on my dairy—on my behind."

"Then you're saying someone else put the gloves in your pocket?"

"Not while I had those pants on. Believe me, I'd have noticed that. But I never use food-service gloves. I don't understand where they could have come from."

"You don't use them at the shop?"

"I don't help make the chocolates at all. If it's real busy I may work in the front, putting chocolates in boxes for customers. And up there we use little tongs."

"The tongs keep the heat of your hands from melting the chocolate," Aunt Nettie said. "But I did give you a couple of pairs of gloves, Lee. You took them out to the Ripley house with you."

"I remember now. In case the trays full of chocolates shifted and had to be rearranged." I turned to VanDam. "They were in a cardboard suspender—I mean, dispenser. I gave them to the security guard when he unloaded the chocolates. But there were bunches of food-service gloves out there. Herrera Catering uses them."

VanDam gave a deep sigh. "I think we've established there were plenty of those plastic gloves available at the Ripley house the night of the murder. What we need to know is how this particular pair wound up in your pocket."

"Let me think." I sat down on the edge of Uncle Phil's old recliner. "When I got out there, Mike Herrera told me to help set up the bar. Then Marion came by looking for the cat. I kept working behind the bar. Anyway, the cat jumped onto Jason, then onto the bar and tried to eat the olives, so I grabbed him and took him back to the office. Oh!"

"You remembered something?"

"When I got to the office, Marion was in there. The cat scratched Marion. Then he ran under the desk and turned the wastebasket over. He knocked trash all around the floor. That's when Marion stepped on something that crunched. Something plastic."

VanDam and Underwood looked at each other. "Maybe the syringe," Underwood said.

"Maybe," I said. "Anyway, I bustled around picking up trash, and then Marion told me rather pointedly that I should go back to my regular duties, and she asked me to take some glasses back to the kitchen as I left. But as I was picking up the glasses, I saw this wad of plastic in one of the chairs. It was a pair of food-service gloves."

"You recognized this wad of plastic as a pair of food-service gloves?"

"Sure did. I guess a couple of the fingers were sticking out or something. I thought one of the Herrera employees had left them there. I grabbed them and stuck them in my pocket so I'd have my hands free to carry the glasses."

This story sent all three detectives into a significant silence. Meaningful looks were shooting around the room and ricocheting off the walls.

"So I guess that's how they got in my pocket," I said. "I meant to take them out and throw them away when I got back to the bar. But when I walked into the main room—well, Clementine Ripley fell off that balcony, and I never gave the gloves another thought."

More meaningful glances bounced, and VanDam finally spoke. "It keeps coming back to Marion McCoy, no matter how you look at it. She must have realized that Ms. McKinney walked off with the gloves."

"So what?" I said. "Like you said, there were bunches of gloves out there. Why not just let me take them?"

"Because Marion McCoy was the personal assistant to a defense attorney," Chief Jones said. "She'd know about scientific evidence."

"You mean the traces of cyanide on the gloves?"

"Yes. Plus, if she used the gloves to handle the cyanide, her fingerprints might be inside. That might have made her desperate enough to break into your house trying to get them back."

"The lab just started working on the gloves," VanDam said. "I might have some more questions for Ms. McKinney in the morning." He got up and led Sergeant Underwood toward the door.

"Wait a minute," I said. "Did Joe tell you about the black nightgown?"

The words "black nightgown" definitely got their

attention. I told the story of how I, or rather Champion Yonkers, found the gown in the wrong closet and what Joe and I had deduced from its size and style.

"So you think it belonged to Marion McCoy," VanDam said.

"It wouldn't have been shaped anything like Ms. Ripley," I said, "but it would have fit me. And since Marion and I were much the same height and both on the skinny side . . ."

"So you think this proves she had a boyfriend."

"That, taken with the boob job and the new clothes she got in Dallas—well, it means she either had a boyfriend or was after one," I said. "Or that's the way I'd interpret it."

VanDam glared. "But why would she hide the gown in Ms. Ripley's closet?"

"I have no idea," I said. "I don't understand why Marion did a lot of things. Blaming Marion gets Aunt Nettie and me off the hook. I guess we should count ourselves lucky and shut up. But I think there are still a lot of unanswered questions here. Everyone agrees she was so devoted to Clementine Ripley that it wasn't healthy. So why did she steal from her? Why would she kill her?"

"She stole because she wanted money. She killed to avoid being sent to prison."

"Over the credit card use? I'll bet Clementine Ripley wouldn't have prosecuted."

"Why not?"

"Because it would have made her look stupid. A person like that would lose tens of thousands of dollars rather than look stupid."

VanDam stood up. "Well, that's your opinion."

"Oh, dear," Aunt Nettie said. "It's your opinion, too, isn't it?"

VanDam dropped his eyes. "We won't drop the

investigation until we've exhausted all avenues of inquiry," he said. His voice was flat, and his expression sardonic.

Then he did go to the door, followed by Underwood and the chief. I sat on the edge of the recliner and thought. Did VanDam really think there was a chance Marion hadn't killed Clementine Ripley? But if she hadn't, who had? It fit so nicely.

Almost as if it had been designed that way.

Drat! Now I really did doubt it. I got up in disgust and followed Aunt Nettie as she saw the detectives out to the back porch. It had gotten chilly, and I still felt stupid about getting caught in those flannel pants and stupid about feeling stupid.

I arrived just in time to see VanDam's unmarked car pull out of the drive, followed by the one marked WARNER PIER POLICE CHIEF.

"Now, Lee," Aunt Nettie said, "you get in the house. Standing out here in your pajamas, with wet hair—you're going to catch your death."

"It is a bit chilly," I said. "But I mainly feel real unattractive. I guess it's all that talk about the black lace nightgown when I rely on flannel for Michigan summers. I don't know why Marion even brought that nightgown to Warner Pier," I said. "She didn't bring any of these other fancy new clothes she had bought."

"I guess she planned to wear it," Aunt Nettie said.

I stared at her. "Of course!" I said. "Marion brought the gown because she planned to wear it. Because she was going to see the man who gave it to her. Marion's boyfriend was someone she saw in Warner Pier."

The two of us sat down and speculated about that for a while. Who could Marion's boyfriend have been? Who did she know in Warner Pier?"

"How about Mike Herrera?" Aunt Nettie said. "He

and Marion had to work together a lot, because of all the entertaining Ms. Ripley did."

"Oh! Lindy said . . ." I stopped, then went on. "Don't repeat this. But Lindy said she and Tony thought he was dating someone. Tony thought she might be an Anglo."

"I guess Mike is fairly attractive," Aunt Nettie said. "Marion could have been drawn to him. Of course, the only really attractive man in Warner Pier—older man, I mean—is Hogan Jones."

"The police chief?" I was scandalized. "You think he's good-looking?"

"Not good-looking, Lee. Attractive. Good company, friendly, and masculine, without . . ." Her voice trailed off.

"You mean he's masculine without hitting you over the head with a bag of testosterone," I said.

Aunt Nettie laughed. "That sums it up. And this boyfriend has to be someone who was out at the house Friday afternoon."

"Well, I think we can eliminate Greg Glossop." Aunt Nettie and I chuckled. "Hugh was there—the security guard. So was Duncan Ainsley. But he swears he didn't even like Marion much. Besides, he shows up in *People* magazine with starlets."

"Yes," Aunt Nettie said, "I think he'd go for a more glamorous type than Marion."

"I guess so. Plus, he bad-mouthed Marion. Called her 'Ms. McPicky.' Even if they were trying to hide their relationship, I can't see him actually insulting her behind her back.

"In fact, I wouldn't want to be cross-examined about the boyfriend's existence. A sexy black nightgown isn't really firm evidence. Maybe the police can trace where it was bought and who bought it. If it was a gift, we'll find out then."

Aunt Nettie said she was going to take a shower.

We said good night, and I checked the doors and windows, then went upstairs. It had been a long and eventful day.

As I climbed into bed and pulled my blanket up to my chin, I allowed myself to hope that things were going to calm down.

"Poor Marion," I murmured. "I don't want to wish you ill, but I hope you actually were guilty. So the rest of us can get on with life."

Poor Clementine, too. She and Marion had had a strange relationship. Yet they'd both seemed to be intelligent women. How did their lives, and apparently their deaths, become so intermeshed? Some weird emotional quirk in Marion had complemented an equally weird emotional quirk in Clementine.

Which sounded like a description of my marriage.

I rolled over and thumped my pillow. I did have one thing to feel satisfied about. If I'd done anything right that day, it was telling Rich where to get off. I reached for my bedtime book. The next thing I knew it was an hour later. I'd been sleeping with the light on. My book had fallen off my chest and hit the floor. Or I guess that was what woke me up.

The house was quiet. I turned off the light. The next thing I knew it was morning, and Aunt Nettie was calling up the stairs. "Lee! Lee! If Joe's bringing that cat at seven-thirty, you might want to get up!"

I poked my nose out from under the covers. "I'll be right down!"

I went downstairs and brushed my teeth, combed my hair into a ponytail and climbed into a pair of jeans and a sweatshirt. I didn't bother with makeup. I was not trying to impress Joe Woodyard, I told myself. Then I put on a little mascara. Maybe I did want to impress him a little. I tossed my flannel pants and T-shirt onto the stairs, to remind me to take them up sometime, and poured a cup of coffee. By then Aunt Nettie was going out the back door.

"If you get cold at night, there are some blankets in the closet of the other bedroom up there."

"I know. But I've had plenty of covers. Why?"

"Oh, I wondered about the afghan," she said.

"The afghan?" She kept one in the living room, draped over the back of the couch, but I hadn't used it.

"It doesn't matter," Aunt Nettie said. Then she went out the door. "Don't worry about being to the shop on time. Take care of the cat; we'll handle things until you get there."

"Taking on this cat doesn't seem like a good idea this morning," I said. "I'm bleary-eyed, and that cat's likely to be wide awake."

Aunt Nettie left. I barely had time to drink the coffee and eat a piece of toast before Joe and Champ showed up. I walked out to meet them, and Joe rolled down his window and leaned out.

"I feel like a jerk over this," he said.

"Over what?"

"Asking you to cat-sit. Taking advantage of our brief acquaintanceship."

"I'm a big girl. I could say no."

I walked around the truck and opened the passenger door. Yonkers's carrying case was in the seat next to Joe, and the cat was lashing his tail like a tiger.

"I really do appreciate your taking care of him," Joe said. "You can leave him in the cage if you want to."

"Until eleven o'clock? He'd be mad as hops, and I wouldn't blame him. Does he have a leash, some way I can let him outside? I wouldn't want him to disappear into the woods and run off with the deer."

"I brought his litter box," Joe said. "I think he'll be all right if you let him out inside. But I warn you, he loves to explore."

"I already know he can open doors."

"He hasn't learned to turn door handles. Yet."

Joe carried Champ, cage and all, into the kitchen and told me the name of the breeder and that she would be at TenHuis Chocolade at eleven o'clock.

Joe knelt and opened the door to Champ's cage. The cat walked out and looked around the kitchen regally. He gave a disdainful meow.

"Welcome," I said. "Where's your water dish, Champ?"

Joe took the dish from a sack I'd carried in, and I filled it and put it on the floor near the basement door.

"If you need to chase Yonkers down, there's a can of cat treats in the sack. He'll usually come if you rattle the can." He looked at his watch. "I'd better hit the road. I've got to stop and see if the ATM is still speaking to me before I head out."

We managed the whole conversation without looking each other in the eye. Joe got clear to his truck, then turned and came back. "A house this old—I guess you've got a Michigan basement."

"Sure do."

"You might want to keep Yonkers out of there. He'd probably think it was a big sandbox. You might be fighting the odor for quite a while."

I waved good-bye and made sure the basement door was shut. Champ was prowling around the living room, exploring behind the television set and under the coffee table. He seemed content. I gave him a toy from the sack Joe had brought, then went into the bathroom to put on makeup. I left the door open, ready to respond to any unusual noises.

As I curled an eyelash something began to gnaw at my mind. Something Joe had said. Something about the house.

Michigan basement. That was it. "I guess you've got a Michigan basement."

Well, so what? Joe grew up in Warner Pier—home of the Victorian cottage and the 1900-era West Michigan farmhouse. There were also lots of newer houses in Warner Pier, of course. But Joe himself could well have been raised in a house with a Michigan basement. No, it wasn't what Joe had said that was bothering me about the Michigan basement. It was something else. Something to do with pizza.

"Oh, my Lord!" I jumped and nearly yanked my eyelashes out. Then I whispered, "Duncan Ainsley." I stood there staring into the mirror in horror, remembering my chat with Duncan Ainsley after eating pizza the night before.

As I was leaving Dock Street, I'd made a joke about the Michigan basement, and Duncan had said something like, "Is that what those sand-floored basements are called?"

If Duncan Ainsley hadn't known what a sand-floored basement was called in Michigan, how had he known what I was talking about? How had he known that our basement had a sand floor unless he'd been in Aunt Nettie's house?

Duncan Ainsley had been our burglar. I was sure of it.

Or perhaps he'd been one of them. He must have been Marion's boyfriend, the person who bought the black lace nightgown. And he'd helped her kill Clementine Ripley and break into Aunt Nettie's house to find the food-service gloves. He'd even mentioned plastic gloves later.

I ran to the telephone, ready to share my latest deduction with somebody, anybody. Then I realized that the phone wasn't working. The repairman was due that afternoon.

The cell phone. I could use it.

But all of a sudden I didn't want to call. I didn't even want to stay at Aunt Nettie's. It simply seemed too spooky. There were too many trees, too many bushes to hide behind. And Duncan Ainsley had already found it easy to break in. I had no reason to think he would be coming back, but I wanted out of there. I wanted to be around people. I decided to load Yonkers into his carrier and go to town.

"Champ!" I yelled. "Yonkers! Here, kitty, kitty!"

I ran into the living room. No sign of him. I went back into the bedroom and checked under the bed and in the closet. I closed the bedroom door tightly so I'd be sure he wouldn't circle around me and go back in there. Then I started to search the rest of the house. I got down on the floor and looked under things. I looked in closets and behind furniture. And I called, "Here, kitty! Here, Yonkers! Com'on, Champ."

When I got to the kitchen I grabbed the can of cat treats off the cabinet and rattled them. "Here, kitty!" There was still no response. I went into the back hall. "Darn you, Champ," I said, "if you've crawled behind the washing machine . . ."

And I heard a meow.

It wasn't behind the washing machine. It was behind me. I whirled. The basement door was ajar.

"Oh, no! I thought I checked that door! Champ, if you've gone down in that basement—"

I pushed the door open and turned on the light. I tried to make my voice enticing. "Here, kitty! Here, Yonkers. I have a nice treat for you." I rattled the can.

Again I heard that meow. It was back in the corner, behind the brick pillar that held up the fireplace.

If I went back there, that darn cat might dash around the other side of the pillar and beat me to the stairs. That would be okay, I decided. He'd be easier to catch upstairs. I started after him. Champ had evidently been having a big time down in the basement. The sand floor was all churned up.

Then I noticed Aunt Nettie's afghan. It was lying in the middle of the basement, wadded up into a sort of nest.

"Darn you, Yonkers! You dragged that afghan down

here. I hope you haven't ruined it." I rattled the treat can. "Nice kitty. Nice Yonkers. Come to Lee, sweetie."

Now I could see him. He was digging at something. "Well, Joe warned me," I said. "We'll have to scoop the poop. But we'll worry about that later. Come on, fellow."

"Meow!" Yonkers batted at something on the floor, behind the brick pillar. But he didn't run away from me.

"What have you got?" I leaned over to look.

And I saw the toe of a tennis shoe.

I hesitated just long enough to take a deep breath before I jumped for the stairs. But that was long enough for Duncan Ainsley to jump after me.

He caught me before I got to the top.

Chapter 18

"Lee? Lee! It's me, Duncan!"

I knew that. Duncan had his left arm around my chest and his right hand over my mouth. And he was trying to tell me who he was?

"I didn't mean to scare you." His voice was right in my ear. "I came to the kitchen door. I called out, but you didn't answer. Then I saw the cat. He pawed the basement door open and went down. I was sure you wouldn't want him there, so I went down after him."

The words were rolling off his tongue glibly, but he hadn't relaxed his grip. "I feel like a fool," he said. "I'm going to let you go now. Okay?"

The guy was unbelievable. He expected me to swallow this story?

But maybe if I hadn't already figured out that he must have been our burglar, maybe I would have bought it. I decided I'd better play along with him. I nodded my head, and he let go of me. Slowly, beginning with the hand over my mouth.

It was time for my dumb blonde from Texas act. "Oh, Duncan! You skeered me! We've had two burglaries, you know. Besides a murder. Ah was just sure the murderer had gotten in here."

He chuckled. "You're safe, honey."

I didn't like the way his eyes narrowed. I moved away, up two steps, dropping my eyes and trying to look demure. Actually I was looking to see if I could kick him where it would really hurt and shove him back down the steps. But he moved with me, staying too close for me to try it.

"Why didn't you jes' call out?" I said. Let him answer that one.

"I'd gone down after the cat on an impulse, and I knew I was going to feel stupid. I thought I'd wait until you went to another part of the house and sneak back up."

He came out into the back hall and flashed that broad, country-boy grin, then dropped his head to give me the look that had charmed millions out of his celebrity clients. "Oh, Lee, I do feel like a fool!"

He was a strong fool. The grip he'd had on me had proved that. And he wasn't letting me get far enough away from him to feel sure that he might not grab me again.

I sidled into the kitchen, and Duncan stayed right on my heels. "I'm sorry I didn't hear you. What can I do for you? I mean, why did you come by?"

He looked really blank for a moment. Then his tongue got right to work. "I had a piece of business I needed to take care of before I could leave this mornin', and I had to wait a few minutes. And I just thought I'd like to see you one more time. So I dropped in." He grinned triumphantly.

I tried to look as if I believed him. "Would you like some coffee?" I said.

"Oh, that sounds wonderful."

I reached for the pot—yes, I was picturing pouring the scalding coffee over him—but he reached around me and grabbed it before I could.

I took a mug from the cupboard over the pot. "We used up all the crook—the cream," I said. "But I can get you some milk."

"No. I take it bank." Duncan's face looked furious for just a moment. Then he forced a parody of his country-boy grin onto his face. "I take it black," he said. He filled the mug, and the two of us stood there, looking at each other. Neither of us was being successful at pretending this was a social occasion.

When Champion Yonkers came up out of the basement and walked past Duncan, tail lashing, it was a welcome distraction. "There you are," I said. I scooped the cat up and held him in front of me, like a shield, or maybe like a weapon. If Duncan came closer, would the cat claw on command? The idea was laughable, but I wasn't laughing.

Just then I heard a strange ringing noise.

"Is that a cell phone?" Duncan said.

"It is!" I'd almost forgotten the cell phone Chief Jones had left for Aunt Nettie and me.

"Shouldn't you answer it?" Duncan said.

"I don't have to."

"I think you should." He wasn't smiling now.

I put the cat down and followed the sound into the bedroom. I found the phone on Aunt Nettie's bedside table. Duncan was right behind me. As I reached for the phone, he grabbed my arm. "Don't tell anyone I'm here," he said. He didn't even try to hide the threat that time.

I picked up the phone and punched the right button. "Hello." Ainsley held his head close to mine. I knew he would be able to hear what was said.

"Lee?"

"Chief Jones?"

"Yeah. Has your aunt left?"

"Yes, she's probably at the shop by now."

"I'll call her there. But I thought you ladies might want to know about those gloves."

"Oh?"

"The lab found one fingerprint inside." He paused for dramatic effect. "It belonged to Duncan Ainsley."

I couldn't say anything. And somehow I couldn't look at Duncan.

"Yep. The state police are on their way out to that B-and-B where he's staying," the chief said. "With any luck he'll still be there."

The chief hung up.

So Duncan Ainsley had used those food-service gloves, the ones with the trace of cyanide on the outside. At this point, that was no surprise.

The surprise was that the chief had hung up so quickly I hadn't been able to give him a hint that the state police were not going to find Duncan Ainsley out at that B-and-B. And I was sure that Duncan had heard every word the chief said.

For a minute I was sure that he was going to kill me. But I decided to give the good ol' Texas girl act one last effort.

"Oh, my!" I said. "I'll call the chief back and tell him there's some mix-up. They're actually suspecting *you* in the death of Clementine Ripley. We all know Marion McCoy did it. She even confessed!"

A smile played over Duncan Ainsley's mouth, and for the first time in my life I was grateful for my dumb blonde reputation and for the twisted tongue that kept that reputation intact. I lowered my head and batted my eyes. Then I held up the phone, ready to punch it.

Ainsley, of course, snatched it away. "No, not now."

"But, Duncan, you've got to talk to the detectives, to get all this straightened out. There's obviously some mistake."

"You're right, Lee. I do have to do that. But I can't do it yet. I have to get hold of a piece of evidence first."

"Evidence?"

Ainsley nodded. I could almost see his brain churning, trying to come up with some explanation simple enough for a dumb blonde to accept.

"The police probably know about one thing," he lied. "Marion and I had a business arrangement. When I reveal the details, it will clear me completely. But Marion had the—the papers. I told her to put them in a safe place, and the id—" His voice broke off, and he gulped twice before he went on. "She put them in a bank box."

"Oh, Duncan!" I almost squealed. "Now she's dead! That means you can't get hold of them. You'll have to tell the authors—the authorities—right away. They'll have to find her key and open the box. Will they have to get a court order?"

Ainsley smiled more confidently. Apparently he did think I believed this wild tale. "Actually, we held the box jointly."

"Oh, good! Then you can get into it yourself."

"Yes, but not until the bank opens."

Suddenly I believed that Duncan was telling me the truth. "You mean it's here in the Warner Pier bank?"

"Right down the street from TenHuis Chocolade."

"Oh, my goodness."

"So I need your help, Lee."

"But what can I do?"

"Let me stay here. Just for an hour. Until the bank opens."

"Of course, Duncan." I maneuvered past him. "Let's go back in the kitchen and sit down. I bet you haven't had any breakfast."

The next hour was the strangest I've ever spent or hope to spend. Duncan followed me into the kitchen. I tried to make him believe that I was cooperating, but maybe I tried too hard. He never eased his vigilance. He never let me get more than an arm's length from him, no matter how stupidly I prattled away.

I was able to get in a few self-protective remarks. "In a practical sense," I said, giving him my dumbest smile, "your timing is good. I have to have that cat downtown at nine a.m."—I moved the time back by a couple of hours—"or the cat breeder will come out here looking for him. And that's when the bank opens." I resisted saying we could kill two birds with one stone. No sense giving him ideas. But maybe I had given him the idea that I'd be missed fairly quickly.

I glanced out at the empty driveway casually. "Where did you park your car?"

"I hid it down the road, Lee. In some bushes. Like I said, I feel like an idiot over all this, but that car's too noticeable. The cops would pick up on it the minute I drove down Dock Street. And I do need to get to that bank box before I deal with them. I'm afraid you'll have to drive. You do have a car here?"

"Oh, yes. Like you, I decided my van was too noticeable. It's hidden at the neighbor's house so the reporters can't find it."

Duncan looked relieved.

A little later I tried one more ploy. "Marion's suicide certainly left you in a mess. What kind of deal were y'all involved in?"

He didn't bother to answer that one. He just shrugged.

By the time we'd sat there, eyeing each other, for forty-five minutes, I was a nervous wreck and about to wet my pants. But I wasn't about to say I needed to use the facilities. I knew Duncan wouldn't let me go into a room with a lock on the door alone.

At quarter to nine, Duncan asked me where my car was and how long it would take to get it.

"Oh, maybe five minutes," I said. "Are you ready to go?"

"Sure 'nuff."

We both stood up, and I called out, "Here, kitty, kitty!" Then I realized that I had no idea where to find the can of cat treats, the key to catching Yonkers. I'd probably dropped them in the basement.

Miraculously, the cat came without them. He seemed to be tired of our house and ready to move on. I enticed him with a piece of deli-sliced turkey and he allowed me to pick him up. When I tried to stuff him in his carrying case, he kicked and yowled, but he went in. Neither Duncan nor I mentioned the litter box or the sack of Yonkers's belongings. I just left them in the corner of the kitchen.

In fact, I don't know why I even insisted on taking the cat. I guess it was because I'd made such a point in telling Duncan I was supposed to deliver him in town, just so he'd think someone would come looking for me if I didn't show up.

There were a lot of bushes between Aunt Nettie's house and the Baileys'. The path on the way over there, I decided, was the best place for an escape attempt.

I latched the cage and picked it up. Then I turned to Duncan. "Here," I said.

Miraculously, he took the cage.

But he didn't let me get very far away from him. He walked beside me, his hand gripping my arm, as we went out the back door and started along the path.

I had my spot in mind. It was a low place in the path, one which was nearly always damp and muddy, with dense brush on either side. When we got to that spot, I'd pretend to fall, shove against Duncan, yank my arm out of his grasp, and leap into the bushes. With the cat cage to throw him off balance—well, it might work.

I led the way, with Duncan's hand on my arm and the cat cage bumping into the back of my thighs, and pretty soon we were close to the low spot. *Relax,* I told myself. *Keep your muscles relaxed. Don't let him know you're planning something.*

The low spot was there. I stepped in it, then threw myself backward at Duncan. I squealed. Then I yanked away and jumped sideways, between two bushes. I heard Duncan swear and Yonkers shriek.

The next thing I knew I was flat on my face in the blackberry stickers.

I thrashed around, trying to get free of the brambles. Suddenly I was yanked to my feet. I was standing up, but Duncan's arm was around my neck, and a silver pistol was pointed at my right eye.

"I didn't want to show you this little gadget while you were being so nice and cooperative," Duncan said, "but you've got to believe that I'm serious as a heart attack."

Chapter 19

Well, I tried. I might have gotten away with it, if the blackberries hadn't tripped me up. I've always hated blackberries. They're so seedy.

Duncan yanked me back onto the path. "Now you get to carry the cat," he said.

I was relieved to see that Yonkers appeared to be unhurt by his rude treatment. He was glaring out the door of his carrying cage, but he wasn't yowling or acting injured. I picked up the cage, and trying to ignore Duncan's fingers digging into my arm, I again led the way toward the Baileys' house.

When we got to the garage, I felt something sharp against my side. "I've still got the gun, honey," Duncan said. "Just don't try anything."

I led the way around the garage, then unlocked the old van and slid the side door open. I put the cage on the floor of the backseat.

"Slide it over to the other side," Duncan said. "Behind the driver's seat."

I obeyed.

Then Duncan opened the right-hand front door. "You can get in here." I saw that he didn't want me going around to the other side of the van.

I hesitated, and he poked me with the pistol again. "I'm determined that I'll get to that bank before the police. So I want you to understand that you have to do exactly what I tell you."

My heart seemed to be alternately racing and coming to a complete standstill. I didn't have a single doubt that Duncan Ainsley could shoot me down in a heartbeat if he took a notion.

And I also realized that no matter what I did, Duncan planned to kill me as soon as he got an opportunity. My only chance was to cooperate until we got where there were people. Then I'd just have to take the chance of being shot and make a break for it.

"So," Duncan said, "you get in, and I get in after you. Then I get into the back of the van—thanks to these bucket seats, it'll be real easy—and I'll sit on the floor. And I'll have this pistol pointed at you every minute, Lee. So you do exactly—exactly!—what I tell you to do."

We arranged ourselves, and I started the van, backed out from behind the garage, then turned onto the road. When I got to the Lake Shore Drive, I stopped. "Which way?"

"To the bank, Lee. Just like I said. And drive carefully. No sudden moves."

All the way to Dock Street I could see the pistol out of the corner of my eye. Duncan scrabbled around, doing something, but every time I glanced sideways I saw that pistol.

As I turned onto Dock Street—I guess Duncan knew where we were when he saw the two-story brick buildings go by the windows—he spoke. "You'd better park in the alley," he said. "It might look a little strange for me to climb out of the floor of the backseat in front of the bank."

It was going to look strange wherever he did it, but I wasn't pointing that out. I turned down Peach Street, then swung into the alley and parked behind TenHuis Chocolade. Duncan eased between the seats and sat down in the front passenger seat. His appearance surprised me; now he was wearing a hat and a jacket.

It took a second to realize they were mine. The khaki-colored rain jacket and billed Dallas Cowboys cap had been tossed into the third seat. Duncan had managed to put them on as we drove along. The sleeves of the jacket were a little short, but it wasn't a bad fit. And the hat hid most of his noticeable gray hair.

He showed me the pistol. Then he put it in the pocket of the jacket. "I'll be keeping my hand on this," he said. "Now let's concentrate on getting out of this van safely."

He opened the front door on the passenger side and sort of oozed out, then stood partially hidden by the van's open door. "Now you scoot over and get out on this side."

Maybe this would be my chance. I moved slowly, but I tried to get in position to kick.

I had just eased over into the passenger seat when the back door to TenHuis Chocolade swung open.

"Lee? What are you doing here?"

It was Aunt Nettie.

Instantly Duncan had his hand on my arm and was pointing the gun in his pocket toward her. He didn't need to say a word. The threat hung in the air like a balloon.

Aunt Nettie looked perplexed. "You're not due until eleven, Lee. How come you're here now?"

I tried to think fast. "Something came up. I had to come down early."

"What became of the cat?"

"I have him. I'm afraid I'll have to leave him here for a little while."

"Here?" Aunt Nettie looked horrified. "But I can't have a cat around."

"He's in his carrying case. He can just sit in the

break room. I don't think the health department will throw the book at you."

Aunt Nettie looked doubtful. Then she looked at Duncan Ainsley. A hat wasn't going to keep her from recognizing him. Suddenly I remembered that Chief Jones had planned to call and tell her about the fingerprint in the glove. So she must know Duncan was involved in Clementine Ripley's death, even if she hadn't figured out that he had been our burglar.

If she said the wrong thing, Ainsley would kill her. I had to keep that from happening.

"I'm helping Duncan," I said frantically. "He's trying to get hold of the state police to straighten out a misunderstanding. If I can't put Champ in the break room, I'll have to leave him in the van."

"All right. I guess there's no help for it."

I eased over and got out the passenger side of the van, then slid the side door open, crawled in, and pulled out the cat cage. Duncan didn't speak to Aunt Nettie, or offer to lift the cage out of the van, and Aunt Nettie didn't seem to notice his lack of courtesy. We were all acting extremely oddly, but none of us wanted to mention it.

As Aunt Nettie took the cage, she squeezed my hand. For a moment I thought she was going to yank me inside the back door. And for a moment I desperately wanted her to do that. Then Duncan poked me with the pistol in his jacket pocket, and I pulled my hand away.

"I'll be back as soon as I help Duncan," I said.

Aunt Nettie nodded. She closed the door. Duncan Ainsley and I were alone in the alley.

Of course, it wasn't exactly private, since cars and pedestrians were passing either end of the alley. But it sure felt lonely right then.

"Well done," Duncan said. "Now let's head on down to the bank."

He held my arm as we walked back toward Peach Street. Would I have a chance to get away from him when we turned out onto the street?

I abandoned that idea as soon as we were there. Warner Pier was just waking up. The half block between the alley and the bank was empty except for a teenager sweeping out Mike's Sidewalk Café, on the opposite side of the street. If I ran for it, Duncan could shoot me down at will, and maybe shoot the kid with the broom as well. I led the way to the bank.

The bank had just been open ten minutes, and there was no rush. Only one teller was on duty, and the only customer was just leaving. No one was in the manager's office. Duncan guided me over to the teller.

"I need to get into my safe-deposit box," he said.

"I'll call the branch manager," the teller said. "You can wait by her desk."

The manager—Barbara—came from the back. "Lee? What can I do for you?"

"I'm the one who needs attention," Duncan said. "Lee's just along for the ride." He poked me with the pistol, but I knew Barbara couldn't see what he was doing. "I need to access my safe-deposit box."

"Of course."

I thought of crossing my eyes, throwing up on her desk—anything to keep Duncan out of that safe-deposit box. But it went off routinely. Barbara led us back to the cage that closed off the safe-deposit boxes. Duncan, still keeping his hand clenched on my upper arm, signed in, and Barbara opened the gate. She looked surprised when Duncan shoved me in ahead of him.

"Miss McKinney should wait outside," she said.

"I need her to sign something," Duncan said. "Can't you make an exception?"

Barbara's face clouded, but she didn't argue. "I guess it's okay, since I know who it is," she said.

She took a key Duncan produced and her own key, opened the box—it was one of the small ones—then locked us in.

At least Duncan let go of my arm. Since neither of us was going anyplace, he evidently didn't consider it necessary to hold me.

He flipped the box open and took out two manila envelopes. He peeked inside the top one, and I got a glimpse. Cash. For some reason I wasn't surprised.

Then he peeked inside the second. I craned my neck, and I got a glimpse of something navy blue and flat.

A passport.

All of a sudden I wanted to laugh. Duncan was ready to fly the coop. Leave the country. Go to Texas, as the old-timers used to say. And Marion McCoy had stashed his passport and the cash for the trip in a bank box that he couldn't access on the weekend.

Well, it explained why he'd sneaked into Aunt Nettie's house, then spent the night lurking in the Michigan basement, huddled in an afghan he'd snitched from the living room, afraid that the cops would pick him up before he could leave Warner Pier. But it didn't do me any particular good. I was still a prisoner.

Unless . . . I moved toward the gate. Maybe I could yell at Barbara, tell her to leave us in the cage and call the cops.

But Duncan was right behind me, his fingers pressing into my arm again. His voice came out as the sort of whisper you hang the phone up on. "Don't even think about it. I could kill both the bank people, plus you. Then me. I'm not going to jail."

He'd won another hand. I stood there while he called to Barbara, and she came and opened the gate. The box was replaced, and Duncan and I walked slowly toward the outside door of the bank.

And once we were outside, I decided, I was going

to make a break for it. If only there were no innocent bystanders on the street. I breathed a silent prayer for Peach Street to be empty.

But there was somebody coming. And darned if it wasn't someone I knew. It was one of Aunt Nettie's teenage employees. Tracy? Or Stacy? I still didn't have them straight. The one with the stringy hair was passing the bank.

She seemed delighted to see me. "Hi, Lee."

"Hi." I pushed on past her. Please let her go into the bank, get off the street. But she lingered. When I looked back, I could see her standing there, staring after Duncan and me as we crossed the street.

What was I going to do?

Just as I reached the point of despair, a miracle happened. A bright blue miracle.

Joe Woodyard's pickup came around the corner of Peach and Dock, and Joe began honking madly.

Duncan clutched my arm even harder, but we both stopped in our tracks. Joe stopped right behind us, opened his door, and got out.

"Duncan! You're the guy I've got to see!"

Duncan moved his hand. I saw that he was going to pull the pistol out of his pocket.

"Look out!" I screamed the words at the same time that I shoved Duncan sideways. He lost his grip on my arm and fell into the little white railing in front of Mike's Sidewalk Café.

Joe was still standing in the door of the pickup, gaping at me. I ran to him and grabbed his hand. I screamed, "Run! He's got a gun!" Then I turned and ran toward TenHuis Chocolade, dragging Joe with me.

Joe yelled, "What's going on?"

I heard a shot, but I kept running. The TenHuis sign was less than half a block away. I dropped Joe's hand, ready to pound on the door to the shop because I knew that it was still closed.

And I heard more feet pounding behind me. I knew it was Duncan. I was shrieking, but I'm not sure words were coming out.

Now I was nearly to the door, and another miracle happened. It swung open.

Aunt Nettie was standing there, her white-blond hair forming a halo. If I ever get to heaven, I'm sure the first angel at the gate is going to look just like she did then.

I ran in the shop, with Joe right behind me, and Aunt Nettie and I slammed the door. But we weren't fast enough. Duncan hit the plate glass and knocked the door open. Aunt Nettie fell back, and he was inside.

"Give me the keys, you little idiot!" He came for me.

I ran past the showcase and through the door into the workroom. I was still screaming, and Duncan was yelling, "The keys! The keys!"

I circled the first stainless worktable, and I saw that Joe was right behind Duncan.

One of the hairnet ladies loomed up right in front of me. I dodged and went back the other way, trying to get to the break room and the back door. I couldn't get past Duncan.

But Duncan couldn't get past Joe. Since he was concentrating on me, he didn't see Joe coming up fast. Joe grabbed Duncan in a hold that reminded me Joe had been a high school wrestler.

They grappled, and I looked for something I could use to hit Duncan. The first thing I saw was a ladle in a big bowl of dark chocolate on the table. I snatched the ladle up and whacked at the struggling pair.

I hit Duncan squarely in the temple. Unfortunately, the chocolate in the ladle hit Joe squarely in the eyes. He automatically threw up a hand, and Duncan wriggled away.

But now he was running away from me. I chased him with the ladle. He turned, and again he yelled, "The keys! Give me the keys!"

I flailed the ladle again. "What keys?"

Duncan ducked. "The van!"

If I'd known where they were, I think I would have given them to him. But someplace between the van and the bank and the chase down Peach Street, I'd lost my purse. So I screamed, "They're in the van!" And I swung the ladle.

Duncan turned and ran to the break room door. He yanked it open. Then the third miracle occurred.

Champion Myanmar Chocolate Yonkers jumped.

He had somehow gotten out of his carrying case, and according to his usual habit, he'd climbed, this time to the top of the oak china cabinet. When Duncan ran in the door, he saw one of his jumping partners, and he pounced.

Duncan screamed. Yonkers jumped from his shoulders to the back of the couch. Duncan ran toward the back door again, and this time I thought he was going to make it.

It was time for the fourth miracle. A river of chocolate.

About five gallons of chocolate—warm, melted, medium brown milk chocolate—flowed past like a flash flood down a Texas creek. It caught Duncan and left him ankle-deep in a lake of chocolate.

He tried to run again. His feet went up, and his body seemed to hang in the air, parallel to the floor. Then he fell flat. His head, his feet, his butt, his shoulders—he landed like a two-by-four dropped out of a truck. Chocolate splashed everywhere.

Duncan's eyes rolled around. He made terrible gasping sounds, but he didn't move. I realized that the breath had been knocked out of him completely.

Joe appeared at my right shoulder, and Aunt Nettie appeared at my left. She was holding an empty steel mixing bowl that had shortly before been full of chocolate.

The three of us stood there, looking down at Duncan.

And Champion Myanmar Yonkers delicately walked over and licked Duncan Ainsley's face.

CHOCOLATE CHAT

CRIME

- Counterfeiting may have been the first crime connected with chocolate. The ancient Aztecs used the beans as currency, and early on some sneaky traders learned to take the meat—the part that makes chocolate—out of its shell and replace the good stuff with dirt.

- Europeans refined this practice, adulterating chocolate with starches, shells, and occasionally brick dust. Brick dust gave the chocolate a realistic red-brown color, and the chocolate of the day was pretty gritty anyway.

- In Mexico in the late 1600s an even more serious crime was linked to chocolate, which was then used only as a drink. Young ladies fell into the habit of having their maids bring them a cup during worship services. They claimed it prevented fainting and weakness. The bishop did not approve and forbade the practice. The ladies, aghast, began to attend a different church. The bishop refused to relent—and then he died. Rumor blamed a cup of chocolate laced with poison. Scandal followed.

- Chocolate was even linked to corporate espionage in 1980 when an apprentice of a Swiss chocolate firm tried to sell trade secrets to several foreign countries.

Chapter 20

Chief Jones ran in almost immediately, and as soon as he and Jerry Cherry had hauled Duncan Ainsley away, Aunt Nettie began to explain. The chief had called her earlier, as he'd promised, to tell her that Duncan Ainsley's fingerprint had been found in the food-service glove. When she'd seen Duncan and me getting out of the van, she'd been sure that all was not as it should be.

So she called the cops. Then she sent Tracy down to the corner to see where Duncan and I were going. But Duncan had transacted his business and started back to the van—which he probably would have forced me to drive away—before the chief had time to get there.

Joe had happened on the scene almost coincidentally. When he met the lawyer from Clementine Ripley's office, the first thing the lawyer had told him was that he'd heard rumors that Duncan Ainsley's financial empire was about to go under. Joe had rushed back to look for Duncan, but he ran into the police—looking for Ainsley. So he headed for town, apparently to warn Aunt Nettie and me.

We figured that Duncan had sneaked into Aunt Nettie's house while she, Chief Jones, and I had gone to look at the van. He probably intended to search for the gloves some more, but when we came back he heard us talking. There are no secrets in that house—you can hear anything said anywhere—and he realized the authorities had the gloves. He decided to skip going back to his B-and-B and hide out in the basement. If Yonkers hadn't found him, maybe he would have come out and stolen my van. Who knows?

"Anyway," I told Aunt Nettie and Joe, "it explains why he paid a peon like me so much attention."

Joe frowned. "Lee, a guy doesn't need an excuse to pay attention to you."

"Thanks, but let's be realistic. The first time he called me—at the shop the night Clementine died—he managed to quiz me about my hours. He was figuring out when the house would be empty, so he could search for the gloves.

"Of course, he didn't find them, because I'd neglected to check my pants pockets before I headed to the cleaners."

"Marion must have decided to give the search a try that night," Aunt Nettie said, "but we caught her."

I nodded. "Then last night I saw Duncan's car down the street as Aunt Nettie and I left the shop. He just happened to run into us at the Dock Street Pizza Place—well, he must have followed us, trying to figure out if we'd found those gloves. And incidentally, to tell me that Joe left law because he was in danger of being disbarred."

"What!" Joe looked horrified. "Where'd he get that?"

"I think he wanted me to regard you with suspicion, Joe. He wanted to make sure we didn't trade too much information. But the gossip backfired, because it made me so curious I went straight out to the house to ask you about it. Though a lot of other things came up before I could work it into the conversation."

"Well, if there was a disbarment in the wings, I didn't know anything about it," Joe said.

It took the hairnet ladies most of the day to clean up the chocolate that had trapped Duncan Ainsley. But no one seemed to mind. I told Aunt Nettie it taught everyone a new use for chocolate. "Chocolate stun guns. You should put them on the order sheet."

It was a few days before we understood just what had been going on with Duncan, Marion, and Clementine, and those days were crazy. The news media—tabloid, television, and every other kind—came back to Warner Pier. Aunt Nettie and I tried another news conference, but Alec VanDam and the state police got most of the attention.

Lindy even called me with one piece of information that surprised everybody. Her uncle ran into Mike Herrera at the movies in Holland. And he was with—tah dah!—Joe Woodyard's mom. Lindy said Tony was vindicated; his dad was dating an Anglo. But Tony couldn't say much, since he and Joe were old friends.

Chief Jones came by and told us he believed Duncan had convinced Marion that whatever he was putting in the chocolates would merely make Clementine Ripley sick. "You remember how she screamed, 'Clementine can't be *dead!*' " he said. "It would have been hard to fake. I think she'd left the estate because she didn't want to be there when her boss took ill. I think she was genuinely surprised when she died."

Joe and I avoided each other like poison. The reporters were asking enough questions about why we'd both been there when Aunt Nettie felled Duncan Ainsley with a bowl of milk chocolate. I certainly didn't want to add any fuel to their speculations about our big relationship.

I had a lot of questions about that relationship myself.

Such as, did I want it to be a relationship? Did Joe want to see me? Did I want to see him? Had the circumstances in which we met ruined any chance we would have had at getting together? Can a girl from rural Texas find happiness with a boatbuilder from western Michigan?

I saw him at the Superette a couple of times, but we both shied off from speaking. I think we were afraid even to get together and explore the question.

Finally, after a week, I was balancing the cash register and Tracy and Stacy were finishing the cleanup for the night when the phone rang.

"Hi," Joe said.

"Hi."

"Nice moon tonight. You interested in a boat ride?"

"Maybe. When?"

"In about an hour."

"I guess so."

"Do you mind meeting me?"

"Meeting you? Where?"

"At the public access area down from your aunt's house. I'll pull the boat in at the creek."

"Oh."

"There's still a reporter staking out my shop, but he doesn't seem to have a boat. I think I can dodge him."

I laughed. "Okay. I'll meet you at the creek."

I went home and got a sweatshirt, since the Lake Michigan shore isn't too balmy on moonlit nights, even in late July. Then I walked down to the beach. I'd been there only a few minutes when I heard a motor and saw the lights of a boat coming from the north. The boat putt-putted along and landed at the mouth of the creek.

I hopped in without getting my feet wet. Joe was

sitting at a steering wheel on the right side of a bench seat, rather like a car's front seat. The seat was upholstered in vinyl. I could see a similar seat behind us, and varnished mahogany decking glowed in the moonlight.

"This is beautiful," I said.

"It's a 1949 Chris-Craft Deluxe Runabout," Joe said. "This may be my last trip in it; I think I've got a buyer."

"I'd love to own it. How much are you asking?"

"He's offered twenty thousand five."

I laughed. "Well, don't wait for me to top that offer."

"I won't. I need the money too bad. The bank gave me an extension, but they're going to get impatient when the word gets out about what a mess Clem's estate is."

"Are you going to get anything out of it?"

"Maybe a few thousand. Which I don't plan to keep. But it'll be months before everything's straightened out."

"Had Duncan taken her for everything she had?"

"Duncan and Marion. The two of them just about cleaned her out. And the money's abroad. We may never track it down."

"It's hard to see how they did that."

"Duncan was running a classic Ponzi scheme," Joe said.

"But he was written up in all the magazines and everything," I said. "Somebody must have looked at his record."

"I think people did, at first," he said. "He probably made legitimate investments in the beginning. But after the market went nuts, he got in a hole, and he couldn't get out. So he began to pay interest to old investors with new investors' money. Apparently most of his high-profile clients were like Clementine—too busy to worry about the details."

"But Marion figured it out," I said.

"She must have. But she was mad at Clem. Apparently I'd put a permanent wedge between Clem and Marion."

"And Duncan, well, seduced her."

"I guess so. Marion had devoted her life to Clem. But Clem had married me, which made Marion feel rejected. At the same time, Duncan was worming his way into her favors. So if she figured out there was something wrong with Clem's investments, at least she was ready to give Duncan the benefit of the doubt. Eventually, she must have thrown in with him."

"But Ponzi schemes eventually collapse."

"Apparently that's what was about to happen. So Duncan and Marion were ready to leave the country. They had fake passports."

"And cash."

"Yeah. Of course, the cash in the safe-deposit box here wasn't enough to keep them going a week. There's got to be more stashed abroad. But the fiasco over ordering the chocolates tipped Clem off to Marion's thefts."

"The Visa card!"

Joe laughed. "Yeah, you did it with the check on her Visa card. I saw Clem when she heard that her Visa was maxed out. She was furious. Marion panicked, and she and Duncan poisoned the chocolates. Chief Jones may be right—Marion may not have realized the stuff they injected was deadly. What the cops haven't figured out is where they got the cyanide."

"I've wondered if Duncan didn't provide it. In fact, I've wondered if he hadn't meant the poison for Marion."

"That would make sense," Joe said. "Marion wasn't really Duncan's type. Which might be why she insisted on holding the passports and getaway cash. She was smart enough not to trust him, even though she bought a slinky black nightgown for him."

"Or he bought it for her."

"The cops traced it. It was one of those Dallas purchases. My theory, by the way, is that Marion left it in Duncan's room, and he sneaked it into the office closet. Marion would have put it in Clem's dressing room."

"Or just left it in her own room. But how could the two of them think they were going to get away with this?"

"I don't think they intended to get away with it. They just wanted to buy time—keep out of jail until Monday morning, when they could get the passports out of the bank box and split."

I stared at the lake. "It's a sad story."

"True, but I hope it's going to get happier."

Joe stretched his arm along the back of the boat's seat, and his hand found the back of my neck. I looked at him. "Joe . . ."

"Yeah?"

I didn't know what to say, so I didn't say anything. So Joe leaned over, and I could see that he was going to kiss me.

And I really wanted him to. He was leaning closer, and the thought of our bodies stretched out together was absolutely wonderful, and . . . I gathered all my strength and remembered what a rat Rich Gottrocks turned out to be. "Joe," I said.

Before I could say anything more, Joe sat back and leaned against his side of the boat. "I didn't really ask you down here to make a pass at you."

"I *think* I'm glad to hear that. Just what did you have in mind?"

"First I wanted to apologize for acting like such a jerk the first couple of times we met."

"You already did that."

"Yeah. But I finally figured out why I did it. See, when Clem and I split up, I was really mad at the world. So I just went out to the boat shop—and sulked. I hadn't looked at another woman. I hadn't wanted to."

He leaned over and took my hand. "Then I saw you standing up to that stupid Hugh, and you were beautiful and spunky, and I knew I liked you right away. But that didn't fit my picture of myself as a woman-hater. So I tried to act as if I didn't like you."

"You were quite convincing."

"Well, it only took me a couple of days to get over it!"

We both laughed. Then Joe went on. "I guess I wanted to say that I'd like to go out with you, but—well, the next couple of months are going to be a mess."

"I can see that you're going to be really busy, both with your own business and with tying up Ms. Ripley's estate."

"It's not just the time factor. It's—well, I thought I'd gotten out from Clem's shadow, and now here I am back under it." He banged his fist against the boat's side. "I like you, Lee. I like you a lot. But if Clem's hanging over us, I might not be very good company."

I considered that for a few moments before I replied. I could see his point.

"I think I understand, Joe. You feel as if you have to get uninvolved with the first woman in your life before you can think about getting involved with a second one."

"Yeah. Only . . ." He banged the side of the boat again. "Only if I sit on my duff, some other guy is going to come along and beat my time!"

I laughed. "Thanks for the compliment! But so far you have nothing to worry about."

Joe looked at me then, and he smiled. "Well, I did

bring you something. Something that might convince you I'm serious, even if I'm not able to move too fast."

He turned and reached over behind us and brought out a plastic Superette sack. I caught a whiff of mothballs as he shoved the sack into my lap. Something heavy and bulky was stuffed inside.

"What is it?" I opened the sack, and the mothball smell grew. Inside was a heavy wool jacket. It was dark in color and had light leather trim on the shoulders. I held it up, and I saw the letters WPHS across the back. It was a Warner Pier High School letter jacket.

I laughed for five minutes before I could say a word. "Joe! I'm thrilled!"

Joe was laughing, too. "I went over to my mother's house and dug it out of the attic. You're the first girl ever to get my letter jacket."

We both leaned into the middle of the boat, and our lips met. It was a lingering kiss, full of promise, but a little fearful.

When we finally moved apart, I was the first one to speak. "I think you've got the right idea, Joe. We both need to move into this a little at a time. And for now, I guess I'd better get on home."

"I'll walk you up."

"Sure."

Joe jumped out of the boat, then turned around and held his hand out toward me. He laughed again when he saw that while he was stepping onto the beach I had put the jacket on.

He lifted me out of the boat, and we kissed again, standing there at the edge of the water. Then we turned and walked across the beach, holding hands in the moonlight.

Test Your Candy Knowledge

How much do you really know about the sweet facts behind this favorite?

1. How much candy do Americans consume in one year?
   - A) 10 pounds
   - B) 25 pounds
   - C) 50 pounds
   - D) 2 pounds

2. What is the biggest holiday for candy sales?
   - A) Halloween
   - B) Easter
   - C) Valentine's Day
   - D) Christmas season

3. Chocolate comes from cocoa beans. How do cocoa beans grow?
   - A) On bushes
   - B) On trees
   - C) Underground

4. The people from which country eat the most candy?
   - A) United States
   - B) India
   - C) Denmark
   - D) Switzerland

5. What is the favorite flavor of American consumers?
   A) Strawberry
   B) Cherry
   C) Chocolate
   D) Lemon

6. Which food contains the most fat?
   A) 15 jelly beans
   B) 1 plain bagel
   C) 2 cups of cooked pasta
   D) 1 lollipop

7. Where was milk chocolate invented?
   A) United States
   B) Switzerland
   C) Canada

8. Which food is more likely to cause tooth decay?
   A) A chocolate bar
   B) A slice of bread
   C) Pretzels
   D) None of these

Turn the page for the answers . . .

Answers

1. B) Americans consume a little more than 25 pounds of confectionery per year.
2. A) Halloween is the biggest candy holiday, chalking up almost two billion dollars in sales.
3. B) Cocoa beans come from cacao trees, which grow in tropical regions of the world.
4. C) While Americans love candy, they are no competition for the Danes. The people of Denmark consume approximately 36 pounds per person per year.
5. C) Chocolate, according to an industry survey. Berry flavors came in second.
6. B) The bagel. The pasta comes in second. Neither jelly beans nor lollipops contain fat or cholesterol.
7. B) Switzerland—a man named David Peter devised a way of adding milk to create the world's first milk chocolate back in 1876.
8. D) None is more likely than the other to cause tooth decay. Whether or not you get cavities depends on several things, including how frequently you eat and how long foods and sugary drinks stay in contact with your teeth. It's most important to brush and floss every day.

Quiz brought to you by the National Confectioners Association and the Chocolate Manufacturers Association. For more information visit www.CandyUSA.org.